# Fringe Girl

# Fringe Girl

## Valerie Frankel

nal
jam
books

NAL Jam
Published by New American Library, a division of Penguin Group (USA) Inc., 375
Hudson Street, New York, New York 10014, USA • Penguin Group (Canada), 90
Eglinton Avenue East, Suite 700, Toronto, Ontario M4P 2Y3, Canada (a division of
Pearson Penguin Canada Inc.) • Penguin Books Ltd., 80 Strand, London WC2R 0RL,
England • Penguin Ireland, 25 St. Stephen's Green, Dublin 2, Ireland (a division of
Penguin Books Ltd.) • Penguin Group (Australia), 250 Camberwell Road, Camberwell,
Victoria 3124, Australia (a division of Pearson Australia Group Pty. Ltd.) • Penguin
Books India Pvt. Ltd., 11 Community Centre, Panchsheel Park, New Delhi - 110 017,
India • Penguin Group (NZ), cnr Airborne and Rosedale Roads, Albany, Auckland
1310, New Zealand (a division of Pearson New Zealand Ltd.) • Penguin Books (South
Africa) (Pty.) Ltd., 24 Sturdee Avenue, Rosebank, Johannesburg 2196, South Africa •
Penguin Books Ltd., Registered Offices: 80 Strand, London WC2R 0RL, England

First published by NAL Jam, an imprint of New American Library, a division of
Penguin Group (USA) Inc.

First Printing, April 2006
1  3  5  7  9  10  8  6  4  2

NAL JAM and logo are trademarks of Penguin Group (USA) Inc.

LIBRARY OF CONGRESS CATALOGING-IN-PUBLICATION DATA:
Frankel, Valerie.
  Fringe girl : the revolution starts now/Valerie Frankel.
    p. cm.
  Summary: As part of a class project on political revolutions, sixteen-year-old Adora
Benet devises a plan to overthrow the popular clique at her school and establish a
new social order.
  ISBN 0-451-21772-1
[1. Popularity—Fiction. 2. Interpersonal relations—Fiction. 3. Schools—Fiction.] I.
Title.
PZ7.F8553Fri 2006
[Fic]—dc22         2005022878

Set in New Caledonia
Designed by Elke Sigal

Printed in the United States of America

*Dedicated to*

# The Big Sister's Club

# 1

"I am hot. My heat could melt the belly of an airplane. I am only slightly less on fire than the surface of the sun."

Such were the (hopeful, idealistic) things one had to say into the mirror when dressing for the first day of school. Not that I believed them, of course. But I said them anyway.

It was the first morning of junior year, eleventh grade, and my twelfth first-day at the Brownstone Collegiate Institute in Brooklyn Heights, New York City. My initial first-day, at age four, had been no less fraught with anxiety. I needed parental assistance then to pull a shirt over my head, and I eagerly listened to Mom and Dad's advice: "You only get one chance to make a good impression! Start the year the way you want to finish it!"

For a while now, I'd been able to dress myself—although I did struggle with knot adjustment on my wrap half-sweater. I continued to hear the echoes of ancient advice, as if I were still four years old in Velcro-strap sneakers and snap pants. But I wasn't. I was sixteen, almost seventeen, in camouflage cargo pants, a white tank top showing a discreet inch of belly, one of Dad's silk ties for a belt, kitten-heeled plastic flip-flops and the above-mentioned pale yellow sweater. My hair was trapped in a painstakingly haphazard ponytail, clipped in the back with a single gold barrette.

"I am hot. I crackle like bacon in a pan," I told myself.

Truthfully, I was tepid. My hair was my best feature—thick, chestnut, straight, trademark bangs. Eyes: hazel, alternately greenish, bluish and grayish depending on what I was wearing (today, greenish). I'd often thought of my eyes as mood indicators. When I was sad, they were blue; happy, green; angry, gray. I'd given up searching for signs of my emotional state of mind in my eyes, though. It seemed like the preoccupation of poets, middle schoolers and self-help gurus.

Where I was "decent," my friend Eli (short for Elizabeth) Stomp fell on the exotic end of the attractiveness spectrum, with jet-black hair, mysterious dark brown eyes, red lips. Her ghostly pallor and rail-thin body gave her a certain (granted, Chinese) vampirish air—the possible explanation for why boys seemed to reel back in fear of her rather than assuming a rightful, worshipful posture in her presence. My other best friend, Liza (short for Elizabeth) Greene, was classically cute, a California blonde in Brooklyn, where she'd been born and raised. Liza's rounded edges, her pleasant cushion, had thus far prevented her from hypnotizing every boy in school with her glass blue eyes, but it was only a matter of time before she gained (1) a couple of inches and (2) the devotion of the entire male species.

Boys had not yet discovered me, either. But, as I took one last glance in the mirror, I felt (viscerally, intuitively) that this would be *my year*. That I'd finally get the attention and admiration I'd been waiting for, dreaming of, fantasizing about. I didn't need a fan club. Just one boy would be fine. My lips turned upward, thinking of him, and suddenly I did feel hot, as steaming and explosive as all the kettles in England.

I went downstairs to the first floor in my family's duplex apartment in an 1861 town house on a tree-lined street. Those trees you might've heard about growing in Brooklyn? They were all on my block, Garden Place—an optimistic name for a city stretch of asphalt, concrete and bricks, along with the abundant sidewalk foliage. That said, as city streets went, ours was as suburban as one could find in New York. The kids on the block played on the street, moms yelling out the window to call them in for dinner. The older residents sat on their stoops for hours, greeting passersby. No litter, no honking. Glorious (almost competitive) flower boxes added splashes of color, even in September.

Our building was at the head of the block, our apartment on the top two floors of our building. My parents—Gloria and Ed Benet—and my thirteen-year-old sister, Joya, were in the eat-in kitchen downstairs, already busy with breakfast. My mother sipped from the mug of coffee that might as well have been fused with the flesh of her hand. She was wearing a bathrobe, blue with yellow embroidered cats. Dad was wearing his, yellow with blue embroidered dogs. They had his-and-her everything. Their lives—professional and personal—were matchy-matchy. Mom and Dad looked up from the *Times* (in unison), showing off toothy his-and-her smiles.

Mom said, "You look so pretty!"

Dad, rising, asked, "What can I get you for breakfast? Eggs? Pancakes?"

Mom followed with, "Big day. It's only natural to have some anxiety about junior year. If you want to talk about anything—anything at all—I'm available. Sex, drugs, peer pressure, SATs, social ambition. Any topic is open for discussion. Your father and I will reserve judgment. We'll just listen."

Dad added, "But only if you want to talk. We wouldn't think of intruding on your privacy. So. Food? Whatever you want. I'll make it fresh. Just name your pleasure."

All this before I'd said a single word.

Why couldn't I have normal parents with normal jobs? I thought, looking at them study me as if I were a hundred-ten-pound lab rat, their teen (and team) project.

I said, "I'm meeting Eli and Liza at Grind."

We'd had a ritual since second grade, holding a first-day-of-school meeting to map the upcoming greatest-year-of-our-lives-thus-far. We used to gather in one of our apartments (before the Great Dispersal, our three families lived in apartments on consecutive floors of a town house on Hicks Street, just around the corner from where I lived now). In seventh grade, when we'd been permitted to roam the streets without a parent or babysitter, we started meeting at Grind, our favorite café on Montague Street.

Joya asked, "Can I come, Dora? I won't talk. I'll be invisible. You won't even know I'm there. I'll blend into the wall. I'll be human wallpaper."

My kid sister was, on the attractiveness spectrum, ethereal. She had an airy-fairy light around her, soft and glowing, mink brown hair, saucer-of-chocolate eyes, dusting of tawny freckles across the bridge of her button nose, sky-high cheekbones, a heart-shaped face. She had the large head and lithe body of a dancer on the verge of explosive growth. Joya caught attention lazily, effortlessly, like a butterfly in a net, without seeming to be aware of her automatic appeal. She acted oblivious to stares, oblivious to everyone and everything, except her best (and only) friend, Ben Teare, and her precious art projects, the comic books she'd been writing and illustrating since she was six. Even if Joya *wanted* to be human wallpaper, she was, perhaps unintentionally, a centerpiece at any table. She'd asked me every year if she could come along to the first-day meeting at Grind. And every year I refused.

I said, "Tell you what, Joya, this year, if you want, you can stand outside the café and watch us through the window."

"Adora!" snapped Mom.

"Why are you so mean to her?" asked Dad.

Mom and Dad often predicted that, when we're twenty-five and twenty-eight, Joya and I will be best buds. That remained to be seen. At thirteen and sixteen, as we were now, I could barely stand her. She was the happy humming machine I wanted to turn off. Only a few days ago, I'd accidentally (on purpose) spilled OJ on one of her drawings—and she forgave me instantly, which made me furious. Joya was pathologically forgiving, helpful and sweet. Mom and Dad always said she filled their hearts with joy. Which filled my mouth with vomit.

According to an article I read in *Time* magazine, every person was born with a set point of happiness. Life events—ecstatic and/or tragic—could move the needle to the right or left, but eventually one would revert back to her set point. Joya's needle was pinned to the right of the dial. She was born happy.

My born disposition? I liked to think of myself as cynically optimistic.

To Mom and Dad, I said, "I want to be alone with my friends! Is that so hard to understand? Can't I say or do anything without the guilt trip, or emotional harassment, or your looking at me like I've just grown a second head?"

The three members of my family absorbed my outburst.

Then Dad said, "Is that my tie?"

Mom asked, "Do you need money?"

## 2

"Open it," said Liza at Grind fifteen minutes later.

"Can I use my teeth?" asked Eli, holding up the cube, as awed as I was by the impressive wrapping job.

The package had been at my place at the table when I arrived at Grind. A small square box, one for each of us. Liza had brought them, and even wrapped her own, just so we could unwrap them together. Liza was a gift-giver, surprising Eli and me with small packages, tiny tokens of her unflinching, undying devotion to our threesome. I loved it. Eli, though, was slightly uncomfortable about receiving. She didn't want to be indebted to anyone, even Liza. We all tore off the wrapping and beheld her latest offering.

Liza said, "I saw these at a novelty shop in the Village and knew we'd all want one for our very own."

I examined my denuded box. "The Sarcastic Ball?" I asked, opening the lid to find what looked like one of those black Magic Eight Balls, with the message-bearing decagon floating in blue fluid inside.

"Ask it a question, shake and read the answer," said Liza, excited and eager.

Eli held her black sphere and asked, "Will Liza ever stop wasting her money on junk?" She shook the ball and waited for the decagon inside to surface and show the message in the round window. It read: "Yeah, right."

I laughed. "Will Vin Transom finally fall sway to my wiles, after three years of active crushing, aggressive flirtation, and sharing dozens of what I hoped would be witty conversations that usually ended up as the mutual exchange of long, uncomfortable silences?"

Liza said, "That's too broad. You should keep the question as specific as possible."

"Will I see some action this year?" I asked, shaking the ball and waiting for the answer.

It read: "You wish."

"I already knew that," I groaned.

Eli said, "So far, the Sarcastic Ball is one hundred percent accurate."

Liza shook her ball and asked, "Would it help if Dora stopped running *after* Vin, and ran *alongside* him?"

"'You've got to be kidding,'" I said, reading the message aloud. "I second that. I'm not a masochist." Vin Transom was a runner, a tracklete, the only member of the Brownstone Institute community to finish the New York City Marathon two years in a row. In the full bloom of my crush last year, I'd attempted to jog across the Brooklyn Bridge, which was a three-mile round-trip from Garden Place. I got as far as Grind (three blocks from my house) and decided to stop for a restorative iced coffee.

"I was referring to running in a metaphorical sense," Liza said, then asked another question: "Will I get over Max Lindsey and move on to bigger and better things?"

"You can't possibly move on to smaller things," sneered Eli.

Max Lindsey was just five feet tall, scary scrawny (which made him and Liza look like the number 18 walking down the street together). He was also chess king at Brownstone, the borough champ and runner-up in a citywide competition last March. In any suburban town, being a chess genius might doom a boy to perpetual geekdom. But chess was, as far as New York private schools went, the true measure of a kid's mind. Max Lindsey, if lacking in stature and girth, had the beefiest brain in school. He knew it, and he strutted around the halls, all five feet of him, with the cockiness of a pro wrestler. A mite in size, Max was mighty in confidence. Like Napoleon.

I sipped my iced coffee, extra sugar and cream. Despite the sweetness, the beverage had a bitter aftertaste. Liza and I shared the bad habit of chasing after boys who didn't seem to care about us. Vin barely registered me as a living, breathing life-form. Max strung Liza along, cruelly, I thought. Calling her once in a while, going out maybe once a month. Nothing consistent, but just often enough to be maddeningly regular.

Liza shook the Sarcastic Ball and said, "Again, will I free myself from the romantic goggle-vision of Max Lindsey and see him for the loser he truly is?"

The sphere read: "Yeah, and I'm the Pope."

The three of us snort-laughed, and a dribble of iced coffee leaked out of the corner of my mouth.

I said, "Come on, Eli. Ask something real."

She said, "Real, meaning *what*? A question about boys? Is that what's real to you?"

I whispered to Liza, "Here it comes."

"Don't you want to know if the year ahead will be a turning point, an accumulation of insight and understanding of the bigger picture? Don't you guys care about world hunger? Endangered wildlife? Global warming?"

Liza and I looked at each other, eyes rolling. I said, "Ask about Jack Carp."

Eli sighed (exasperatedly) and said, "Fine. O, Great Sarcastic Ball, cosmic all-seeing and all-knowing entity disguised as a cheap piece of plastic made in a Hong Kong factory by five-year-old orphans, will Jack Carp and I have sex soon?"

Jack Carp was Eli's boyfriend of six months. When they'd started dating, I had given them two months. They'd lasted through the summer, much to my surprise. He existed on the dark side, wearing all black, all the time, including black Chuck Connors and a black hoop earring in his left lobe. He had a nose pierce, which, frankly, disgusted me, and a small tattoo of a goldfish (aka, a carp) on his right bicep. Like Eli, he was a piano prodigy, excelling at creepy and morose sonatas by Bartók and Prokofiev. Eli and Jack had spent years together in after-school piano lessons with Mr. Yamora, the Brownstone instructor, competing with each other fiercely, glaring at each other across their face-to-face uprights in the music room. Last March, while pounding out a Stravinsky duet, everything changed. They looked over their instruments, into each other's eyes, and heard high notes of a different sort.

I said, "If you want to have sex so badly, why don't you?"

"It's not as easy as you think," said Eli, shaking the Sarcastic Ball. "It requires planning—birth control, a place to go. He'd do it standing up in the basement bathroom at Brownstone. But can you imagine me losing my virginity in such gross surroundings?"

Honestly, I didn't want to imagine my friend having sex at all. But, if forced, I agreed that Eli wasn't the basement-bathroom-quickie type.

Eli repeated her question: "Me, Jack, a bed, a condom,

sometime before lines appear on my face and my hair turns gray?"

The ball read: "Ask me if I care."

Eli shook the ball again and said, "Are you punishing me for saying Liza wasted her money on you?"

The ball replied: "What*ever*."

# 3

The Brownstone Collegiate Institute was founded in 1855 as an academy for aspiring teenage nuns. The main building (which annexed several of the neighboring structures over the decades) showcased a chapel with stained-glass windows and a huge organ. Sometimes, I swear, I heard ghost nuns shushing through the halls in their black wool habits and wimples.

For the past seventy years, the classrooms had been filled with secular students, grades pre-K through twelve. Brownstoners (as we called ourselves) were culturally diverse—multiethnic with a smattering of religious backgrounds. The majority of the students' parents had sufficient wealth to float the tuition, along with the sideways liberal logic of gleefully paying taxes to support public schools but lacking the gumption to send their kids to one.

This was by no means a snarky complaint. I became a student at the school long before I understood why "Brownstoner" was funny. Graduates were funneled into the nation's top colleges. Alumni included scholars, authors, politicians, and scientists. I should be grateful to attend.

I really should be.

Pushing any negative thoughts from my mind, I recited my mantra: "This is *my year*" as Liza, Eli and I approached the massive, arched, twelve-panel oak front door.

Eli asked, "What are you muttering?"

"Am I as hot as the surface of the sun?"

"You are whatever you want to be," intoned Liza, whose looks *and* philosophies were decidedly Californian.

We inhaled deeply and entered the uncharted world called Eleventh Grade.

We were not two feet inside when Eli said, "Oh, shit."

Unavoidably, we'd stepped right into the viper's nest. Sondra Fortune, unofficial head of the Ruling Class in the unspoken-but-understood Brownstone social hierarchy, was holding court by the security desk in the front hall. Evil twins Lori and Micha Dropov bookended Sondra as she greeted incoming students like the social director on a cruise ship.

All smiles and kissy-kissy and "You look amazing!" and "I missed you so so so much this summer!"

That *bitch*.

I tried to hustle by unscathed, but Sondra's gaze fell on me like a hammer. She beamed, huge white smile splayed across her caramel-colored face.

"Fringe Girl!" she hollered.

I cringed, but obeyed my summons. "Hey, Sondra!" Grinning like an idiot, I went over to kiss her cheek.

She said, "I haven't seen you all summer! I missed you, girl! Why didn't you call me?" She actually pouted. Lori and Micha Dropov giggled.

"I was out of town," I said. "On a Teen Tour."

"What the hell is a Teen Tour?" asked Sondra.

"You fly to Denver and then travel across the American West in a bus with thirty other kids, visiting giant holes in the ground, huge piles of rocks and loud geysers. We stayed at campgrounds and slept in tents. It was deeply, grubbily enlightening."

Sondra gasped at my gritty tale. The evil twins seemed shocked—shocked!—by the filth. I should have stopped there, when they were speechless, but I went on. Why? I asked myself, even as my lips flapped. Because being ignored by Sondra was worse than being ridiculed by her.

"Yeah," I continued. "The highlights of the summer were when one boy got busted for shoplifting a T-shirt in Calgary and was sent home to Long Island. Another girl was bitten by a scorpion in Arizona, and her arm blew up. And one girl swallowed water at the Great Salt Lake and had to be rushed to a Mormon doctor, who gave her two prayers and told her to call God in the morning."

Eli and Liza, who stood behind me, laughed.

Sondra didn't. She said, "My God, Fringe! I thought I had a grand adventure interning for Anna Sui, helping design her fall collection."

Eli said, "Really? Tell us more. We're dying to hear all about it." She had her straight face on, eyes flat and dark as coal. Sondra didn't know how to reply, clearly wondering whether Eli was making fun of her. (YES!) Sondra never knew what to make of Eli, and, like many others, she was a bit intimidated by her.

Liza let slip a giggle at Sondra's bafflement. Mistake. Sondra focused her antipathy on poor Liza, who hadn't invented a coping strategy for dealing with Sondra. I had my make-her-laugh ploy. Eli used the ironic-confusion gambit. Liza had nothing.

Sondra asked, "And what did you do this summer, Ms. Liza?"

Liza replied, "I visited my father in Bermuda, and then my mom and I spent a few weeks on Long Beach Island."

Micha said, "Your surfer dude dad?"

Lori said, "Long Beach Island? That's in *New Jersey*, right?"

Sondra supplied the kicker: "Come on, now, guys. Don't make fun of Ms. Liza on the first day."

And that was all she needed to say.

For the record, downtown Brooklynites were not snobs. Our quaint borough, at least this corner of it, was overrun with lefty organic urban hippies who cared less about "things" than "issues and ideas." Sondra was an exception. She lived on Columbia Heights, the most desirable block in Brooklyn. Her building sat on the edge of the Promenade—a walkway on the rim of the borough overlooking the East River. Out of her bedroom window, Sondra had a front-row view of Manhattan, two rivers, four famous bridges and the Statue of Liberty. Sondra couldn't help her snobbery, having been lavished with praise for her unusual beauty (she was half black and half Japanese) since birth. When we were in second grade, Sondra appeared in a Gap Kids ad wearing an orange scarf and a striped blue and green sweater. Her face appeared on every bus shelter, Gap store window, even a billboard in Times Square. It was then, when we were eight, that Sondra's superiority was sealed.

Lori and Micha's snobbery came, in part, from their address, too. They lived in Tribeca, in Manhattan, in a huge loft on Franklin Street. Their parents, both Russian diplomats, were mysterious and sexy. Whenever I saw Madam Dropov (about three times in ten years), she was wearing four-inch sandals, even in the dead of winter, and a sable coat. Lori and Micha had never been models, although they were identically gorgeous, with Slavic bone structure, light blue eyes, shiny straight sandy hair and neat ballet bodies. Second tier to Sondra, the evil twins outclassed their leader in snideness, and they showed off their viciousness for her pleasure.

A fresh group of students came through the front door, momentarily distracting Sondra. I tried to slip away, but the ex-Gap model ensnared my wrist and said, "Don't go anywhere, Fringe Girl. We *have* to talk more."

I faded a few steps back. Eli hissed in my ear, "When are you going to tell her to stop calling you Fringe Girl?"

"I don't mind it," I said. The truth? I did mind, but I was used to it. I'd had the nickname since sixth grade when a new girl from London, Cosima, informed the class that in England they called bangs "fringe." I had bangs, as did Eli and Liza then, and Cosima started calling us the Fringe Girls. Eli had only to give the Brit one drop-dead eye glare to stop the taunts to her. Liza took to the nickname with good-natured surrender, which didn't make teasing her any fun and therefore a waste of time. I bristled, protested, complained, however, and the nickname stuck on me like Gorilla Glue. Around eighth grade, I tried embracing it (I was on a pop psychology binge then), and I bought a suede jacket with strands of soft fringe that hung from the arms. But just when I started to get into the Fringe Girl thing, most everyone stopped using it.

Except Sondra. She wouldn't let it go. I had a theory why: Sondra recognized that my erstwhile nickname fit, not just for the bangs (which I still had) or the jacket (ditto). I was, then and always, on the fringe of the social order at Brownstone. I counted myself not among the lowly ranked Teeming Masses, nor an exalted member of the Ruling Class. I hovered on the edge, on the fringe. I was a Fringe Dweller. The most unstable rung on the social ladder.

Eli was above social posturing. Liza downplayed the significance. They gave up caring in middle school, safe and secure on our island for three. My parents repeatedly espoused, "All you need are two close friends." For Eli and Liza, that was true. But I was haunted by my precarious placement, craved approval from girls like Sondra and was afraid of slipping off the fringe into oblivion. Like a shark in bloody water, Sondra could smell my fear. And she didn't want me to forget it. Hence, she reminded me by calling me Fringe Girl.

Liza whispered, "There's Max."

Max Lindsey strutted through the front doors, his backpack bursting with who knew what, his dirty brown hair too long, his jeans riding low. He looked exactly the same as the last time I'd seen him, with one enormous change: Over the summer, Max had grown five inches.

Eli said, "He's tall enough to go on rides at Disney World now."

I added, "Max Lindsey: a tower of power?"

Liza beamed with secret pride at his growth. She gave him a modest half wave. He cocked his chin at her in silent acknowledgment but no enthusiasm. A blow-off. My curvy friend's face fell. Clearly she'd been expecting more from him. A lot more.

Eli and I squinted at each other in puzzlement. I asked, "Liza, when you told us you'd been good and hadn't called, e-mailed, IMed, text-messaged, paged or staked out Max all summer, were you lying?"

"I checked in with him a few times," she admitted.

"How many?" I asked.

"A dozen," she said. "Give or take a dozen."

Eli and I groaned. And then the three of us watched in shock and horror as the newly tall chess king Max Lindsey made his move. He strutted over to Lori Dropov, leaned (down!) and kissed her on the lips in front of everyone.

"That is the most disgusting thing I've ever seen," said Eli.

I was looking at the saddest thing I'd ever seen: Liza fighting back tears. For a crazy half second, I wondered if Sondra had held us back so Liza would witness the spectacle.

I said, "Let's go." Eli and I started to push through the congested front hallway to get Liza out of there before she lost it.

But Sondra had other plans. She said loudly, "Fringe Girl, wait up. I wanted to ask you something."

My blood froze. Instinct told me she would not be asking, "How can I make your life easier?"

I stopped. Waited for it.

Sondra produced a copy of the latest *Cosmo* magazine, and flipped to the page she'd folded down. She opened to a spread that featured a hot couple lying on a rumpled bed together, showing it to the crowd around her. She cleared her throat dramatically, and waited for the clustered people to give her their attention, which they did, slavishly. She read the title of the article aloud. " 'How to Get a Man to Notice You, by Gloria and Ed Benet, excerpted from their new book, *His-and-Her Seduction*.' "

Randy hoots and chuckles from some boys behind me. I felt my face flush. My throat went dry.

Sondra read on: " 'Ever wanted a man so badly that you'd do anything to get him? Well, why are you doing nothing? Below, ten no-excuses swear-by tips and tricks that make getting the man you crave as easy as snapping your fingers.' "

Lori and Micha were outright howling at this point. Raising one eyebrow, Sondra asked, "So, Fringe Girl, with seduction experts for parents, you must know how it's done. Any luck this summer? Get to use any of their no-excuses tips and tricks on your *Teen Tour*? Or was the highlight of your vacation really watching some stupid girl get stung by a bug?"

Micha mocked, " 'As easy as snapping your fingers.' "

And then she started snapping. Lori and Sondra joined in. As did the twenty people who'd witnessed my humiliation. I stood at the center of this crowd of snapping assholes and took it. I was great at taking it. Taking it with a smile was my special skill, what put me on a higher moral ground. I smiled and nodded as the snapping died down.

Then I said, "It wasn't just any bug. It was a scorpion."

Sondra laughed and said, "I stand corrected."

I could tell by her expression that she was done with me and was ready for a new victim. Released from my punishment, I spun around and found myself inches from Vin Transom.

I nearly gasped out loud. He was with his tracklete friends. I suspected they'd been the horny hooters behind me. But Vin couldn't have been one of them. He wasn't a crass idiot. We made eye contact, and then he looked over my shoulder. He was embarrassed for me.

I blinked, I sputtered. I nearly lost the cool I'd been fighting to maintain. Eli, fortunately, never lost hers, and she put an arm around me and guided me out of hostile territory. Liza was still furtively checking out Max and Lori. I glanced back at Sondra as we were hurrying away. She smiled brightly at me and waved as if to say, "No hard feelings!"

"Hard" did not begin to describe my feelings . . . No. Correction: It did *begin* to describe my feelings about Sondra—and the rest of the conversation would last all night long.

## HOW TO GET A MAN TO NOTICE YOU
*by Gloria and Ed Benet*
*(excerpted from* His-and-Her Seduction*)*

Ever wanted a man so badly that you'd do *anything* to get him? Well, what are you waiting for? Below, ten no-excuses swear-by tips and tricks that make getting the man you crave as easy as snapping your fingers.

I got Ed to notice me by sitting in front of him in our college poetry class. Despite positioning myself directly between his chair and the professor's lectern, I might as well have been invisible to him. But then he dropped his textbook, and I leaned down to pick it up . . .

Ahem. If I, Ed, may interject. I dropped my book on purpose to get Gloria to speak! She'd been purposely blocking my view all semester, but she never talked. I feared she might be pathologically shy.

Amazing but true: A man hopscotches from a woman's nervous passivity to her having a mental defect in one quick jump. Make sure that doesn't happen to you. We suggest starting soft, but keeping the sledgehammer in your back pocket for emergencies.

### Gloria's Subtle Stealth Maneuvers

1  Block his view. I stand by my own success. Put yourself directly in his line of vision. This is especially useful at a concert, play, movie theater, or sports event. He'll ask you to move. You should: (a) apologize and ask if the seat next to him is available, or (b) beg forgiveness with such sincerity that he'll want to make it up to you by buying you dinner.

2  Give him the eye. The wink has a cheese-ball reputation. But if you play it for ironic/comic effect, you can get more bang for the blink. Do your thing—a purposeful, two-second lid-flicker—and then rub your eye as if something

was irritating it. Do it with a wicked half smile, and he'll be confused—and intrigued—by your action.

3   Remove your sandals. You'd be surprised how many men are foot fetishists. Dangling a sandal by the toe, or removing it and then rubbing the arch of your foot against the back of your calf. Every man in the room will be fixated. FYI: Pedicures are required.

4   Sneeze. A cute, delicate, dainty nasal exclamation into a clean and embroidered cotton handkerchief will turn heads. He'll be immediately concerned for your fragile health and impressed by your accessories. This is a staged event. Real honking, juicy sneezes are NOT sexy.

5   Stumble. A charming little tangle with your hem when he's nearby will guarantee notice. Men love a woman who's a bit of a klutz. They think it means she's distracted by thoughts of sex. If he catches you before you fall, he'll feel like a hero, and you will have wound up in his arms.

## Ed's Bold Breakthroughs

1   Compete for a seat. If he's just entering a taxi, slide in next to him and suggest a share. If he's grabbing the last seat on the bus or subway, make like you went for it at the same time and plop down on his lap.

2   Steal a fry. This works for (forgive me, world!) slender women only. You see him eating lunch alone in the park, at the office cafeteria, at a restaurant. Sit down next to him and snag a French fry. Or a pickle. Any neat morsel will do. Pop it in your mouth, chew with zeal. Smile and be sure to say, "Thank you."

3   Whistle. Loud. Use your fingers. Then, when he turns around to see where the noise came from, pretend to be looking around, too. Ask, "What was *that*?"

4  Accidental brushing. Use your assets. Good for crowded elevators.

5  Crash. If all else fails, go for a big, ugly, purse-and-briefcase-flying collision that puts both of you on your arses. The guy simply can't help but notice you (and, ideally, your gorgeous legs) if you're sitting on the sidewalk, or in the hallway, or on the floor of the conference room together. Two friendly warnings: Timing is key. Also, this is a one-time-only move. Do it twice, and he might take out a protective order against you.

# 4

Gloria and Ed Benet, my parents, were advice columnists for the *New York Moon* weekly newspaper, contributors to all the major magazines and authors of self-help books, including their latest, *His-and-Her Seduction*, and previous best sellers *His-and-Her Dating*, *His-and-Her Weddings*, *His-and-Her Marriage* and *His-and-Her Divorce*. (Only in their world was divorce an opportunity to grow closer as a couple.) They'd appeared on *Oprah* three times, and did monthly NPR segments. Mom and Dad weren't shrinks or therapists, just good writers with a gimmick. As far as I could tell, they were unqualified to dispense advice to anyone, since they were so bad at giving it to me. But readers loved their trademark kooky common sense, and I shouldn't complain, because their book sales and column fees had made them—us—comfortable. Money was distorted in Brooklyn Heights. Anywhere else, our family would be considered loaded. But here, in the richest section of the hottest borough in New York City, we were doing just all right.

Usually, Mom and Dad wrote about emotional issues ("My husband is a shit. Help!" or "My girlfriend is a bitch! Help!"). Sometimes (the times I wished I were an insect under a rock), my parents doled out sex advice. This was beyond mortifying. Adults shouldn't have anything to do with sex. And no daughter on earth should have to contemplate the fact that her parents . . . Honestly, I didn't even want to finish the sentence. The luxury of blissful ignorance was beyond me. My parents advised about—granted, other people's—sex in the *Moon*. (If only they were ON the moon.) Clearly, they had *some* experience. And anyone with two quarters to scratch together could buy the paper and read all about it. If their byline wasn't bad enough, a cutesy picture of Mom and Dad ran alongside the *Moon* column. At fifty, Mom was a grown-up version of Joya—dark, petite, wide-eyed and pointy-chinned. Dad, who was fifty-one, was the masculine grown-up version of me—devastatingly attractive, a genius, hilarious. Seriously, he wasn't fat, and he still had his hair.

When I got home from school that first day, Mom and Dad came rushing out of the home office to greet me.

I said, "Mountains of homework," stopping them midstep, and rushed up the stairs to my room before they could bombard me with questions.

Ten minutes later, however, Mom pawed at my door like a lonesome puppy. "Adora? Are you all right?" she asked.

"I'm fine," I snapped.

"Where are Eli and Liza?"

"Eli has piano and Liza has to help her mom with something."

"You usually don't come home at three fifteen, run up to your room and lock the door," she observed.

Should I tell her the truth? That their *Cosmo* article was the source of my abject mortification, ruining my first day of school of what was supposed to be MY YEAR? All day long, kids snapped their fingers at me in the hall between classes. I dreaded the idea that this little joke would plague me for months, if not years, to come. I wanted to tell Mom what she'd inadvertently done. To blame her, to make her feel so horrible that she'd have to drown her sorrows by eating an entire quiche.

I sprang off my bed and flung open my bedroom door.

Mom flinched, not expecting my sudden movement.

"Why did you name me Adora?" I asked, not sure where that came from. "Good gravy, Mother! Did you want to embarrass me every time I filled out a form?"

Mom regained her composure and said, "Odd as it might seem now, you were an absolutely adorable baby."

"I suppose you think I should see a shrink." Mom and Dad had been trying to get me in therapy for years, offering a shrink like cake on a plate, as in, "Here, darling, have a yummy psychologist. So delicious, and good for you!"

Mom smiled and asked patiently, "Do *you* think you need a therapist?"

In return, I uttered an impatient "ARGHH!!&#$!" and shut the door again. I didn't slam it. My mother had created the ideal environment for my cynicism (albeit optimistic), but she hadn't raised me to be rude.

Eventually, hunger set in. I ventured downstairs in search of food. Mom and Dad were still in their office, working on *His-and-Her Reconciliation*, and Joya was alone at the dining room table, eating a sandwich of her own construction.

She smiled brightly at me. I scowled at her. "Want half?" she asked, already reaching for the knife.

I shrugged and got a plate. As she sliced into the whole wheat bread, through the turkey and Swiss, the tomato, lettuce, slaw, Russian, chopped liver and pickles, she asked sunnily, "How was your first day of school?"

Her innocence and lack of ironic inflection galled me. I said, "Fine. And you?"

"Great! Ben and I are in three of the same classes, and I placed in Ms. Gligman's invitation-only advanced drawing seminar. I'm the only eighth grader in the class—by special permission."

She rambled on and on, and I realized, uncomfortably, that Joya really did live in her own shiny, sparkly world. Nothing as mundane as snapping fingers and social torment would put her on edge. I respected her (grudgingly)—and pitied her for it.

"Doesn't it bother you that people think you're a flake?"

"People?" she asked. "Meaning you?"

"Forget I asked."

"I don't care what you think about me now. When we're twenty-five and twenty-eight, we're going to be best friends. Until then, I can take whatever you throw at me."

This made my temples throb. I took my sandwich and went back upstairs, violating my own no-food-in-room policy (my shag carpet plus crumbs was a recipe for disastrous vacuuming). When I finished eating, I lay back on my bed and rubbed my full belly. I reached into my backpack and found the Sarcastic Ball.

Giving it a good shake, I asked, "Will Joya and I be best friends when we're twenty-five and twenty-eight?"

It read: "Duh."

Which made me throw the ball across the room.

# 5

The French Revolution, FYI, was largely defined by the lopping off of people's heads via the swift and thorough guillotine. The guillotine was a dastardly invention. How it worked: The victim would be forced to get on his knees, lower his head onto a curved slot of the guillotine's base. The executioner released a blade hanging above, which careened down at great speed, chopping off the victim's head in one deadly slice. The body remained in the same kneeling position. The liberated head dropped into a basket.

"And here's the really creepy part," said Mr. Sagebrush, one of the upper school's social studies teachers. "After decapitation, the brain continued to function for up to ten seconds. Meaning, the head would continue to see and hear after it'd been chopped off. You'd see the inside of the basket! You'd hear the roar of the crowd, thousands of Parisians cheering your execution."

After sharing that indeed creepy interlude, Mr. Sagebrush bored into the eyes of the front-row students. He loved theatrics—and meaningful eye contact. His intense gaze demanded a reaction. Whenever it hit me, I gave him an expression of "amazement!" or "disbelief!" or "enriched by learning!" Only then would he move on to someone else.

He said, "Yes, question, Mr. Kepner."

"Could the head *smell*, too? And taste?" asked Noel Kepner, center on the soccer team, sax player for the jazz duo Lump (they had actual paying gigs), star as Gandalf in the upper school stage adaptation of *The Hobbit* last year. In class, he was constantly raising his hand to offer an opinion, as if his ideas were golden rays, shedding the light of truth on all those lucky enough to bask in them. Noel was tall, over six feet, blue eyes, shaggy brown hair, rolling walk. He nodded at people as they passed him in the hallway, like the leader of the pack—or king of the Ruling Class, which he was. By all appearances, he was a snotty, conceited overachieving show-off. He changed girlfriends like T-shirts, but was currently unattached. Maybe that was because he'd worked his way through the entire Ruling Class dating pool, including (on and off) Sondra Fortune and (for five minutes) Micha Dropov.

Mr. Sagebrush said, "I don't know for sure, so I'll say yes. The decapitated head could probably smell and taste the blood."

The class made a collective "Ewww."

Mr. Sagebrush quieted the room by raising his arms. "Okay, okay. We've been talking about violent revolution for a week already. And it's been very gory, all the beheadings and disembowelings and bodies crushed with tanks and whatnot. But now I want to shift to nonviolent revolution. The bloodless coup d'état, or relatively peaceful overthrow of state."

Eli, seated a few rows back to my right, caught my eye and held up her phone.

I turned mine on. A text message appeared. "Major news."

I squeaked. Mr. Sagebrush gave me his most penetrating eye contact. I offered him a look of "insatiable thirst for knowledge," and he turned his back to the class and started scribbling on the whiteboard. At Brownstone, the whiteboards were digitized. Students didn't have to take notes during class, because anything on the board could be uploaded onto our laptops.

At the lull, half the students checked their e-mail and text messages.

I texted back to Eli, "How major?"

She wrote, "Übermajor."

It was 11:50 on Thursday. In ten minutes, we'd be free for our lunch hour. I texted, "Grind?"

Eli gave me the high sign (a mime of drinking a hot beverage). I nodded. Mr. Sagebrush, meanwhile, turned back toward the class (resulting in the instant hiding of phones) and said, "These are the three tenets of bloodless revolution." He'd written:

1 Undermine authority.
2 Present an alternative government.
3 Enlist the masses.

"We'll talk more about examples in history next week. But for now, I want you to think about how revolutionaries might attempt to achieve the undermining of authority. Also, start thinking of a term project. Proposals should be e-mailed to me by a week from Monday. Pick any revolution in ancient or modern history and chart its course. Yes, Mr. Kepner."

"Can we team up with partners? Like, if we wanted to reenact scenes from a revolution?"

"That would be great," said Mr. Sagebrush, who practically bathed in fake blood every Halloween for his infamous Dracula costume.

Noel and Stanley Nable looked at each other and said, "Sweet."

Stanley was a bass player (the other half of Lump), also a soccer genius, Ruling Classer, tall, handsome. He had perfectly smooth brown-colored skin and a nearly shorn head, warm deep dark eyes that had transfixed me since kindergarten. Liza had a brief make-out session with him in ninth grade. She said he was delectable indeed. She'd gotten just the one sample, though. As soon as Sondra saw him with Liza, she took him for herself. That lasted all of ten minutes, but it was enough to intimidate Liza away from Stanley for good.

Mr. Sagebrush let us leave two minutes early, but not before assigning us a hundred pages of reading for the weekend. We'd see him again on Tuesday. Less than two weeks into the new school year, social studies was shaping up to be the best class of the semester. Penetrating eye contact aside, I liked Mr. Sagebrush and his sweater vests. More importantly, I could tell he liked me. He'd been feeding me a steady diet of looks that said, "dazzle me." And I shot back tart glances that said, "I dazzle at my own pleasure."

In any event, he was the one teacher of the year who hadn't asked me about my parents' latest appearance on the *Today* show.

Liza was waiting for us in the hallway outside Mr. Sagebrush's classroom. She was gnawing on a Snickers bar like a gerbil. Eli said, "What's wrong?"

Our sunshine blond friend pointed her candy bar down the hallway. Under an archway (the halls were full of high arches and columns, holdovers from the nunnery days), I spied a couple in full snog, sucking face as if they would find gold on each other's incisors. I recognized the stick-figure silhouette of one of the Dropov twins. Lori, judging by the slightly shorter hair. I couldn't see the boy's face clearly. But he looked vaguely sexy.

Liza said, "Lori is after something from Max. It's obvious!

Maybe she's using him to get an in with the chess club? I have to protect him. She'll eat Max alive!"

Eli said, "Looks like she's already started."

That was Max? My, he *had* changed. I said, "I doubt Lori Dropov is campaigning for a spot in the chess club. And so what if she is? That's their problem. You don't owe him help or protection or anything."

At that moment, Sondra and Micha paraded by. They smiled sweetly at us, as they always did (part of their subversive insidiousness to make Fringe Dwellers feel comfortable only to pull the rug out from under them when they least expected it). They went straight over to Noel Kepner and Stanley Nable. What a pretty foursome they made. The two highest-ranking junior Ruling Class girls and their male counterparts.

Kids in the hallway watched the quartet—waiting and hoping to see something good. They were the movie stars of the school, and everyone else was a worshipful, lowly fan.

Well, not everyone. I ground my teeth, brushed aside my bangs. I hated this spectacle. Why did they deserve so much notice and attention? I wondered. I turned my back on Sondra's klatch. Out of sight, out of mind.

Envy was abhorrent. Really, I had no idea why I felt this way, and I detested myself for it.

Eli said, "Weren't we just leaving?"

"Yes," I said. "To Grind! Away!" I pointed Liza's shoulders down the hall, and we made for the rear stairway.

"Hey, Fringe Girl!" sang Sondra, making my neck hairs salute.

I stopped, plastered a smile on and turned around. Sondra made a beeline for us. Her demeanor was sweetness and innocence.

That *snake*.

When she and henchgirl Micha were upon us, Sondra asked, "Are you guys going out for lunch?"

"To Grind," I said. "Want to come?"

Eli growled under her breath.

Sondra said to Liza, "Yum, Snickers."

Liza handed Sondra her candy bar, assuming she wanted a bite. Sondra took it, but instead of giving it a nibble, she made a *tsk-tsk* sound and patted Liza's pleasantly plump belly. Then Sondra threw the candy in the garbage can behind her, as if she were doing Liza a favor.

"We're going to Monty's for pizza," said Sondra. The invitation was implied, but unspoken. She'd drawn an invisible hoop, and was daring me to jump through it.

My two real friends were stone silent. Eli would skin me alive if I went with Sondra. Liza was still in shock over the Snickers incident.

How did she do it? I wondered. Sondra could turn a simple lunch invitation into an emotional high-wire act.

Noel Kepner interjected, "Let's all go to Grind. I'm sick of pizza."

Stanley seemed to be looking at Liza when he said, "Sounds good to me."

Eli said, "Actually, the three of us wanted privacy."

Sondra and Micha laughed at her brazen rejection. "Message received," said Sondra in high snark. She spun on her heel and headed down the hall, Micha and the boys in her wake. Along the way, they collected Lori and Max and disappeared down the front stairs.

I felt my lungs empty with relief. Eli said, "For a sickening nanosecond, I thought you were going to choose them over us."

"That is sickening," I said. "I've lost my appetite.'

We ended up eating in the school cafeteria, Chez Brownstone, a Gothic, cathedral-like, buttressed cafeteria that looked a lot like the dining room at Hogwarts, complete with stained-glass windows and twenty-foot-long tables. The food choices were all organic and healthy. The lower school parents' association held a protest a few years ago, demanding that every item on the menu be nutritionally sound. The quality of the food went up, as did the prices, and the upper school cafeteria traffic declined. The only popular cafeteria lunch day for juniors was Thursday, wrap sandwich day.

We threw our backpacks on one of the few private tables in the room. Liza and I got wraps. Eli chose a bagel and two hard-boiled eggs.

Once we were seated, I said, "If Sondra took away my candy, I would rip her arm off."

Liza shrugged. "I shouldn't be eating Snickers anyway."

Eli said, "But no one has the right to tell you what you should eat. Except the lower school PA."

"Tell that to my mom," said Liza. "The way she acts, it's like she gains five pounds whenever I eat a cookie." Liza's parents divorced four years ago. Ryan Greene moved to Bermuda and now ran snorkeling tours. He was the ultimate absent father. He never came back to New York. Stephanie Greene, Liza's mom, had to sell the Hicks Street apartment in the building we grew up in (the Greenes were the last of our three families to relocate) and move to a smaller place in Cobble Hill, a neighborhood one over and less expensive than Brooklyn Heights. Liza's older brother, Matt, had started college by then, so the last several years had been the Stephanie and Liza Greene show.

"Vin Transom just walked in," whispered Liza.

"Does he see us?" I asked.

"Not sure," said Liza. "He's walking down our aisle. He's getting closer."

I took a sip of coffee to distract myself.

Then Eli said, "I had sex last night."

I spit the coffee. Right on the floor, inches from Vin Transom's feet. He stopped and looked at his New Balance sneakers. A few drops of regurgitated brown liquid had marred the pristine white laces. I dared to look up at him, in shock for what I'd done, and what I'd just heard.

I blinked and said, "Sorry. Hair ball."

He bobbed his head (a nod?) and walked on, away from me and my secret love for him and into the food service area.

Liza said, "Spit on him. Was that a tip or trick from your parents' *Cosmo* article?"

Eli was chuckling. "Sorry about that."

"Next time you announce that you had sex, give me a warning," I said.

"Okay. I'll make the signal," she agreed. "Like this."

I won't describe the explicit pantomime Eli performed for us, but it included the bagel and her index finger.

"I trust Jack Carp is larger than your finger?" I asked.

"Dora!" shrieked Liza. "That's none of your business." To Eli: "Well? Is he?"

"Significantly," said Eli. "We did it in my bedroom. Ravel's *Bolero*, vanilla-scented candle. All according to my specifications. But sex was *not* what I expected. It hurt and Jack was a fumbling idiot with the condom. And the worst part: He wants to do it again."

"That bad?" I asked, disappointed by her negative review.

Eli chewed her bagel. "My mother swears it'll get better, but I'm not so eager to find out." I must have looked horrified and/or disgusted. "What's the face?" asked Eli. "I promised my mom that I'd tell her when it happened, so I did."

Mrs. Anita Stomp was a type A, take-no-prisoners lawyer

for Viacom. She was around sixty years old now, had been in her midforties when she and her husband, Bertram Stomp, went to China to adopt Eli. Anita Stomp did not do heart-to-heart. She didn't suffer fools, and she was not the person I'd go limping to after I'd just lost my virginity.

Liza said, "When you say 'hurt,' do you mean still? Like, are you sore right now?"

Eli shook her head. "It stopped hurting as soon as it ended, and since the whole thing lasted about two minutes, the pain was tolerable."

"What about the psychic pain?" I asked. "Do you feel upset?"

Both of them blinked in my general direction. "I don't understand the question," said Eli.

"Why would there be emotional pain when you do it with someone you love and trust?" asked Liza. "Jack and Eli love and trust each other."

"I wouldn't say *that*," countered Eli. "Shut up. Here he comes."

Jack Carp, goldfish tat visible on his upper arm, hair spiky and stiff, in black jeans and black sleeveless T, sauntered toward our table. I examined him, hunting for signs in his appearance that he'd changed. He seemed slicker somehow, sharper. He got to our table and shifted his backpack (black) to his other shoulder.

"You can stop staring at me, Dora," he said. To Eli: "You told them?"

"Like you didn't tell your friends," she said.

He smiled. Which is something I'd hardly seen on him before. He said to Eli, "Want to skip practice? Go to my house?"

Eli said, "And have sex *again*?"

He blushed, poor bastard. On his pallid skin it was painfully obvious. Eli took pity on him. "Okay, okay," she relented. "But you know Mr. Yamora wants us to practice for States."

Jack said, "I though you weren't going to compete this year."

"Of course I am," said Eli. "I'm going for a three-peat."

"You were complaining about your fingers," he said.

"They're better now," she snapped.

The boy Eli allowed to enter her body scratched the back of his head, then pointed his tattooed arm down the aisle and said, "Snapple."

And he left us in search of his beverage. As Jack entered the food service area, Vin Transom, tray loaded with complex carbs, exited. I watched him take a seat at a table across the room.

I said to Eli, "Have you consulted the Sarcastic Ball about all this?"

"I don't dare," she said. "It's still mad at me."

Liza took hers out of her backpack and shook it. "Will sex deepen the connection between Eli and Jack?" she asked.

The message: "Dumb question. Ask another."

"Okay," I said, taking the ball. "Will it complicate their relationship in ways they can't imagine or predict?"

"Get a clue," said the ball.

Eli laughed. "It knows you're a virgin, Dora."

"Don't rub it in," I said, sipping my coffee, my eyes floating over the rim of the cup, fixed on Vin Transom's red lips as he put a fork between them.

# 6

Juicy Bar opened on super-happening Smith Street last summer, catering to the health-conscious and the explosive population of underage drinkers at the epicenter of gentrified Brooklyn. The nonalcoholic bar offered a menu of freshly juiced drinks, smoothies, sugar-free treats and power bars. Ergo, as you might easily guess, we didn't come for the food.

Lump, the jazz duo of Noel Kepner and Stanley Nable, was making its Boerum Hill debut at Juicy Bar. Attendance was mandatory for members of the Ruling Class and select Fringe Dwellers. If one wanted to be relevant in the social hierarchy at Brownstone, he or she had better show up to support Noel and Stan. At school yesterday, Sondra and a dozen other Ruling Class groupies passed out flyers advertising the event. The understood message: Get Lumped or get dumped.

Liza and I sat in a booth, sipping strawberry smoothies. For the record, I hated smoothies. But I hated "high-protein, low-gluten Juicy fruit/granola shakes" even more. On the other side of the booth, Eli and Jack were checking each other for cavities with their tongues.

I said, "So you're up to, what, five or six times by now?"

Eli broke for air. "Jack, how many times?"

"Eight," he said, grinning, which was becoming a habit for

him, and a stark contrast to his usual dark scowl. I had to say,
the smile was growing on me. Like a fungus.

"Eight times. Almost into double digits," said Liza.

"It's getting better," said Eli. She leaned over the table and
stage-whispered, "I haven't had an orgasm yet, though."

Liza and I laughed.

Jack's jaw dropped to the tabletop. "I'm doing my best," he
grunted.

She replied, "I was getting close last time."

With the small morsel of encouragement, the couple resumed their mutual dental exploration.

I sipped my smoothie and looked around. Juicy was packed,
overflowing with Brownstoners and kids from the other private
institute of higher education in the Heights, St. Andrews, deri-
sively referred to as "the school for gifted parents." I scanned
the crowd, hunting for Vin Transom and his posse of trackletes.
Liza spotted Max Lindsey immediately despite the fact that,
with Lori Dropov on his lap, he was partially obscured.

Noel and Stanley were glad-handing and high-fiving all
over the joint. Eventually, they drifted their way to our booth.
When they stopped to say hello, I felt like we'd been granted
an audience with the president(s).

Stanley said, "I had no idea so many guys on the soccer
team liked jazz." He smiled at Liza.

Noel said, "If we embarrass ourselves up there, pretend not
to notice."

I said, "Oh, we won't."

Eli and Liza smiled at him to compensate for my tart-
ness. I had no idea why I was so dismissive with him. Something about Noel made me do it. Like he represented every
cute boy who'd ever ignored me, and he had to pay for their
sins. He hardly seemed to register my obnoxiousness any-

way. The duo of Lump left our booth to continue their pre-victory lap.

Eli asked me, "Not that I'm in love with the guy, but what has Noel Kepner ever done to you?"

I said, "He just bugs me. He's so sure of himself, I feel compelled to sprinkle a little shit on him."

Eli nodded. "Yeah, that, or you're jealous of him."

"Not jealous," I said. "*Envious*. There is a difference."

"Why envious?" asked Jack. "He's a guy."

"Not of *him*—of his place," I corrected. "Not even his place. His *assumption* of his place. It's hard to explain. I know that I feel envy, but I don't know of what or why."

Jack said, "Aren't your parents professional advisors? You should ask them about this."

Eli and Liza laughed at his insane suggestion.

"They're the last people I'd ask for advice," I said.

The door of Juicy opened, letting in a blast of autumnal wind. Sondra, Micha and three other Ruling Class girls made their entrance. Their arrival seemed to be in slow motion, each strut of long leg lasting forever. Each flutter of their sheer Saturday-night shirts hung in the air.

Eli said, "Gang haircut. Fucking lemmings."

True enough, the five girls had matching haircuts, a deviation from last year's long and stick-straight style. The new cut was cropped layers, random, flipping outward, and framing wisps along the cheeks. The tip of each cropped flip was three shades lighter than the layers. Sondra's tips were auburn. Micha's were platinum blond.

Liza said, "They look exactly like Bratz dolls."

Living Bratz. How appropriate, I thought.

Sondra swept by our table almost upon entering. She stopped to air-kiss, and said, "You like?"

"Love," I said. "Just when I think I've gotten the approved school style figured out, you go and change it."

Sondra laughed. "We went to Pomme de Hair together this afternoon. They call the cut Freestyle." Pomme de Hair was a pricey Smith Street salon a few blocks down from Juicy.

"It's gorgeous. I'm seething with envy." I piled it on, feeling Eli's disgust from across the booth.

Liza had to agree. "You look beautiful."

Sondra knew the truth when she heard it. She smiled at our blond friend and said, "You should get this haircut, Ms. Liza. It'll make your cheeks look slimmer."

And Sondra was off, accepting the compliments of the entire room. Liza sucked down the remainder of her smoothie in one gulp.

Eli said, "She acts like I'm invisible."

"She's afraid of you," said Jack wisely. "The twat."

I laughed. Thankfully, so did Liza, but she started to subconsciously pinch her cheeks (which, if chubby, were pink and kissable) while furtively stealing glances at (cheek-fat-deprived) Lori, still seated upon Max.

Jack said, "Should I ask why Ruling Class envy makes you bitchy to Noel Kepner but ass-lappy to Sondra Fortune?"

"No," I said.

Eli whispered, "Don't try to figure it out, Jack. You'll only confuse yourself."

Liza, meanwhile, snapped out of her cheek-pinching self-consciousness and gasped suddenly, her blue eyes bugging. I instantly turned to where she was looking.

Stephanie Greene, Liza's mom, had just stepped into the Juicy Bar. A man was at her side, his arm around her waist. Stephanie said something to him. The man smiled smugly at her. Then he kissed Stephanie. On the lips.

Our view: half of Stephanie's face and the back of the man's head. Their mouths still touching, Stephanie opened her eyes, as if instinct drew them to our table. When she spotted her daughter, Stephanie pushed the man back and smiled extra wide.

Liza recoiled.

Stephanie came over to our booth. With her date.

"Hi, honey," said Stephanie. "This is a surprise."

"What are you doing here?" asked Liza, her tone flat and hostile, which I'd never heard on her before.

"We were walking to Patois for dinner, and saw a flyer for live jazz. Gary thought it'd be fun to pop in."

The man said a rote "Hello, Liza."

She answered with a crisp and contentious "Hello, Gary."

Silence.

Eli and I blinked at each other. I hadn't heard any news of Liza's mom taking a boyfriend. Apparently, neither had Eli. I smiled nervously at Stephanie and checked out this Gary. For starters, he was nothing like Ryan Greene, Liza's dad, who was a blond, perpetually tan, shorts-and-flip-flops-wearing snorkel boat captain. Liza thought of her dad as a hero, grabbing life by the drawstring, having had the courage to drop out of the city and chase his dream. Gary, on the other hand, seemed like he'd been born, raised and reared on Wall Street. He was the embodiment of the Man, in casual Saturday khakis and dry-look brown hair, teeth as white and straight as a picket fence.

Stephanie asked, "Is that Max Lindsey over there?" She pointed. "He looks huge!" Lori Dropov, seated next to Max now, was attempting to increase his bulk by sticking the straw of a powershake between his lips. Then she licked an errant drop off of his chin. I watched Stephanie's face as the information processed—the boy Liza loved was being licked by another, far skinnier, girl.

"Are you all right, honey?" asked Stephanie, turning back to examine her daughter closely.

Liza nodded, but tears were pooling in her blue eyes. It'd been too much, the fat crack from Sondra, her mom with Gary, Max and Lori, Stephanie finding out about it. Liza, a sensitive girl, could take only so much.

Stephanie tried to rub Liza's back as if she were a little girl in need of comfort. Liza shook her off. The gentle maternal touch uncorked the bottle, though. Liza started crying.

I had always loved Stephanie Greene for her homemade chocolate chip cookies (unlike Mom and Anita Stomp, Stephanie would break out the mixing bowl whenever we asked) and for letting us watch PG-13 movies when we were ten. And I loved her right now for lifting Liza out of the booth, tucking her into a protective wing and getting her out of there before anyone noticed a thing. Gary, meanwhile, followed the mother and daughter out of Juicy, a slight shadow of disappointment—or was it sympathy?—on his face.

Eli said, "Should we go, too?"

"I don't know," I said.

From the back of the bar, Noel spoke into the microphone. "Welcome to Juicy," he said. "Stan and I are going to play an original piece now, called 'Nails on Blackboard.' One, two, one, two, three, four . . ."

The music started. If you could call it music. The crowd surged closer to watch, but we stayed in our booth. Eli and Jack listened carefully to the chaotic jazz riffs.

Eli said, "Atonal."

Jack sneered, "Amelodic."

"No time signature," Eli added.

They looked at each other and said, "Crap."

Even to my tin ear, I knew the sounds coming from Noel's sax and Stanley's bass were cacophonous, grating, a hash of wobbly notes and thumps that made my brain ache and my ears bleed. And yet, the Ruling Classers swayed and bopped as if they were listening to John Coltrane in his prime.

I said, "Lori looks pissed off that she wasn't in on the haircut junta."

The three of us watched as Lori made her way over to Sondra and Micha, Max Lindsey at her heel like an obedient dog. We could see their mouths moving, and I took it upon myself to supply Lori's dialogue from our booth.

I mocked, " 'Sondra, how you could get your hair cut without me? Just yesterday, you went to the bathroom without me. Are you trying to tell me something?' "

Eli took over for Sondra. " 'Well, Lori, the truth is, you're too thin. You make me look fat by comparison, and I can't have that.' "

I said, " 'I will shovel food into my mouth to please you. I will consume the meat of an entire elephant.' "

We watched as Max Lindsey started talking. The girls looked at him politely. Jack supplied his lines, saying, " 'Excuse me, but you two make me sick with your vanity and stupidity. Would it be all right with you, Lori, if I went back to our table and picked my nose for a while?' "

Amazingly, at that moment, Max walked away from the girls and sat down alone at his table. We laughed uproariously. Max looked over at us. He had to know we were laughing at him. Feeling a bit guilty (just a bit), I slid out of our booth, walked over to Max's table and sat down next to him.

I said, "How's it going?" Up close, I saw that he'd not only grown inches but had beard stubble as well. His face had also elongated. It appeared stretched, like the rest of him.

Max, who'd never had much use for me (or me for him), barely acknowledged my intrusion.

"You like the band?" I asked.

He said, "I guess I don't understand jazz."

"I guess I don't either."

Common ground established, I figured I'd done enough to make up for laughing at him. I started to stand up.

He said, "I saw Liza leave with her mom. Was she crying?"

"She had something in her eye," I said.

Max nodded, deciding to believe me. Deciding that he couldn't be at fault. That if Liza cried, it was not his problem.

Naturally, this enraged me. I said, "What she had in her eye was the sickening sight of you with Lori Dropov."

"That's my business," he said with a strength I hadn't known he possessed. "It has nothing to do with Liza."

"Except that you were stringing her along all last year," I said.

He paused, calmed himself down. "It's obvious that there's a lot you don't know about me and Liza."

"She tells me *everything*," I insisted.

"If you say so," he said snidely.

I stood. So did everyone else who wasn't already on his or her feet. "Nails on a Blackboard" had ended, and Lump was receiving a standing ovation (for stopping?). I rushed back to our booth. Eli and Jack were making out again. I grabbed Eli by the arm and said, "We're leaving now."

Jack said, "My parents are out tonight. Charity benefit for the Brooklyn Museum of Art."

The same party my parents were attending, as were Eli's.

"I'm not going to your apartment to watch you two have sex," I said.

"Actually," said Jack, grinning, "that could be good."

"Honestly, Dora," said Eli, "anything would help."

Jack blushed. I put the brakes on their lovers' spat. "I'm going home."

Before Lump could torture us with another song, we slipped out. We walked together toward the Heights and then went our separate ways.

I called Liza as soon as I got home.

Stephanie answered. "She went to bed, Dora."

It was only ten o'clock. "Is she asleep? Should I come over?"

"That's not a great idea," she said. "Liza wants to be alone, and Gary's here." Meaning, Stephanie wanted to be alone with Gary.

I said, "Please tell her I called."

"I'll put a note under her door right now."

Assuming Liza was awake and was hiding in her room because Gary was over, I figured she'd call any minute.

While I waited, I watched *Return of the King* with Joya and Ben until midnight.

The phone rang twice. Each call was from Mom and Dad. Just checking in. Every hour. On the hour.

# 7

By Tuesday, the Freestyle had spread like a virus to the sophomore and freshman classes. By Thursday, a few eighth graders were sporting the new do. By Friday, Liza, Eli and I were awed and disgusted to see a gaggle of girls from the lower school—they couldn't have been more than ten years old—strutting into Chez Brownstone in boot-cut low-rise jeans and Freestyling hair. They ordered decaf cappuccinos and waited for them with their flat chests sticking out.

Eli sipped her coffee, turning away from the frightening fourth graders. "Does Joya want a Freestyle?" she asked.

"No bloody idea," I said. "You have to admit, it is a flattering cut."

"Don't. You. Dare," warned Eli.

Liza said, "I'm thinking about it, too."

"Because Sondra said it would make your face look thinner?" Eli ventured. "If the two of you give in, I'm moving back to the orphanage in China."

"China isn't the place to go for freedom of choice," I reminded her. "Speaking of which, social studies revolution project. I'm thinking Bolsheviks." The entire grade had to do a revolution project, for one of the three social studies teachers.

Liza was in Sondra and Max's class, with a different teacher than Eli and I had.

"I'm thinking Belgian Congo," said Eli.

"Max is doing the Bolsheviks, too," said Liza.

Part of his sudden interest in all things Russian, I suspected. I bit my tongue. Despite my gentle inquiries, Liza continued to insist that she had no secrets about what happened between her and Max this past summer. I wanted to believe—like a convert, I wanted to believe—but the look in Max's eyes at Juicy and Liza's intense reaction to the Lori Dropov affair made me wonder.

Eli announced, "A week since I lost my virginity, I have not yet had an intercourse-specific orgasm. What's more . . ."

"There's more?" I asked.

"For the first time in three years, Jack and I are competing at the same level in States." Previously, Eli was in a higher tier for the New York State student piano competition. "He's been dropping hints that he wants me to play an easier piece of music than the one he's preparing."

"What kind of hints?" asked Liza.

"He keeps saying, 'But you *love* Beethoven,' " she said.

"Max loves Beethoven," said Liza limply.

I bit my tongue, again. If I had to keep biting it like this, I might draw blood.

"So. No intercourse-specific orgasms," I said, trying to get the conversation back to something less embarrassing. "What about non-intercourse-specific?"

"A distant memory. Jack only wants one thing now," Eli said, "And therein lies—lays?—the irony of losing your virginity: Since I started having sex, I stopped having orgasms."

That depressed the hell out of me. But it didn't keep me from thinking about Vin Transom, and how different our sex life would be, once he finally noticed that (1) I was alive, (2) I was a female and (3) I was perfect for him.

After school, I told Eli and Liza I had a doctor's appointment and couldn't go to Grind. I met Joya on the corner outside of Brownstone, and we walked as fast as our legs would carry us for our clandestine 3:20 appointments. I had two hundred bucks, cash, from Mom in my jeans pocket. We got to Pomme de Hair with three minutes to spare.

I would catch boatloads of shit from Eli tomorrow, but I was going Freestyle. I felt like a sheep—I'd soon look like a sheep—about caving in to a trend. But every time I saw a Freestyled head in the hallway at school, the locks shiny and layered, my insides turned green with envy. So I had plotted my *coup de tête*.

Last night, at dinner, I stabbed a piece of steamed broccoli and said, "I HATE my hair."

"You have beautiful hair," said Joya sweetly, which irritated me like sand in the bathing suit.

Mom said, "You loved your hair a week ago. I heard you talking to your bedroom mirror about it."

"You were eavesdropping on me?" I asked. The violation! How dare she?

"I was putting away your laundry," she said. "You were so wrapped up, you didn't realize I was there."

"How do we feel about Adora talking to herself?" asked Dad.

Mom and Dad had a nice little laugh at my expense. I waited, grimly, for them to finish.

The truth was, I did talk to my mirror. Sometimes, I impressed myself with my wit and insight.

"Can I have money for a haircut or not?" I cut to the chase.

"And a real haircut. At Pomme de Hair. I'm too old for Super-cuts. They always ask if I want the booster seat. Need I remind you, Mom, that you spend hundreds of dollars a month on your hair."

"Since I earn the money," she said. "I should be able to spend it in any way I see fit. And I need maintenance for appearances. We do have a book out."

Yes, *His-and-Her Seduction*, as I knew only too well. I tried to take a page from their book. "Of course, you have every right to spend your money. Women don't spend nearly enough on themselves. And, whatever you're paying for maintenance, it's worth it. You look gorgeous, Mom. Better than you have in years. It's like you're growing younger. And thinner."

"I agree with every word you just said," concurred Mom. "And I'll give you money for a haircut. On one condition."

"What?" I asked nervously.

"Joya is old enough for a real haircut, too," said Mom.

"*Really?*" trilled Joya.

"No, Mom!" I protested.

"You can go to Pomme de Hair if you take Joya."

How could I argue? I'd rather not be seen on the streets with my sister. But, then again, no one noticed me when she was around anyway. Walking side by side with Joya was like wearing an invisibility cloak.

"I'll do it," I said, rushing off to schedule appointments.

Joya was so excited by our upcoming sister-sister beauty bonding adventure, she floated upstairs after dinner to do her homework. She didn't bug me for the rest of the night, either.

And now, as we stood together on the threshold of Pomme de Hair, I didn't have the luxury of privacy.

Joya said, "This is gonna be *great!*"

I rolled my eyes. "Let's just go in."

We pushed through the door, and were greeted by the salon maître d'. Her name was Gabrielle, and she had a thick French accent.

I said, "Dora and Joya Benet. Three twenty."

"Oui," she breathed. "Please wait ici." She pointed at a leopard-skin couch. Once seated, I looked around. Along with exposed brick walls and plush furniture, the place looked more like someone's living room than a salon. The hair-cutting chairs were sleek architectural designs, not the pleather foot-pump kind that Supercuts had. The mirrors were oval, in gilt frames. The floor was wide wood planks, like those in the most coveted brownstone apartments in the Heights. I felt like I belonged in this opulent setting, as if I already had a fabulous new look just by breathing the perfumed air.

Joya dug in her backpack and took out one of her sketch pads. She flipped the cover over and showed me the first page. She'd sectioned it into eight panels, like her weird comics.

She said, "Okay, this is me with a bob. You like?"

I took a closer look. Each of the eight drawings was Joya, a remarkable likeness of her, with a different haircut. I had to admit the sketches were impressive. The kid could move a pencil. I'd tuned out her art since she'd produced "Unicorn Princess Meets the Lake Monster." But that was several years ago. She'd matured, thematically speaking. I tapped the panel of Joya with a short pixie do.

"It takes a brave girl to have short hair," I said.

"I don't know if I have the guts," she said.

She flipped the page and showed me another eight panels. The girl in these sketches was me, with eight different cuts. Joya had rendered my face carefully. Obviously, she'd worked harder on my likeness than she had on her own self-portraits. She'd drawn me pretty, too. Lashes, blush, with smoky gray eyes. The styles were also in elaborate detail, including tints and streaks. Joya was watching me examine her work. She wanted my approval so badly, I could hear her begging for it telepathically.

"Nice," I said. "Very nice."

I tapped the panel of me with a Freestyle. "What do you think of this one?"

"Not you," she said bluntly. "But this one. Wow!"

She pointed at the panel with shorter hair, windblown and loose, bouncy and full, my bangs artfully softened and brightened with coppery highlights.

"I can't believe you did this," I said.

"It was fun," said Joya. "Much better than watching TV."

Ben, Joya's best friend, burst into the salon. He looked harried but well put together in jeans, the long-under-short T-shirt combo, and New Balance sneaks. He had the floppiness of a Doberman pup, with big hands and feet, the rest of his body only just starting to catch up. He and Joya had been inseparable since preschool. As a little kid, Ben cried over stains on his clothes. He could play with dolls for hours. He loved cooking projects. I'd privately thought of him as soon-to-be-gay Ben Teare. So imagine my surprise when he kissed Joya hello. On the lips. And then looked (deeply, soulfully, romantically) into her eyes.

He said, "Are you going for the pixie?"

Joya crinkled her button nose. "I'm thinking about bangs."

"*Don't*," I warned.

Gabrielle came to fetch us. "D'accord," she said. "Avec moi."

We were escorted through her cloud of Chanel No. 5 to meet Nicole and Simone, our stylists. Neither of them spoke English. Both wore Hermès scarves around their dainty throats, tied in perfect knots I could never duplicate even if locked in a room for ten years with nothing but yards of silk. What was it about French women and neckwear?

After a washing and conditioning that was so soothing and divine that I almost started to drool right there in the chair, Simone gestured to me to follow her to her station.

A curt, pert grin on her lips, Simone sliced the air a few times with her scissors, as if to warm up. She asked me, with a nearly impenetrable accent, what I wanted.

"Freestyle," I said.

I knew she was thinking exactly what I was thinking: another sheep. Another mindless follower who went along with everyone else and didn't have a willful, independent thought in her banal little brain.

Simone said, "Non, non, non." She clicked her tongue, pulled at my bangs and shook her head. She was attempting to explain that Freestyle didn't work with fringe. And since I couldn't grow out my bangs in the next five minutes, and she couldn't shave them off, the cut of the moment would not work for me.

I said, "Simone, I was born and raised in Brooklyn. I'm not easily fooled. I'd bet my life that you understand every word I'm saying. Correct?"

Simone of the Frenchified scarf and striped boatneck sweater, Simone with the clicking tongue and skinny eyebrows, leaned close and whispered, "Yeah?" in a decidedly Flatbush accent.

I said, "Work with the bangs."

"It'll look like shit," she predicted.

And then I admitted something that shocked and embarrassed me then—and now. "I don't care if it's bad," I said, "as long as it's right."

"Okay," said Simone, snipping away. "You're the boss."

*        *        *

Later that night at dinner, I stared at Joya across the table with her smashing new do. Ben had convinced her to go pixie, and the close-cropped hair with her huge brown eyes and tiny nose and red lips was mesmerizing. I simply could not take my eyes off her. She looked exactly like she had in her drawing.

And I looked exactly like Joya's portrait of me with a Freestyle. Joya and Simone had been right. The cut made my face seem too thin, my nose too long. The swishy layers were an odd contrast to my heavy bangs. To say the cut added nothing to my appearance would be inaccurate. In fact, it subtracted. I'd knowingly, purposefully, STUPIDLY, made myself appreciably less attractive. The new me was a disaster.

That meal was also a travesty. My parents complimented both of us on our hundred-dollar cuts, knowing full well that Joya's was magnificent and mine a horror.

When I went to hide in my room after dinner, I toyed with product, trying mousse, gel, spray. Experimenting made my hair even worse (amazingly, that was possible). I wanted to call or IM Liza and Eli, but I was afraid of telling them just how low I'd sunk.

"I am cold. I am the frozen tundra. I am the contents of the Sub-Zero freezer," I told my mirror. "I should check out rental listings in Siberia."

I imagined bumping into Vin Transom in the hall, having a classic nonconversation with him. All the while, he was staring at my head, his jaw unhinged with disbelief.

In a haze of self-pity, I took out the Sarcastic Ball and asked, "Will I die a virgin?"

It said: "Not a chance."

That's when I decided the Sarcastic Ball was my very best friend in the whole entire world.

# 8

"Very nice, Fringe Girl," said Sondra.

Micha and Lori (who'd secured her Freestyle earlier in the week) were standing with Sondra on the steps by the front door of Brownstone. And all three of them were twirling my hair with their fingers, oohing and ahhing approvingly.

I felt queasy-yet-happy, aware of the contradiction and helpless to make sense of it. "I want you to know, Sondra, my haircut has nothing to do with yours," I said. "Or yours, Micha. Or yours, Lori."

They laughed at my attempt at ironic self-deprecation. God, they were easy. Ruling Class girls were not known for their wit. Humor was a defense mechanism, after all. And members of the upper echelons didn't need mechanisms when they had machinations.

Micha said, "God, I'm so bored today."

Was she bored with me? "Oh, yeah," I agreed. "I am beyond bored."

"I'm as bored as a human being can be and still be alive," said Sondra.

Pause. Then Lori, Micha and I laughed like drunken hyenas. Like it was going out of style. Like (because) our social lives depended on it. Sondra laughed, too, at her own not-funny joke. And then we recovered with (shallow, empty, awkward) sighs.

Sondra said, "Here's the thing, Fringe. I'm having one of my Saturday brunches. Very informal. Just Lori, Micha and me. And you, if you can make it."

"I'm there."

"I didn't tell you what time," she said.

"Doesn't matter," I said sycophantically.

They smiled at my subservience.

"You can invite Ms. Liza," said Sondra. "She's always so cheerful—when she's not being morose."

"I'm sure she'd love to come," I said.

Sondra said slowly, lowly, "But don't invite Eli."

I had to bite back a chuckle. Eli would sooner have each of her fingernails torn off, one by one, than go to one of Sondra's fabled brunches. I'd never been invited before and felt flattered, included, part of something larger than myself.

I said, "Should we bring anything?"

"Just yourselves," said Sondra. "And your emotional openness."

I was afraid to ask what *that* could possibly mean, so I didn't. I smiled vapidly, and the three lethal (h)it girls of the junior class tousled my hair, then walked up the steps and into the building.

Following them (in so many humbling ways), I went into the entryway. Immediately, I was pounced on by Eli and Liza.

Eli studied my head and said, "I knew it. Doctor's appointment, my flat ass."

Liza said, "I think it looks nice."

"It looks horrible, and we all know it," I said. "Will one of you stop me before I do something idiotic again?"

Eli said, "I don't know if that's possible. You're pretty determined."

"Would it be idiotic to go to Sondra's brunch on Saturday?"

"Oh, God, yes," said Eli. "You know what they do at those brunches? They sit around, eat Krispy Kremes and shit on everyone who's not there for hours and hours. It's soul-annihilating, Dora. It'll erase your moral infrastructure. You'll forget all the joy and goodness in the world and walk away with emotional scars that'll take years to heal."

"You're probably right." I turned to Liza. "Wanna come?"

"Can I?" she asked excitedly.

"You bet," I said.

Eli whistled a riff from Mozart's creepy *Requiem Mass*. "So you're going to leave me alone with Jack all day long? He's going to want sex again. Sometimes I think he's using sex to get me to stop practicing."

"You're paranoid," I said.

"Better than idiotic," Eli replied.

"She is such a *bitch*," said Micha. "And I can say that after having just one conversation with her."

We lounged on overstuffed couches in the sunken living room of Sondra's town house. The picture windows faced the Brooklyn Heights Promenade and showcased a postcard-worthy view of the Brooklyn Bridge. Sondra, along with being beautiful (her Gap Kids ad of her hung, actually, on the wall behind me), was incredibly, mind-bogglingly wealthy. Her dad was the first (only?) black CEO of a major Wall Street investment company; her mom designed Japanese-style rice bowls and teacups that were sold for obscene amounts at Barneys and ABC Carpet. Unlike my parents—who seemed never to leave our apartment—Sondra's worked long hours, traveled constantly and seemed perpetually absent from the town house they'd renovated and decorated to the last square inch. The

only adult who'd poked her head into the living room all afternoon (before Sondra beamed at her and chimed, "Everything's
under control, thanks so much!" or, in other words, "Leave us
the fuck alone!") was the live-in Jamaican housekeeper.

Much as my family made me crazy, I'd go certifiably
bonkers if I had to ramble around a big house alone. I almost
felt sorry for Sondra. But then I saw her bedroom. It was an entire floor of the four-story house, or half the size of our Garden
Place duplex (which I shared with three other people). Queen-
sized bed, huge walk-in closet, hundreds of CDs in her own
jukebox, thirty-two-inch flat panel iMac, forty-two-inch plasma
TV. The list could go on, and on, but I'd only had a few minutes
to gush about her room before Sondra got bored with my ava-
lanche of praise and led me away.

As well as my parents did, financially speaking, as famous as
they were, they would never net Wall Street–sized bucks. Not
in a million years, or a million books. I felt both pride for their
honest hard work and the familiar thorny prick of envy for Sondra's family's lavish lifestyle.

I nibbled a cream-filled donut and asked, "If you've barely
spoken to Karen"—the senior girl Micha had been vivisecting—
"how do you know she's a bitch?"

Lori said, "Just look at her."

Micha added, "The way she looks and acts. She's such a
know-it-all. She's had five boyfriends in the last year."

Lucky her. She was a nonvirgin, for sure. I'd never spoken
to this accused bitch, but I had seen Karen in the hallway, and
I knew she volunteered to tutor middle schoolers in math. She
seemed like a reasonable person.

Sondra said, "Karen's last boyfriend was Noel Kepner."

"He gets around," said Lori.

"Yeah, he's the slut," I said.

That didn't go over well. "No trash-talking about Noel," warned Sondra. "He's got a place in my heart."

Micha snorted. "Why don't you just admit you want him?"

All this time, meanwhile, Liza sat stone silent, listening to these girls shit all over their "friends" and gossip about boys. I tried to get her to talk a couple of times, but she merely smiled shyly and kept her hands and mouth busy with Krispy Kremes.

"If *he* wants *me*, he can come and get me," said Sondra tartly. "I do not chase any boy." Then she turned her Freestyling head in Liza's direction. "Ms. Liza, what do you think about chasing after boys?"

Liza stammered, "I don't know."

The three Ruling Classers looked at each other, as if verifying a previously agreed-upon agenda. My heart plunged from my chest to my knees. The brunch was a setup. And I'd been duped. Used. They'd played me completely.

Lori said, "Tell me the truth, Liza. Do you still have feelings for Max Lindsey?"

"Because it seems like you do," seconded Micha. "The way you follow him around. And moon over him, and cry whenever you see him and Lori together. Everyone notices, Liza. Everyone thinks it's embarrassing for you, and, frankly, pathetic."

Sondra had a glint in her eye while Micha said her part, instantly replacing it with sympathy when it was her turn. "You need to let him go," she said earnestly. "You have to get on with your life."

I said, "She knows that. You don't need to gang up on her."

"Open your eyes, Fringe Girl," said Sondra, shaking her perfectly shaped head. "This is an intervention. Lori, Micha and I felt like we had to do *something*, since you and Eli Stomp are . . . well, we have no idea what you're doing to help Liza move on, but it doesn't seem like much. We want Liza to be happy. Lori and Max deserve their happiness, too."

So now I understood the whole plan. They'd played on my desire for inclusion to get me to invite Liza, whom they planned to attack. Added benefit: They'd take the high road of "helping her," thereby impugning Eli's and my efforts. I'd been force-fed a triple whammy. And I'd thought I was being invited over for brunch.

Sondra and I glared at each other as if no one else was in the room. I said, "Liza couldn't be happier for Lori and Max. She's thrilled to be rid of him, if you must know. If she seems upset lately, it has nothing to do with Max. It's pure ego on your part, Lori, to assume that your picking up her leftovers from last year would upset her in any way at all."

Silence. Sondra, Lori and Micha seemed to be taking measure of my outburst, deciding whether they were going to tolerate it.

"So why is she crying and pouting all the time?" asked Sondra.

Liza, finally finding the courage to speak up for herself, said, "It's about a boy. A different boy."

Lori said, "Oh, puh-leeze."

Micha said, "What boy?"

Liza looked at me, her eyes imploring me to think of someone, anyone. But I knew that any lie would only lead to bigger problems. The information would become fodder for the Ruling Class rumor mill. Confessing a crush to these killers would be suicide-by-gossip. I couldn't let Liza do it.

"I've got a huge crush on a boy," I blurted suddenly, too loudly. "I've wanted him forever. And he doesn't know I exist."

Sondra's attention returned to me. Liza seemed to slump with relief.

"Don't stop there, Fringe. Who is it?"

"Vin Transom," I confessed.

"Speak of the devil!" Micha was pointing out the picture window at a boy stretching his legs right outside on the Promenade. It was Vin, all right, in running shorts and a T-shirt. He appeared to be trying to peer inside Sondra's house.

Sondra went to the window. He must have seen her, as he suddenly looked startled. He stopped stretching and ran off. His loping gait was perfectly rhythmic. Just the sight of him heated my blood, tightened my chest.

"Look at Fringe!" said Sondra, turning around. "Her face is bright red!"

Lori went to the window to watch Vin's retreating figure all the way down the Promenade and then out of sight. "That guy? He's nobody," she said.

"Vin Transom," said Sondra, rolling his name around in her mouth like a sugar drop. "He flies under the radar, doesn't he? I'm surprised, Fringe. I thought you'd be more attracted to a creative type, like Noel or Stanley. Vin Transom. Well. I might have to take another look at that boy. He does have an excellent body. I mean, he runs hours and hours every single day. He's got a kind of poetic charm. The quiet, contemplative athlete, a loner, a mystery. Yes, Fringe. I'm starting to see the attraction."

Liza said, "But Vin isn't in your league, Sondra."

"Oh, Ms. Liza. I don't pay any mind to arbitrary placement on a random social structure. It's all ridiculous! Means nothing to me."

Sondra's face—the faraway dreamy look as she contemplated the wonder of Vin—was too much for me to bear. Why had he been scoping out Sondra's house? Did he have a secret crush on *HER*? I shut my eyes in pain at that disgusting thought.

I'd served up my heart as a sacrifice for Liza. And she'd just sat there, mute, motionless. Useless. An image appeared on the underside of my lids. Sondra and Vin, in a passionate clench, their lips pressed against each other. I heard the crashing sound of my heart breaking.

I opened my eyes and saw that Liza had dropped a glass on the ceramic tile floor, shattering it.

# 9

"Will Sondra and Vin hook up?"

The Sarcastic Ball said, "What do you think?"

"Does Sondra take sadistic pleasure in pretending to like me, only then to use me as her personal punching bag?" I asked.

"Obviously."

"Do I have a right to be pissed off at Liza?"

"As if."

"What if I am anyway? If she weren't so pathetic about Max and Lori, the brunch wouldn't have happened."

"Ask me if I care."

I threw the Sarcastic Ball on the shag carpet and looked in my mirror. "I didn't own Vin Transom. He isn't my personal property," I said. "He *was* my secret. My well-kept secret. Now everyone is going to take a second look at him."

It occurred to me that I might like Vin simply because he was a hidden treasure. No one else had wanted him, so my chances were better. Even if that was once true, it wasn't any longer.

I lay on my stomach on my bed, the door shut. Okay, yes, I cried. I cried big, heavy tears of self-pity. I'd set myself up like a bowling pin. I replayed Sondra's brunch invitation over and over again. Her: "I didn't tell you what time." Me: "Doesn't matter."

I hated her! I wanted the earth to open up and swallow her whole. It was one thing to torment me with a phony-baloney smile on her beautiful face. I could take whatever she dished out. But I crumbled at the notion of her with Vin.

"He is *not* my personal property," I said again. "I don't own him."

Knock on the door.

"Adora? Time for dinner." It was Dad.

"Not hungry," I whined.

"Can I come in?" he asked.

His voice was soft, gentle. I started crying again. He opened the door a crack. Seeing me sobbing, he came in, sat on the edge of the bed and said, "Oh, honey! A bad haircut isn't worth crying over."

I laughed despite the tears. "Is, too," I said, turning over and sitting up, my arms around my knees. "Dad, I need a male opinion."

"Okay," he said. "I'll go get your mother."

"Very funny," I said. "Why do all the boys at school like the same five girls?"

"Are you one of them?"

"I wouldn't be asking if I were."

"You should be," he said. "You're the prettiest girl in Brooklyn."

He would say that. I looked just like him (granted, a female, softer, *younger* version). "I think you have me confused with Joya," I said.

"You're just as pretty as she is, Adora," he said. "Except, of course, for the hair."

"It seems like some people get everything they want," I said.

"Exactly," he agreed. "It does *seem* like that. But hardly anything is what it *seems*."

"Spare me the *Star Wars* philosophy lesson, Yoda."

He laughed. "It *seems* like you're upset about a haircut. But you're not, are you?"

"Yes," I pouted.

"Well, then, I'm proven wrong," he said. "And if you'd like to tell me about anything else that might be bothering you, I'm available."

"So I've heard."

"Those five girls, the ones all the boys like. I bet there's something or someone they want and don't have," he said.

"Yet," I said.

"Ms. Benet," said Mr. Sagebrush after social studies on Tuesday. "A word."

The rest of the class was leaving for lunch. I told Eli I'd meet her at Chez Brownstone and shuffled up to Mr. Sagebrush's desk.

He gave me a "cautious but intrigued" look, and said, "About your project proposal."

I said, "I know it's unconventional."

"It's also highly inappropriate," he said. "You want to stage a political revolution *in this school*? To 'dismantle the existing social order'? Where did you get these phrases, 'Ruling Class,' 'Fringe Dwellers,' 'Teeming Masses'? There are no masses at Brownstone. The entire junior class has only eighty students!"

I defended my idea. "I'm going to use the operating procedures of bloodless coup d'état—the ones you taught us, brilliantly, I might add—and see if I can effect change. Nothing scary. Just a little restructuring of the social hierarchy and establishment of a new governance that would benefit the downtrodden."

"Yes, I read the proposal already," he said. "And there are no downtrodden at the Brownstone Institute."

"I'm speaking hyperbolically."

"Look, Ms. Benet, I appreciate your creative impulse. I respect it. And I'm agreeing with you that it would be a fascinating term project to stage an actual, real-time revolution, one that we could study and deconstruct later. It could open up a huge vein of classroom discussion, supply a way to connect historical events to students' personal lives . . . "

I said nothing. Why speak when Mr. Sagebrush was talking himself into agreeing to my plot?

"I need to ask you something," he said suddenly. "And you have to give me a completely honest answer." He shot me a look that said, "I want to trust you."

I said, "You can trust me."

Mr. Sagebrush held up my one-page proposal, the one I'd stayed up until two a.m. writing. "There's a lot of passionate rhetoric about the Ruling Class getting everything it wants, and how everyone else has to settle for scraps and leftovers," he said. "Forgive me if I'm wrong, but I wonder if all this is about a boy."

"Absolutely not!" I protested. "I'm insulted you would even think that. I'm motivated solely and purely by intellectual curiosity."

He telegraphed "I'm not convinced" with his eyes, but he said, "Okay, Ms. Benet. I'm going to let you do it. But I'm keeping you on a tight leash. I want a report on your plans and progress on my desk every Wednesday."

"You are the greatest teacher *ever*!" I said.

He held up his hand, silencing me. "A word of warning, Ms. Benet. You should do some reading on the political fallout of bloodless revolution. The historical precedent does not favor the revolutionaries."

I said, "I will."

"Action plan e-mailed to me by tomorrow morning. You do not take a step without my knowing what shoes you're wearing."

"Clogs," I announced.

"Excuse me?" he said.

"I'm wearing clogs."

"You'd better walk those clogs out of here, before I change my mind."

"Leaving!" I yelped.

# 10

$\mathcal{S}$eptember 21st, Wednesday

To: Mr. "Risk Taker" Sagebrush
From: Dora Benet
Subject: Action Plan, Week One

According to your wisdom, and our large and informative Revolutionary History text, the first step toward peaceful overthrow of an entrenched government is: Question Authority. So, this week, I plan to take subtle yet drastic measures to challenge the policies of the authoritarians at Brownstone. To do so, I'm going to use time-honored tools of defiance, those being:

1 Use the power of the press
2 Reject established codes of appearance
3 Reject established codes of behavior

To wit, Mr. Sagebrush, I'm going to write an editorial for the *Brownstone Brief*, as well as change how I dress and boycott events and parties that would otherwise be required attendance, thereby risking my social banishment in the process.

I just want to say again how much I appreciate the opportunity to put theory into action. And just think about the many valuable, life-altering lessons we'll all learn in the process. I swear to you, Mr. Sagebrush, you won't regret it.

9/21, 11:30 A.M.

Ms. Benet:
This outline is not nearly as specific as I'd expected. Please redo, and give me precise details of your plans, including the draft of your editorial. I want it by Friday.
That is all,
Mr. Sagebrush

### Editorial Submission
*A Modest Proposal, By Dora Benet*

I've done it! I've figured out the key to happiness, harmony and health. Gaining this insight and wisdom (at such a young age), happened quite by accident. I was having lunch at Chez Brownstone, minding my own feta wrap sandwich, and I looked out, from table to table, at my fellow students. What struck me—and would strike anyone— were the small pockets of variety. Some people (you know who you are) had a stubborn contrary air about them, flagrantly flaunting a disregard for the approved demeanor and dress code of our fine school. It hurt me to see these people being different (an ugly word, I know). It hurt me deeply.

I never want to experience such pain again. Here at Brownstone, we are lucky, lucky ducks. We are blessed—blessed!—with student leaders who dictate style, taste, decorum so the rest of the rabble doesn't have to think at all. Those ingrates who reject the determinations of our student leaders, whose interests and passions aren't socially acceptable, those "people" are spitting in the face of convention. And that's just sad. Sad, disrespectful, and wrong. Their nonconformity threatens everything conformists hold dear! These isolationist heretical individualists are mucking up the good thing we've got going. They're clogging the conformist flow. Dressing, acting, speaking, *thinking* for yourself are evil and must be stopped. Society functions only as long as everyone does what he or she is supposed to.

The key to health, harmony and happiness, as I alluded to above, is to stop this disturbing rebellion. Which brings me to my modest proposal: Those people who veer outside the mainstream should be corralled and brought to the courtyard garden behind the main building. They should then be lined up along the wall and (Brown)stoned to death. Thank you for your time and attention.

9/22, noonish

Ms. Benet:
You've got guts. I'll give you that. I think your "Modest Proposal," in the great Jonathan Swift tradition of social satire, deserves to be published in the *Brownstone Brief*. But if you use this note to convince Ms. Shatsky, the paper's faculty advisor, or Mr. Brainard, the student editor, to run it, I'll shut you down quicker than you can say "irony" five times fast. Part of the process is the struggle. Good luck!
Mr. Sagebrush

"I'm begging, Eli!" I said. "My grade depends on this!"

"You're asking me to whore myself," she protested. We were standing outside the basement-level offices of the *Brownstone Brief*.

"That is so not true," I defended.

"I hate Eric Brainard!" she said, way too loudly, since he was on the other side of the closed office door. "He repulses me. Him and his sick Asian fetish."

Everyone knew Eric Brainard had a thing for Asian girls. He'd dated every Chinese adoptee in the senior class, and a few in the junior class. He'd asked our Eli three times, and finally gave up when she punched him hard in the chest and told him to leave "me and my people" alone.

"This isn't whoring," I said. "We're using every tool at our disposal to start a revolution!"

Eli said, "Calm down, Pancho Villa." She was silent for a second. I held my tongue, let her think. "I'll help you. But I want it on record that this goes beyond the usual friendly assist."

"Noted!" I whooped. "Thank you so much, Eli! I love ya."

"You know, Dora, despite the hair, you are looking good lately. Revolution becomes you."

I felt good, too, like I was breaking out of a cocoon. Ever since I'd come up with the idea to overthrow the Ruling Class, I'd been energized. Excited, fully charged.

"I'm going in," said Eli, one hand on the doorknob of the *Brief* office. She looked over my shoulder. "Vin Transom is behind you."

"Right behind me?"

"He's walking down the hall."

I got a flash. That excerpt from *His-and-Her Seduction*, from Dad's list of Bold Breakthroughs. I wanted Vin to notice me, and I wasn't going to let an opportunity slip by.

"Tell me when he's two steps away," I said, cool and calculated.

Eli whispered a countdown. "Eight, seven, six, five, four, three . . . now!"

I spun around, and crashed into Vin Transom, bounced off him, and landed on my butt on the carpet. Backpacks flew, papers fluttered. Vin was on his ass, too. We looked at each other from our seats on the floor, him stunned, me pretending to be. It was the longest eye contact we'd ever had in ten years of going to school together. In my peripheral vision, I saw Eli slip into the newspaper office.

My heart leapt into my throat as I stared at Vin on the floor. He gathered his things and then sprang, tigerlike, to his feet. He reached down to me. I inserted my hand into his, we made skin-to-skin contact, and he pulled me upright with Herculean strength.

I said, "I am so sorry!"

He said, "No big deal."

How succinct he was. What economical diction! I said, "You're right. Life is too short to get upset about a little accident. Why waste another second on negative emotions, like regret and guilt?"

Vin smiled—if thinly. He seemed to understand. How philosophically in sync we were.

He said, "Can I have my hand back?"

I let go. Must have turned steamed-lobster red. But, the miracles of the week had only just begun to unfold. Vin smiled—plumply! He even made a smallish chuckle sound.

I amused him. He enjoyed my company. The chuckle was at my expense, but a chuckle is better than silence. I said, "I saw you running on the Promenade last weekend."

"I'm there every day, almost."

"What are you doing this weekend?"

I couldn't believe my own balls! I'd asked him out! Vin's eyes widened. He said, "I'm training for the marathon in November," he said. "So I've got to do two ten-mile runs. I usually go to bed early."

"Of course you do! You need your rest! My God, running all those miles on just this one pair of legs. It's got to be exhausting. If only you had a spare pair."

He smiled again. I was on a roll. "I'm late for calculus," he said.

"You'd better run. Ha," I said.

"Yeah," he agreed.

He loped on his magnificent legs down the hallway, and then up the stairs, taking two or three at a time, bouncing as if he were on springs. High on the contact and a real conversation with Vin (many sentences! a chuckle!), I poked my head into the *Brief* office.

Eli was standing with Eric in front of his desk. An iMac blinked behind him, framing him as he read my editorial. He lowered the page, and smiled up at Eli. I didn't know if the smile was for her Chinese beauty or for what he'd just read on the paper.

I pushed the door all the way open. They both turned to look at me.

"Benet," said Eric Brainard. "Nice work."

"You dig?" I asked.

He nodded and said, "Oh, yeah."

I have to say, Eric was a fine-looking specimen—short brown hair, dark green eyes, luscious red lips, too-much-time-in-the-basement ivory skin, and the gangly body type I found most appealing. Too bad he wasn't available to all girlkind, not only to the Asian variety.

Eric parted those red lips and said, "Nice change of pace for the *Brief*. This year, it's been wall-to-wall mystery hacker and sports scores. E-mail the piece to me and I'll run it next week."

"Done," I said. "And, forgive my ignorance. Mystery hacker?"

"Someone has been posting dirty jokes on the home page of the Brownstone Web site," said Eric. "We did a big story on it in the latest edition of the *Brief*."

"Now I remember," I lied. "I read that article." I hadn't looked at a copy of the student paper all year.

"Right," mocked Eric. "I know my paper isn't exactly a hot sheet. Maybe this piece will help change that. I need a digital photograph of you to run with it."

I stammered. "I don't have one."

"I can take it now." He reached into his jeans pocket and took out his cell phone. Opening it, he said, "Say cheese."

I put my hands over my face and said, "No! I need makeup. Major hair help. A red shirt with a scooped sweetheart neckline."

"Girls are so vain," he said, shaking his head. "E-mail me a JPEG by Monday morning. Otherwise, I won't be able to put this in the Thursday paper."

The *Brownstone Brief* was a four-page broadsheet published entirely in-house, meaning from within the school building. Eric was the senior student editor. He created the paper on the school computer and ran copies on a special broadsheet printer that a Brownstone alumnus had donated to the school a few years ago. It was quite an operation for him, to put out four pages of original content every week. Eric had a staff of one faculty advisor and three junior editors, none of whom were present.

He said, "Now that that's settled, how about having dinner with me tonight, Eli?"

She said, "I'm sure Jack Carp would object."

"I bet he wouldn't mind extra practice time. I can hear him playing every night until eleven," said Eric, whose apartment was directly across a rear courtyard from Jack's on parallel blocks. Eli told me once she'd seen Eric in his kitchen from Jack's living room window.

Eli's eyes (and nostrils) flared like a dragon's. "I've got to go," she said, and ran out of the newspaper office.

# 11

On Saturday morning, Joya and I sat on her bed as she flipped through her sketchbook to find the right page. I was tossing the Sarcastic Ball from hand to hand, rolling it down my arm, catching it in my palm.

My little sister's room was chaotic. She had stacks of books and papers everywhere, paint splattered on her desk, her bed was half made. Mom said Joya's "creative" mind thrived on disorder, and she forgave her the mess. Since my "logical" brain preferred order, I was expected to keep my room clean.

"You ever think about cleaning up in here?" I asked. Mom was right: I did prefer neatness. Chaos made me nervous.

"What's wrong with it?" Joya asked, looking up from her pad briefly and scanning her pigsty.

"Never mind," I said.

"So you, Eli and Liza all have a Sarcastic Ball?" asked Joya. "Is it like a part of being in your club?"

"Our *club*?" I sneered.

"I wish I had a Sarcastic Ball," she said wistfully.

"That's nice," I said. "Okay, right there." I snatched the sketch pad from her, and examined my eight portraits. "When you drew the pictures, which haircut did you like best?"

Joya pursed, she paused, she rubbed her chin thoughtfully and annoyingly. "I guess number four."

"Ben liked number four, too?" He might be straight, but Ben still had great style.

"He only looked at my self-portraits."

"I didn't realize that you and Ben were . . . whatever you are," I said.

"We're not sure what we are either," said Joya. "Sometimes, I think we're friends. But everything has changed in the last year, and I'm not sure what my feelings are for him, or his for me. I mean, we make out a lot. And it feels good. But I don't think I want to do anything else."

I said, "Yeah, well, I've got to go talk to Mom."

Joya sang, "Okay! Come by anytime!" The ruder I was to her, the more she liked me. "By the way, Dora? I'm glad you're going to get rid of *that*," she said, waggling a finger at my Freestyle.

"Thanks, I think," I said, folding her panel drawings and heading down the stairs. I found Mom in the kitchen, in the yellow and blue bathrobe, a mug of the hot stuff in her hand, as always.

"I need a hundred dollars," I announced.

Mom choked on her coffee. "Don't do that to me so early in the morning."

"But I need it!" I said.

"For what?"

I groaned. Would I have to say it out loud? "The truth is, I'm in a desperate situation, Mom."

She looked worried all of the sudden, her brow creasing. "My God, Adora, what's wrong?" I could almost see her sinister thoughts. Did I need the cash for an abortion, a gambling debt, a drug deal gone bad?

"Look at me, Mom."

"You're beautiful," she said.

I sighed (frustratingly). "My hair. Hello. I have to fix it."

Mom visibly relaxed. "I didn't want to say anything, but it is atrocious—and I mean that in the nicest possible way. I'll give you the money, on one condition."

"What is it this time?" Last time, she'd made me take Joya to Pomme de Hair.

"Let me come with you to the salon," she said softly.

Dad and Joya were going to the Whitney. Mom didn't want to be alone. Or maybe she wanted to be alone with me. And she thought bribing me was the only way to do it, which was sad, scary and sweet all at once.

"Can we go shopping after?" I asked. "Buy some new tops?"

"Sounds fun," she said. "Just for the record, I don't expect you to tell me anything too personal about your life. Although, if you did want to share your feelings, or if you have any confusion about anything, or feelings you'd like to get out in the open, I'd be happy to listen."

"Don't ruin it, Mom," I said.

"This one," I instructed Simone, handing her Joya's portrait.

Mom whispered, "Adora, she doesn't speak any English."

"You are so naive," I said.

Simone wielded magic scissors. An hour later, I was a steaming-hot plate of babe. Mom was so excited by the transformation, she bought me five new scoop- and V-necked tops, including a red drawstring tunic at the Brooklyn Refinery that would be ideal for my photo in the *Brownstone Brief*. Mom got three new pairs of earrings, too.

We walked down Smith Street together, rehashing the details of our shopping triumph. Mom leaned over to kiss my cheek.

I said, "You haven't done that in a while."

"I haven't had the opportunity."

She was right. Sometime in eighth or ninth grade, I'd put Mom at arm's length. There she stayed—far enough away, but hovering nearby. Or, as she put it, "respecting my privacy while letting me know she was there for me." Mom was smiling now, looking at the street signals, making sure we didn't walk against the light.

I took her hand.

She started crying.

"You're ruining it," I cautioned.

"I can't help myself," she said, laughing at her own sap. "I miss this." She squeezed my hand.

"Me, too," I said, not sure I meant it, but knowing how much it meant to her to hear me say it (I was a damned good daughter).

"Dora! Over here!"

I looked toward the sound. Across the street, waving like an air traffic controller, Liza was standing on the corner with her mom. By all appearances, they were having a Smith Street shopping binge afternoon, too. With our bags, Mom and I ran across the street (with the light) and greeted them and their bags with hugs and smiles. I'd forgiven Liza for her impersonation of a sack of potatoes at Sondra's brunch. Her inaction was a catalyst. It forced me to motivate myself.

The four of us started walking back to the Heights, falling, naturally, into pairs. Liza and I walked behind our moms. I asked, "You dig the new do?"

"I haven't said anything yet because I'm speechless. You are gorge! I mean a deep, plunging gorge. Not a shallow, superficial, obvious attractiveness like Lori Dropov's. Take away her skinny body, straight nose, perfect hair, blue eyes, puffy lips, and what is she?"

"A faceless skull?"

"She's nothing!" Liza practically spat the words.

The moms turned around at Liza's too loud and vicious outburst. We smiled nicely, and they went back to their conversation. Mom and Stephanie had been pretty close when we lived on Hicks Street. In our years there, the two of them must have swallowed a swimming pool's worth of coffee at our kitchen table. Their heads were close together now. Must be talking about Gary, the new man in Stephanie's life.

"Where's Gary today?" I asked.

"Who the hell cares?" replied Liza.

That floored me. Eli could outswear a sailor on shore leave. But Liza was not a curser. She used to stammer when she said "darn." I took a good look at my blond friend. She seemed rounder. I hadn't noticed the cluster of zits on her forehead before. And, the biggest weirdness of all—her eyes weren't laughing. They weren't even smiling. I felt a chill along my spine: For all her venom, Sondra could be right about Liza. She might be in a worse place than I'd thought.

Two kinds of people in the world: the kind that thought there were two types of people and the kind that didn't. That said, there were the types that let scabs heal slowly and in their own time. And then there was the type that couldn't help but pick and pull at the scab until the wound was ripped wide open.

Guess which type I was.

I said, "I've been meaning to ask you something. About Max Lindsey."

"Max?" said Liza, brightening. "What about him?"

"This is probably insane to even suggest. But"—self-conscious chortle—"I sort of got the ridiculous idea in my head that"—disbelieving shake of the head—"if it's possible"—talking really fast now—"that sometime over the summer, you had sex with Max, and then he dumped you, and you've gone a little nuts from the humiliation and from keeping the secret."

I braced myself, waiting for her to take offense that I could even suggest such an outlandish fiction. But instead of an explosion, Liza sniffled. She snuffled. She fought to hold off the inevitable deluge. I whispered, "It's okay. You're okay."

And that did it. After one loud intake of breath, she started wailing and fell into my arms for comfort. I could make two people cry inside of fifteen minutes. That had to be a record.

The moms spun around. One on each side, they asked Liza what was wrong, what happened. Mom glanced at me imploringly, and I shook my head.

Stephanie said, "Is this about Gary?"

Liza snapped, "It's not about Gary. I'm sick of talking about him! All you think about is fucking Gary!"

Although it was probably an accurate statement, I think Liza meant to use "fucking" as an adjective, and not a verb. Liza fell back into my arms, and wet my shirt with her tears.

Stephanie's lip quivered. She turned to Mom and said, "You see? It's impossible. There is no way I can be happy without making Liza miserable." And then *she* started sobbing, too, and fell into Mom's arms for comfort.

Over the crying Greenes' shoulders, Mom and I looked at each other in bafflement. I couldn't help laughing at the absurdity of the sight: two wailing women, and their shoulders to cry on, surrounded by shopping bags. Mom glared at me for a second, and then she saw the humor in the situation, too.

Laughter was contagious. Soon enough, Liza and

Stephanie caught the disease. The four of us were standing in the middle of the sidewalk, howling, letting out the wolves inside, each of us for her own reason, be it relief, release, frustration, whatever.

After such cathartic emotional depletion, there was only one thing the four of us could do next.

We got coffee.

## 12

Eli had a digital camera. My dad had one, too, but I couldn't possibly pose for him. Imagine trying to look sexy and sweet, desirable and intellectual when your dad was the photographer? Disgusting. Could not be done. So, Sunday afternoon, my hair still perfecto, I walked the three blocks to Eli's house on Clinton Street.

"Hello, Mrs. Stomp," I said formally when she let me in.

"Hello, Adora. You look very nice today."

"Thank you, ma'am," I said with the rote politeness that had been drilled into my head since I could burp. Anita Stomp was closer to my grandparents' age, and as a member of that generation, she came with a stricter set of expectations, besides. I learned early (around age three), that I'd better meet Mrs. Stomp's standards—or else. The "or else" used to be a full detailed report of my offenses to my mom; nowadays, it was Mrs. Stomp's Stern and Withering Look of Disapproval. Although our mothers all liked each other, Mrs. Stomp hadn't joined Mom for coffee on Hicks Street as often as Stephanie Greene had.

Eli's dad, Bertram Stomp, walked into his parlor-floor living room. He was sixty-eight years old, retired. He'd been a family internist in the neighborhood for forty years. On Hicks Street, he was the doctor in the house, always good-natured and willing to do midnight stomachache or ear infection exams.

He said, "Adora! I never see you anymore."

I had to mentally adjust when I saw Dr. Stomp these days. He looked so old. Jurassic. He was older than my oldest grandparent. When they'd adopted the infant Eli from China, the Stomps must have realized that they wouldn't live to see much of their daughter's adult life. They probably wouldn't meet Eli's children, if she had any. Eli was accepting about having much older parents. Considering the life she would have had in China, Eli considered her American adoption a blessing no matter how old her mom and dad were. For their part, the Stomps probably figured that limited time as parents was better than none.

Dr. Stomp came up to me, pretended to look into my ear, and said, "So, where does it hurt?"

This bit was an old (*way* old) joke from when we were little. Dr. Stomp would pull on a stethoscope and ask us where it hurt. We'd point to our arm or our leg, and he'd give us a lollipop to make it feel better.

One source of pain immediately sprang to mind: I suffered from a sharp, aching desire for Vin Transom. "It hurts in the heart, Dr. Stomp. Think a lollipop will help?"

"Absolutely!" he said, and limped over to a jar on a table by the door. He reached in, pulled out a Tootsie Pop and handed it to me. I unwrapped it, and deposited it in my mouth. Chocolate. Maybe doctors did know best. I felt a little bit better. Perhaps I should replace my desires for Vin with candy.

"Eli and Jack are upstairs in her bedroom," said Mrs. Stomp. "Go on up. I'm sure they'll be happy to see you."

She'd left them alone in Eli's room? Mrs. Stomp knew what was going on between them. I supposed she assumed Eli would never do anything untoward with her only three floors below. I wasn't as confident about that as Mrs. Stomp seemed to be.

"Have you forgotten the way?" she asked, perplexed by my hesitation.

I gulped. "No, ma'am. Thanks." I stood at the foot of the stairs. I had a few flights up to make my presence known to them. I hollered, "Eli! Jack! It's Dora! I'm coming up!"

"Volume, Adora," cautioned Mrs. Stomp.

"Sorry, ma'am."

I walked with heavy feet up, trying to be as loud as I could. I shouted my approach at each landing. When I was right outside the door, I knocked. Hard.

They didn't hear me. How could they, with all that screaming?

"You are so selfish!" Jack yelled from inside Eli's room.

"How can you say that, after all I've done for you?" she shrieked back.

"And what exactly have you done for me?" he asked.

"You know what I've done," said Eli. "I *mumble mumble*. And you damn well know that I had no interest in *whisper mumble*, but I did it for you. Many, many times! And that goes for *mumble mumble*, and *whisper mumble*, too!"

"You think I was so psyched to *mumble whisper*? Okay, I really did enjoy that. But what about *whisper mumble*? I wasn't doing that for myself!"

I couldn't take much more *mumbling* and *whispering*. It was just too sordid. I knocked as hard as I could, turned the knob, and pushed the door open.

I said, "Surprise!"

Eli and Jack were facing off in the middle of her room. She was strangling a Hello Kitty doll. Jack had his hands in the pockets of his black jeans, as if he were protecting the contents underneath. I said, "Can't we all just get along?"

Jack practically hissed at me. Turning to Eli, he said, "You can forget about ever doing . . . that thing I mentioned before . . . again!"

"Forget about all of it. I wouldn't touch you with Dora's hand."

"Keep me out of this," I mumble-whispered.

But Jack was already gone, slamming out of the room, thumping down the stairs and out the door without saying good-bye to the Stomps. I wondered what they'd make of his hasty departure.

Eli sat down on her bed, releasing Hello Kitty's neck. "Jack's been practicing Rachmaninoff's Third behind my back," she said, seemingly unfazed by what had just happened.

"Is that bad?" I asked.

"He's plotting to upstage me at States. He's determined to win. Second place isn't good enough for him."

"It's not good enough for you, either," I said.

"The point is, Dora, he deceived me. He said he was preparing Mozart's Allegro in A, but he was practicing Rach Three. He knew I was doing Beethoven's *Waldstein*, that sneaky little shit!"

"Say again, this time in English," I said.

"I never should have slept with him! And definitely not fifteen and a half times!"

I wanted to ask what she meant by "a half."

"I gave myself to him! And this is how he repays me."

"Didn't he give himself to you, too?"

"That concept would be easier to swallow if I'd had one single, solitary orgasm."

I winced. "Maybe that's why you want to beat him at States so badly. To punish him."

Eli shot me a look of pure loathing, and then it softened.

"You bitch. You're right," she said. "But, regardless, I am a better pianist. And I'm going to prove it to him, and everyone else. And if it means I never have sex with Jack Carp again, so be it."

She waited for me to nod in encouragement. So I did, although I thought she was being a bit harsh. I noticed Eli's Sarcastic Ball on the bookshelf behind her bed. I reached for it and asked, "Is love about keeping score?" and shook.

It read: "Stupid question, ask another."

Eli said, "Don't bother. It doesn't matter. Jack walked out on me. You saw it. And for that insult, I'm done with that bastard."

"Great," I said. "Just when I was starting to like him."

Eli was glad to take my picture for the paper. Our impromptu photo shoot was a convenient distraction for her.

She said, "That's good. Give me more lips. Make it pout. Model mouth. Now say 'sexy.'"

"Can you just take the picture?" I asked.

"That hair is amazing. Tousle it. Yes. Now say 'hotcha.'"

"Just take the fucking picture!" I shouted.

*Click.*

# 13

$\mathcal{S}$ept 26th, Monday

To: Mr. "Brain Trust" Sagebrush
From: Dora Benet
Subject: Operation Revolution Update

You will notice, in fourth period, when I enter the classroom, that I have changed my haircut from Freestyle to Me Style. This is a major demonstration of revolutionary procedure number one (Question Authority). I have also traded low-rise flare jeans for medium-rise boot cut. This might seem like a minor shift, but (I'm telling you) it's significant, i.e., the Ruling Class powers that be will notice my flagrant disregard of established style rules.

My editorial runs on Thursday, with a photo of the author (yours truly), flaunting Me Style. Meanwhile, I have operatives collecting intelligence that will be central to my plan as it evolves, providing a window into how the Ruling Class reacts to my tugging, ever so radically, on the fabric of their existence.

Monday, 3:24 P.M.

Ms. Benet:
This may come as a shock to you, but I did not notice that you've

changed your hair. Perhaps if you'd shaved your head or dyed it lime green, the change might have registered. Last time I checked, I am a male, and have not noticed the rise and fall of women's hairstyles or hemlines in my fifty years on earth. But—if you say a new cut is as heretical as beheading the king of France, I'll take your word for it. Ms. Shatsky, faculty advisor at the *Brief*, and I have discussed your editorial and whether or not it is acceptable for publication. You should know that Ms. Shatsky is an admirer of your parents' writing, and has been hoping you'd show an interest in journalism. She's given it the go-ahead. One note of caution, Ms. Benet: You're too cheeky in your weekly updates. Cut it out.

Take care,

Mr. "Loathes Cutesy Epithets" Sagebrush

"I'm following Lori Dropov right now," said Liza via cell after school the next day.

I was walking down Joralemon Street, heading to Garden Place for the non-intrigue of dinner with the fam and homework. Much as I appreciated Liza's volunteering to do reconnaissance work and spy on the enemy, I feared my encouragement only worsened her obsession. I said, "You don't have to stalk her every day."

Liza said, "She's had three grapes, a granola bar and a twenty-ounce Diet Coke. But she stopped into a deli just now. She might be getting something to eat before ballet."

"You are taking this way too seriously," I said. "Lori is clearly an anorexic. Or aspires to be."

"She's too rich *and* too thin."

"What's that sound?"

"I'm crouched behind a cement mixer on Canal Street," said Liza. "Lori's ballet studio is a few doors down. Oh, I wanted to tell you. I saw Vin Transom on the subway into Manhattan. He was with a bunch of his trackletes. They were talk-ing about Sondra, how hot she is, 'get me some of that,' et cetera."

"Did Vin say anything?" I asked.

"No. He laughed along, though."

A kill-the-messenger anger blast shot through me. I switched the phone to my other ear. "Anything else?" I asked curtly.

"Mom, Gary and I are coming to your house for dinner on Sunday night. Your mom invited us."

"Why am I the last to know?"

"More bogus bonding time with Gary." Liza sighed. "Mom doesn't seem to understand that the more time I spend with him, the more I hate him. Oh, God, here she comes. Lori is stepping out of the deli. She's taking a bite of an apple. Another bite. Oh, she just threw the apple in a garbage can. This is great stuff. I wonder if Max knows she's got an eating disorder."

Ms. Shatsky, according to Eli, who heard from Eric Brainard (aka her new best friend), changed the title of my editorial from "A Modest Proposal" (subtle, satirical, literary) to the hammer-blow-to-the-skull Bob Dylan referential "Everybody Must Get Brownstoned."

I kid. Not.

Until Eric explained the reference to Eli, who then ex-plained it to me, I'd never heard of the song "Everybody Must Get Stoned," or any other Bob Dylan song, for that matter. But Ms. Shatsky was a tongue-lolling fan of the guy. Contrary to what I thought initially, the Dylan song was not a rallying cry to all potheads, but it actually meant the same thing my editorial did—that oppressive jerks who wanted everyone to be the same might as well kill people who aren't. The three hundred copies of the *Brief* that appeared in great stacks all over the school, however, did not have a hundred-word explanation of the title of my piece. The confusing but provocative title had the happy result of drawing attention to the front page of the broadsheet. Those who read it were not disappointed with the content.

In short, I was a hit.

And the picture Eli took of me was really quite fetching.

At Chez Brownstone (aka the Epicenter of Revolution), I sat at a central table with Eli, Liza and Eric during our morning free period between ten thirty and eleven.

"Here comes another one," said Eric, as excited as I was by my success.

A dumpy boy I vaguely recognized (a sophomore?) walked up to our table and handed me a folded sheet of newsprint. It was my editorial, and he'd drawn a great big smiley face in the middle of it. He waited for me to look at him—to see him, I think—then shot me a limp demi-smile and moved along.

On the table between us were two dozen copies of the editorial, with hearts, or check marks, or the words "thanks," "cool," "finally," written over the type. Dozens among the Teeming Masses and several Fringe Dwellers had streamed by during lunch to drop a copy on the table or just give me the thumbs-up.

I asked Eric, "Ever seen anything like this before?"

He said, "Never! This is awesome! What are you going to write next? Something even weirder." He pointed at the stack on the table. "Look at this! Just look at it!"

Shaking my head in disbelief, I smiled at the pile of approval—and felt lighter than air.

A Teeming Masser, junior, Kim Daniels, walked up with a copy of my editorial. "You are so cool, Dora!"

I said, "Thanks. The response to my little article, it's been humbling, really. I'm just grateful, and glad to strike a chord."

But Kim lost the second half of my Oscar-worthy acceptance speech because Sondra and Micha had pushed her aside to get to me.

"May I sit?" asked Sondra, cool as an ice cube.

She was already nudging me to scoot over and make room. I wondered if she wanted to sit at our table (for the first time ever) to muscle in, share my glory. Micha preferred to stand, resting her bony hip on the table edge, blocking anyone else who might want to heap praise upon me.

Micha said, "I don't get it. Do you really think the losers of the school should be stoned? Is it a metaphor? That they should start smoking pot or smoke more until they've killed every last miserable, lonely brain cell?"

Eli said, "That's exactly what she meant."

"It's satire," I said. "I'm suggesting that there might be a social culture at Brownstone that prohibits freedom of expression. I used exaggeration to show how oppressive—"

"I still don't get it," said Micha.

"Because you're too literal," said Sondra. To me: "I understand what you're trying to *say*, Fringe. But I don't *agree* with your opinion."

Eric, smelling controversy like a (news)hound, said, "Is that so? You should write a dissent. I'll run a rebuttal next week."

Sondra tore her golden eyes off me, dragging them toward Eric, and said, "And you are?"

"He's the editor of the paper," I said. "Eric Brainard, meet Sondra Fortune."

I watched Sondra size him up, knowing the dilemma she found herself in. Eric was a Teeming Masser, and therefore beneath Sondra's paying him a cent of attention. But he could be of use to her, and she should speak and/or, horrors, spend time with him, thereby compromising her high position.

It was the first time I'd ever seen Sondra squirm. It would not be the last.

She made her decision quickly. Smiling radiantly at Eric, she said, "It's wonderful to meet you, Eric. I would love to talk about writing something. Why don't we take a walk, say, around the block? Get some privacy?"

"Yes," I said. "You wouldn't want to be seen together in school."

Everyone, including Sondra, gasped. She sputtered, "Of course I'd want to be seen—"

I said, "You want to make an impact, so it'd be better to surprise the school with your editorial. People might guess you're writing for the *Brief* if they saw you with Eric. That's why you want privacy, right?"

Eli chuckled. Eric laughed along with her, not sure why any of this was amusing. But he said, "How right you are, Benet." He stood up. "Sondra? Shall we?"

"Meet me outside. I want to say good-bye to my friends," she purred. Eric left, either not realizing or not caring that she'd deftly avoided leaving the room with him.

Micha said, "I'm not walking around the block with that geek."

Sondra ignored her. "All this has been very unexpected," she said to me. "Fringe Girl, have I told you yet how much I absolutely love your hair? Freestyle on you just wasn't working. It was ghastly on you. A real fright. But I didn't want to say anything. I didn't—*don't*—want to hurt you."

Her warning clear, Sondra smiled and walked out, Micha in her wake.

# 14

"The thing about oppressive regimes is that those in power are often just as oppressed as the . . . uh, the oppressed," espoused Noel Kepner in social studies ten minutes later.

Mr. Sagebrush said, "How so?"

Noel said, "They have standards to maintain, and that's a lot of pressure. Plus, they're isolated, in a small population, always worried that everyone secretly hates them. They live in a constant state of doubt that their peers are phonies and liars."

"I'm sorry, are we still talking about Iraq?" asked Mr. Sagebrush. Then, "Yes, Ms. Benet."

I lowered my arm. "Excuse my bluntness, but that is a load of bull." The classroom erupted in snickers. Noel frowned furiously. I went on. "Anyone with two brain cells to rub together can see plainly that the power elite's doubt and isolation are a cakewalk compared to the soul-killing fear of the underclasses, the constant worry that you'd say or do the wrong thing, be exiled or tortured at the whim of the upper class."

When I'd finished my invective, there was a wave of approving finger snaps around the classroom.

Mr. Sagebrush held up his arms, quieting the class. "Ms. Benet, you will not say 'bull' in my class again, unless you are talking about a male cow." He sent me a direct line of eye contact that said, "I have to reprimand you, but I'm with you, sister."

Noel, never at a loss for words, said, "People are born into power. They don't necessarily choose their position, and they can't control other people who thrust them into a role that they might seem suited for, but aren't."

"Then that person should abdicate," I shot back.

More snaps for me. Noel knew when he was beat, and he didn't try to respond.

The class drifted along, but I barely heard a word of the discussion. I was floating on a cloud of confidence and righteousness. This had to be how Sondra Fortune felt every day. I could get used to it, too, I thought.

After the bell rang, I walked to my locker with Eli. When we got there, we both couldn't believe our eyes.

My locker was completely covered, five layers thick, with *Brief* editorial pages. Some were taped on, some folded and stuffed into the slats. Some were placed on the floor in front. All of them had icons drawn on them: smiley faces, exclamation points, hearts, lightning bolts, check marks. One had a sketch of me, with my new haircut, holding a torch like the Statue of Liberty.

The style was unmistakable. Just to be sure, the artist scribbled her initials—J.B.

Eli said, "You're her hero, you know."

"I'm her sister," I said.

Eli said, "When we lived together on Hicks Street, in and out of each other's apartments, it was like *we* were sisters. It was a big adjustment for me when we moved. You're lucky to have Joya."

"When she's twenty-five and I'm twenty-eight, I'm sure I'll agree with you," I said, uncomfortable with Eli's sap. Emotional guilt trips were Liza's territory, not Eli's. "Have you seen Jack today?" I asked, changing the subject.

"Nope," she said succinctly. "And I'm not going to. I told Mr. Yamora that I'm not going to the music room after school anymore. I'll practice at home. I scheduled an extra private lesson each week. And I'm going to start working at the *Brief*."

"What about Eric's Asian fetish?"

"There's nothing wrong with being appreciated for who you are," said Eli.

I decided it'd be vain to leave the newspaper articles on my locker. But I waited until after school to take them down. Actually, I waited until long after school. First, I let some sophomore buy me a cup of coffee at Grind, and then a pair of junior class Fringe Dwellers dragged me to Monty's for a congratulatory slice. I got back to Brownstone to clean off my locker at around four thirty. The hallway was nearly deserted.

I started peeling the pages off, reading the anonymous messages some kids had written, and was hit with a tsunami-like wave of pride. I felt like I could scale mountains, swim the ocean . . . run a marathon.

"Hey, Dora," someone said behind me.

I turned. "Afternoon, Vin," I said casually, though my insides were churning at the sight of him. In all the excitement of the response to my piece, the joy of my Noel Kepner smackdown, I'd temporarily forgotten about my abiding and devoted love for Vin Transom.

He said, "I wanted to congratulate you on your essay."

I said, "Thanks."

We were doing it again. A bona fide exchange of sentences, one after the other.

He said, "I guess I'm the kind of person who should be taken out back and stoned to death."

"No," I said. "You're a special case."

"Because I'm a runner?" he asked.

Because I love you, I thought. "Yeah," I said with a stunning lack of articulation. "I mean, you *are* special. Not in a mentally challenged way, of course."

Silence. Uncomfortable (as usual). Suddenly self-conscious, Vin said, "I've got to get going."

"Would you like to get some coffee?" I asked, despite the homework that awaited me, and the two cups that were already coursing through my intestines.

He hesitated. I instantly fell into my default position when near him—lame and awkward.

But then he blew my mind and said, "Sure."

Our first date—if you could call it that—consisted of sharing a table at Grind, our homework spread out before us, each of us working furiously to finish despite the late start. Occasionally, I'd find myself staring at him, the way his eyelashes fluttered when he blinked, or how he nibbled the end of his pen, his cute frown when he was concentrating hard. He caught me looking a couple of times, but he didn't seem to mind. In fact, he smiled at me and went back to work. For once, our silence wasn't uncomfortable. It was still. Like the surface of a deep pond on a windless day.

We left an hour and a half after we arrived, parting ways at the corner of Henry and Joralemon Streets. He had another half a dozen blocks to go to get to his apartment on Pacific Street.

I said, "Have a good night."

He said, "You, too."

"Thanks for the coffee. I'll never get to sleep tonight." I wouldn't anyway, but it had nothing to do with the caffeine.

Vin shifted his backpack. I thought that was it. But—

He kissed me. Lightly. On the lips. Then he said, "See you tomorrow," and left me there on the street, goo for a spine, noodles for legs.

It was a miracle I could walk the rest of the way home.

# 15

One evening later, Dad and I were pigging out on microwave popcorn, watching the first DVD in our double bill of *Zoolander* and *Dodgeball*.

"Incredible how the Academy of Motion Pictures fails, year after year, to recognize the comic genius of Ben Stiller," said Dad.

"He's robbed repeatedly," I agreed. "A serial robbee."

The landline rang, and Dad paused the movie. Since none of my friends ever called the home number, I was surprised when Dad said, "For you, Adora." Cupping the phone, he mouthed, "It's a boy."

Could it be? After a whole day of waiting and wishing and praying and hoping, had Vin Transom finally mustered the smallest mite of courage to call me? We hadn't seen each other since our sublime mini-kiss on the street, the one I'd relived in my head several (hundred) times.

I bolted out of my couch potato position, fluffed my hair and straightened my clothes. Dad mouthed, "He can't see you through the phone."

Grabbing the receiver, I mouthed, "Just to be sure." Into the phone, I said, "Hello?"

"Dora? Hey, it's Noel."

Noel? Who the . . . Noel Kepner? I said, "Yeah, hey."

"Hey."

Silence. I said, "If this is really Noel, why aren't you talking?"

"You think I talk a lot?" he asked. "I guess I do. But what's the alternative? Most people don't talk enough. They think of something they'd like to say, but don't and then lose the opportunity. See, if more people spoke their minds—"

"Okay, I'm convinced it's you now," I said.

"You got me going there," he said.

"I sure did."

"The reason I'm calling—besides one more opportunity to talk—Lump is playing at the Juicy Bar again tomorrow night. I saw you there last time. A lot of people will be there."

Oh, God. Not another night of sonic torture. I said, "Thanks for the heads-up."

"So you'll come?"

"Possibly," I said.

"Great."

"Okay," I said. "Bye."

"Bye," he said.

I hung up the phone. Last time, I went to Juicy because I felt like I had to, to brush elbows with the Ruling Class, put in face time. But everything had changed. I'd had my first taste of rebellion—and been rewarded richly for it. Being herded like a barnyard animal back into Juicy just because the great Noel Kepner beckoned was just not going to happen. I wondered if Sondra had asked him to invite me so she could mock my obsequiousness to Noel in front of the whole Ruling Class.

Dad said, "So. Boys now. Calling the house. Begging for your favor."

"Sorry to disappoint, Dad," I said. "I know how much you and Mom are dying for me to get a boyfriend so you can crack open a copy of *His-and-Her Dating* and force advice down my throat."

"No, darling. We plan to cram it into your head via the ears."

"Keep the book on the shelf. The overinflated ego who called: He just wants warm bodies and ass-kissers to fill the room at his next gig."

Dad said, "Have we cleared use of 'ass' in the house?"

"We cleared 'ass,' 'damn,' and 'shit' last year," I said. "We cleared 'hell' the year before that. You cleared 'bitch' when I was ten, but only in reference to female dogs."

"I remember," he said. "And every time we walked by a dog on the street, you'd smile at the owner with your adorable little face and ask, 'Is your dog a nice boy, or a real *bitch*?' "

The landline again.

Dad said, "Did the overinflated ego forget to give you directions?"

Or the time. Impatiently, I picked up and said, "Yes?"

"Dora?"

Holy shit (damn ass hell bitch)! I said, "Vin, yes, hi."

To Dad, I mouthed, "Not the ego!"

He took the hint and left the room (although I'm pretty sure he eavesdropped from the kitchen).

"How's it going?" asked Vin.

"Great!" I said. "I mean, pretty good."

"Cool," he said.

I just loved his economy with words. He didn't waste a syllable. I said, "So."

"Want to hang out tomorrow night?" he asked.

"Yes!" I said. "I mean, sure."

"I thought we'd take a walk. It's still warm enough outside."

I said, "I love outside!" I adored outside. I could marry and spend the rest of my life with outside—as long as I was on a date with Vin.

We arranged the particulars. I hung up. Rays of light and joy shined out of the top of my head. Granted, it'd been a long time coming, but I'd finally been asked out by someone I wanted to say yes to. This feeling was beyond the beyond. Floating, heart pounding, the words "he likes me . . . he likes me . . . update in five minutes . . ." rolled across my brain like a news crawl on the side of a building. My limbs felt shaky and I needed to sit, but I also wanted to jump out of my skin and dance until my guts spilled out.

I realized suddenly: All the times I'd said, "I don't need a boy to be happy," I was lying to myself. Now that I had what I said I didn't need, I understood how desperately I wanted it, needed it, could not live without it.

Dad called from the kitchen. "Safe to enter?"

"You bet your ass!" I said.

"You're pushing it," he warned.

We got back to the serious business of watching comedy. *Zoolander* had never been funnier.

Later that night, I consulted the Sarcastic Ball. "Will Vin and I make out tomorrow night?"

It read (not wasting a syllable): "Duh."

I won't hash over the boring details of getting dressed, putting on natural-but-alluring makeup, artfully arranging my hair. Let me just say that as hard as it was to put myself together for the first day of school, dressing for my first date with Vin—the promise of sexual activity (future dates, future sexual activity) hanging in the balance—was excruciating. I decided to go with my favorite jeans, a cute emerald top that made my eyes green, a small-fit inky jean jacket, and the only pair of high-heeled strappy sandals I owned. Man, were they hot. Cobalt blue straps across the arch and a two-inch kitten heel. If Vin happened to catch sight of my feet, and he would (I'd make sure of it), he wouldn't be able to resist me. I also wore a thick layer of bright red lipstick. My lips looked like a target. Just to make sure he knew where to aim.

The buzzer, right on time, at eight. I'd already eaten a snack so that, if Vin took me to dinner, I'd have the charmingly delicate appetite of a tiny bird.

I yelled, "Mom, Dad, I'm gone!" and ran downstairs to the building's front door. Vin was waiting on the other side of it. He looked good. The same. If he'd done anything special, sartorially speaking, I didn't notice it.

He said, "Do you have a curfew?"

"Eleven."

"Me, too."

"Then we'd better get going," I said jauntily, a madcap on the loose.

Traipsing along, we walked toward Montague Street, and the dozens of restaurants and cafés on it. I wondered if Vin had a fake ID, and if he'd use it.

I said, "Nice night."

"Colder than I thought."

Colder than I'd thought, too. With only the jean jacket and my bare toes, I was freezing. But I didn't complain. Good dates didn't complain. I said, "So, what's the plan?"

"I thought we'd walk the Bridge."

The Brooklyn Bridge was beautiful at night. Romantic, goes without saying. One could see everything from the top: Statue of Liberty, Manhattan skyline, South Street Seaport, Staten Island, New Jersey, two rivers, three other bridges, thousands of lights like pearls on a necklace. I'd walked the Bridge about eight hundred thousand times. My first crossing was in a Baby Bjorn strapped to my dad's chest at two weeks old. But this would be my first crossing on a date. And I was going to do it with Vin. In nothing but a jean jacket. And heels that, after two blocks, were already digging into my feet.

I said, "You run the Bridge every day, right?"

"Yeah," he said. "And I always wonder about being up there with a girl."

Ho. Lee. Shit.

We walked. And walked. With each step, the straps of my sandals dug divots in my tender feet. The Bridge's footpath was a boardwalk, wooden planks with a half an inch between them. My kitten heels got stuck about ten times before I adjusted to walk on my toes, which dug the straps in deeper. The upside to pain: It kept me relatively quiet. Vin seemed to approve. We were a quarter of the way across the Bridge when he took hold of my hand.

I loved how silky his skin felt. And, honestly, I needed the support. And the warmth. The air was colder over the East River, and the higher up the Bridge we walked, the windier it got. My hair was whipping around, my jeweled bobby pins flying off and falling into the river below. The upside to the cold: It kept my mind off my pain. Sort of.

I said, "Let's sit."

We were at the Bridge's highest point, between the two towers, one on the Brooklyn side, one on the Manhattan side. Connecting them, strands of crisscrossed steel cables created the illusion of a spider's web. I plopped down on a bench and hugged my jacket closer.

Vin said, "Are you cold?"

"A little," I said.

He sat next to me. Put his arm around me.

I wish I could say I was excited. But I was more grateful for the body heat. I snuggled into his side for more of it, and he edged closer to me.

Okay, now I was getting excited.

He said, "We've been in class together since preschool."

"But we've never gotten to know each other," I said, completing his thought. "Except for those couple of playdates we had in kindergarten."

"We had playdates?" he said.

"You came to my house after school and undressed all my Barbies. I cried because I'd planned their outfits so carefully."

He laughed. "Are you sure you're not confusing me with Noel Kepner? He seems like the Barbie-stripping type."

No, it was Vin. At six, I was insanely jealous of how he'd ignored me in favor of my dolls. That was why I cried when he made the Barbie nudist colony. I wanted to be his doll. Not to be stripped and lined up in a row with the others. He'd concentrated too hard on taking off the little tops and bottoms. I'd wanted him to concentrate that hard on me.

"You do come off as a bit remote," I said.

"You should see me around my friends."

I had. I'd made a study of Vin in various settings. Around his friends, he was just as loud, idiotic and guffawing as they were. I said, "You seem distant otherwise. Around me anyway."

Vin pulled me closer. I got the feeling he had had enough talking. My heart pounded, almost frighteningly hard, as if I might have a heart attack and drop dead in Vin's arms (which would be insanely romantic, like a Russian epic novel, and possibly worth dying for). My mouth went dry suddenly, too.

"Do you have a lot of experience?" I had to know.

"Some," he said.

"With who?" If I knew her, I'd have to kill her.

"Girls in my runners' club. Girls I've met at camp. And, you know, Beth Clomp," he said. Beth went to Brownstone until ninth grade when her family fled Brooklyn for the burbs. She was also a track star, and she and Vin had had—according to the rumors, at least—some interesting bus rides to and from meets. As for how interesting, I would never know (and not for lack of trying to find out).

I said, "I really liked Beth. I wish she hadn't moved." I'd danced in my room for hours when I heard she was leaving town. Vin hadn't had an official girlfriend at school since.

Vin asked, "How about you? Any experience?"

Hardly any. I was kissed at a camp social when I was thirteen. "Yeah, some boys I met over the summer," I lied. "Those Teen Tours were like Roman orgies. If my parents'd had the slightest clue, they'd have locked me in my room."

He seemed impressed, and started rubbing my shoulder, squeezing my upper arm. With his other hand, he touched my chin, and tilted my head up.

To kiss me.

The upside of kissing: I forgot about the cold, the pain, my name, my address, where we were, who we were. I thought about the earliest troglodytes who somehow got the idea in their peanut-sized brains to press their mouths against each other and see what happened. I felt as if I were that hairy-armpit cavegirl who spoke in grunts and had the forehead width of a pencil. One didn't need an intellect to press against Vin's luscious, pillowlike lips with my own.

Channeling my prehistoric ancestry, I may have grunted. Vin pulled back and said, "Are you okay?"

"No," I said.

"What's wrong?"

"You stopped kissing me," I said. "Mustn't do that, Vin."

He plunged into my mouth again, his tongue gliding around mine like a slippery eel.

See, I could go on, for page after page, about this kiss. A snog for the record books, topping the list of "Most Passionate, Stupefying, Mouth-Fusing Kisses of All Time." We sucked face until I wasn't sure I had much of one left. We played tonsil hockey until we'd both scored. He kissed me bone stupid. There was quite a bit of above-the-waist groping as well. And, okay, maybe a little below the waist, too.

Sadly, it had to end. And in dramatic fashion. I didn't hear the puttering of the NYPD security patrol golf cart as it pulled up next to us. But I couldn't miss the flashlight shining in my (closed) eyes.

"You've had enough for one night," said the cop, pinning us on the bench with the light. "Break it up. It's after midnight."

My curfew was eleven. We'd been making out on the bench for three hours. I couldn't believe it. Time had warped.

"Shit," said Vin (succinctly, economically, adorably). "Come on, Dora. Let's run."

He sprang off the bench, and he started running. I stood up, and immediately collapsed from the head rush of kissing and the fear of missing my curfew, along with battered and bloody feet that were now frozen blocks of ice.

The cop helped me up. I said, "Take pity on me, sir."

"If my daughter were on the Brooklyn Bridge with a boy at midnight, she wouldn't get my pity," he said. "She'd get the back of my hand."

O-*kay*, so the cop was a child beater. "Just give me a lift to the end of the bridge," I pleaded.

I sat on the passenger seat of the golf cart. We drove past Vin, and I waved at him as we went by.

At the end of the footpath, the cop kicked me out of the

cart. My feet had warmed enough. Vin caught up, and we walked home. Correction: I limped, he pestered me to please move faster.

While we'd been making out, I'd loved every second of it. But now, under the glare of streetlights with Vin annoyed that I was so slow, it was almost like we'd never touched at all. As if the hours before had been a crazy, sexy dream. The magic of making out didn't linger for ten minutes? I'd thought it would last for days.

Vin deposited me at my doorstep, the stoop light making him squint. He said, "Now I know what the Bridge is like with a girl."

"Was it all you'd imagined?"

"Almost," he said. I must have looked surprised, because he quickly added, "I'd imagined more. But I don't expect any girl to take off all her clothes and have sex in public with me."

I must have looked surprised (if not grossed out) because he said, "I'm a guy. I have bizarre thoughts."

Then he lightly punched me on the upper arm, and we kissed good-bye—too quickly—before he ran off toward his punishment at home.

I unlocked my town house door and crept extra quietly up the stairs to our third-floor duplex, still processing Vin's final confession. Okay, yes, he was a boy. All boys probably had fantasies about having sex on the Brooklyn Bridge. I'd been trained since sex ed in fifth grade to view males as walking erections that thought about sex forty-seven times a day and sized up every female over the age of thirteen as a potential partner. But, I had to say, his comment drained some of the romance out of what had happened between us on the Bridge in the dark.

I unlocked my apartment door with the stealth of a spy.

Opening it, I expected to find my parents waiting, Mom frantically dialing 911, Dad vexed and disappointed, shredding paper napkins to keep himself calm.

But the downstairs floor was completely dark. And quiet. Everyone was asleep. My parents trusted me not to break curfew. But I broke it anyway, without losing their trust, or getting caught.

Sweet.

The kitchen clock said 12:35. I had to eat something. I made a sandwich and took it upstairs to my room. I turned on the light and locked the door. Wanting to see if making out for hours had altered my appearance, I checked myself out in the mirror.

I screamed and dropped the sandwich, which broke the plate. I stared at the revolting sight before me—the hair windswept into a squirrel's nest, the lipstick I'd painstakingly applied smeared halfway up my cheeks like a waxy red mask, my shirt stained with fingerprint smudges of what seemed to be soot. My feet were a disturbing shade of blue, swollen to twice their normal size, with bloody pulp squishing between the straps. I looked like I'd been hit by a truck. Or sat on by an buffalo. Or shot through a cannon.

And this travesty was what Vin saw under the five-million-watt streetlights.

No wonder he'd barely kissed me good-bye.

A knock on the door. Mom said, "Adora? I heard a scream."

"I'm fine, Mom. Don't come in. I'm naked."

"How was the date?"

"Good. Fine."

"Do you want to talk about it?" she asked. "Because I'm here. If you have any questions. No matter how small."

Poor woman. She was downright desperate. "Thanks,

Mom." Exaggerated yawn. "I'm going to sleep. See you in the morning."

She said good night and left. I exhaled, cleaned up the broken plate, ate the parts of the sandwich that weren't covered with floor lint. I washed my face and feet and, finally, tucked myself into bed.

I didn't sleep, though. As soon as I lay down, I instantly forgot about the thirty minutes between the cop kicking us off the Bridge and now. I merely cropped all the negatives out of my memory. That accomplished, the magic of kissing quickly returned. I replayed every second of our three hours on the bench until the first light of dawn came in through my bedroom window.

## CALL WAITING
*by Gloria and Ed Benet*
*(excerpted from* His-and-Her Dating*)*

The date was perfect. It seemed as if the two of you were yin and yang, two parts of a glorious whole. And yet, he hasn't picked up the %$#%* phone to thank you for the lovely time. What is his %$*&@ problem?

### Possible Explanations from Gloria

1  He's a busy guy. This is one of the reasons you liked him in the first place. Maybe he's meeting his fantastic friends, or winning a tennis tournament, or buying a new car. Maybe he's getting a full-body wax so that he'll feel all silky on your next date.

2  He's playing it cool. Most men know the codes of cool conduct. If he were to call or e-mail five minutes after dropping you off, you'd be turned off. He understands the subtle tightrope walk of being interested, but not appearing to be too much. He's giving you a chance to reflect. To look forward. To worry, just a little bit, so that you'll feel that much happier when he does call.

3  He's been mugged/had a heart attack in his sleep/choked on a chicken leg. Far-fetched? Perhaps, but won't you feel foolish when you get a phone call from him in the hospital, apologizing for not contacting you sooner?

4  He feels guilty and/or embarrassed. He let you split the check. Or he didn't walk you all the way home. Or he spilled his soup. On your lap. Perhaps he spoke out of turn, or made a political comment he wishes he could take back. Or he told an off-color joke. Could be he accidentally burped, farted, spit up or vomited, in your ladylike presence.

5   He's not sure you want him to call. Think back. Did he say he would call and you didn't give him the necessary encouragement?

6   He lost your phone number, e-mail address, forgot your last name, the name of the place where you work, the phone number for the friend who fixed you up. Or, perhaps his dog ate his PDA, and his computer blew up.

### Probable Explanations from Ed

1   He doesn't want to.
2   He lacks the balls.

In which case, he's not worth obsessing over, is he?

# 16

"Has he called yet?" asked Liza before dinner on Sunday night, eighteen hours since Vin dropped me off. We were in my room, waiting to be summoned downstairs by the adults, who were, at the moment, guzzling wine and kibitzing. I could hear my mother's voice barreling up the stairs. When she drank, she got loud.

I said, "I'm glad he hasn't called. I respect his stoicism. It'd be a huge turnoff if he called today. Or IMed or sent an e-mail. Besides which, we have an understanding."

"How do you know he hasn't e-mailed?" asked Liza. "You should check."

I'd checked my e-mail approximately five thousand times already. I'd called Sprint to make sure my cell voice mail was working. I'd scanned the skies for carrier pigeons.

"I remember when Max blew me off for the first time," said Liza with wispy nostalgia for the early heartbreak of her enduringly depressing quasi relationship with the former-midget chess king.

"Vin is not Max Lindseying me. That's absurd to even suggest. Vin cares about me. We have romance. We have passion. It's nothing like you and Max."

Liza's face started to crumble. Her forehead furrowed. Lips went aquiver, eyes moistened.

I said, "But I'm sure, in a few months, Vin will turn into just as big a shit as Max is."

That little remark did not help.

My mom yelled, "Kids! Come on down for dinner."

Joya shot out of her room and thundered down the stairs, eager eater that she was. Liza and I took our time about it. She pulled herself together, summoning her game face.

I said, "How's it going with Gary?"

"If I pretend he doesn't exist," she said, "maybe he won't."

At dinner, Gary was polite, with shiny, high-polish manners. I'd never heard so many "pleases" and "thank yous" in my life. My mom was pushing the homemade coleslaw like there was no tomorrow (and there might not be, if one dared to eat the stuff). My dad smiled and nodded like a windup yes-man doll as he listened to (or pretended to) Gary's unending stream of hair-raising tales from the trading floor.

Joya ate quietly and smiled a lot at Stephanie, who'd always had a soft spot for the baby girl of our old building.

"I haven't seen you for at least a year, Joya," said Stephanie just before dessert. "How do you do it? You're even more precious with age."

"Thank you, Ms. Greene," said Joya, blushing and smiling, making Stephanie swoon under the tidal wave of cuteness.

Mom brought out a platter of cookies and pastries from Fongu, an Italian bakery on Montague Street. I snagged a chocolate éclair and took a big, delicious bite.

Gary said, "So, Adora. Liza told us you're staging a revolution at school and have a plan in action to dismantle the status quo and construct a new world order."

The sly smile, the lilting way he said "new world order." He mocked me. He was yet another adult who thought all teens were dumb (i.e., stupid). Fortunately, I couldn't reply with all that custard in my mouth.

"What's this?" Mom boomed (two glasses of wine and counting). To Stephanie, she added, "You're so lucky Liza tells you what's going on in her life. Adora never tells me anything."

" 'New world order' is a bit ambitious," I said finally. "I'll settle for a kinder, gentler eleventh grade." I glared at Liza. I couldn't believe she'd told her mom and step-boyfriend about my project. And now my parents knew, and they'd heap bright ideas on me until I was smothered by them. I'd spent a lifetime listening to them. This revolution was my thing. My personal, private show. And Liza told Stephanie? I couldn't believe it. *God*, she was pissing me off lately.

Giving credit where it was due, Joya, who'd obviously read my *Brief* editorial, hadn't breathed a word to Mom and Dad.

Dad said, "This is a school project?"

"Term project," I said. "For social studies."

Gary said, "I'm quite interested, Adora. If you'd like, I can offer some ideas. I used to be an arbitrator for companies involved in hostile takeovers. You know what that means? A big, powerful corporation wants to buy a smaller, weaker one. The smaller company is against the takeover but usually can't prevent it. I'm brought in to try to make the process as painless as possible."

In other words, he batted for the winning, if evil, team. And this vulture took hold of Stephanie's hand, right on top of the table, for all the world to see. Liza averted her eyes, letting them fall on the plate of pastries, taking two, three, for her own.

Stephanie said, "Do you need all that cake, Liza?"

Liza sighed and put one pastry back. She was the small, weak company in her own hostile domestic takeover.

I said, "That's fascinating, Gary."

If he registered the snark, he didn't let it show. "As I said, I have a lot of insight into these type of situations, if you'd care to hear more about it."

"Thanks, Gary, but no thanks," I said, taking another bite of éclair.

"Adora!" shrieked Mom. "Gary is offering to help."

"And I said, 'No thanks.' "

"I'm sure he'll have some good ideas," said diplomatic Dad. Liza devoured a biscotti.

"I'm doing just fine with my own ideas," I retorted.

"But you can always use more opinions," yelled Mom (three glasses and counting).

"She said no," said Gary, as if I'd declined a dish of manna from heaven.

Stephanie asked, "Liza, aren't *you* curious what Gary has to say?"

Poor Liza looked close to tears. Once again, I was forced to step in to protect her. "Thank you very, very, very, very much, but Liza and I don't want to hear your opinions, advice or ideas. This is my project. Not hers—or yours. If I have to swallow one more piece of parental advice—and you, Gary, aren't even my parent!—I'll puke up my lungs."

I grabbed Liza by the wrist and we ran out of the dining room, upstairs and into my bedroom. I slammed the door and locked it.

We were trapped. No means of escape. Which could be the operative metaphor for my entire adolescence.

Liza said, "Puke up your lungs. I don't think that's physiologically possible. Puke up your intestines, now there's an image."

"I may never leave this room again," I whined. "Why did you tell them about my project?"

She shrugged. "You don't know what it's like at home. Gary is over every night. Mom is always at me to eat less and talk more. Gary makes fun of me in his sneaky, creepy way. I had to fill the void."

Liza's chin went quivery again, and I almost groaned (selfish first reaction). I went to cheap distraction. "Check out my feet," I said, taking off my socks.

They were as mangled and pulpy as hamburger meat. I'd had to use an entire tube of Neosporin and two dozen Band-Aids to patch them up. Liza gasped and poked at my swollen arch.

"Ouch!"

"Sorry," she said. "Dating battle scars. Was it worth the pain and disfigurement?"

I smiled and said, "I'll tell you after he *fucking calls me*."

She laughed. Thank God. I'd broken through to her happy default setting. "Can I make a small suggestion?" I asked. "About this wretched Gary situation?"

Liza said, "Thanks, Dora, but no, thank you."

I nodded, taking the swat with more generosity than Gary. "What can I do?"

"I'm sorry I've been weird lately," she said. "It's just that I'm so mixed up. I guess I should talk about it—"

Ring. Cell phone. I pulled it out of my pocket and saw the caller ID. Vin Transom. He'd finally called.

I answered it. If Liza had asked me to ignore it, I would have. But she didn't.

# 17

S NOG WEEK DIARY

**Monday**
*Noon to 1:00 P.M.:* Met Vin at Chez Brownstone, and then we immediately went into the off-limits, still-under-construction teachers' lounge on the upper level. Made out, groped, clothing on but askew. Arrived *tarde* to French.

*2:00 to 2:30 P.M.:* Vin and I skipped study half hour and went to the deserted basketball court outside the rear entrance to the lower school library. Serious snogging, and some dignified humping against the concrete wall. My tongue was fast becoming the best-exercised muscle in my body.

*3:00 to 5:00 P.M.:* After three seconds of deliberation, Vin decided to blow off track practice. I asked him over to my house, but he said parents made him uncomfortable, especially mine because they would probably "overanalyze me." I explained that my parents were not shrinks and would more likely talk him to death than listen to what he had to say besides. But Vin was adamant, so we got a back booth at Monty's and shared a slice and a large Diet Coke, feeding each other, and licking marinara sauce off our lips. We took turns relieving our bladders ("large" was a gross understatement, in terms of beverage sizing). We also spent some time gazing longingly into each other's eyes and stroking each other's thighs under the table.

## Tuesday

*12:00 to 1:00 P.M.:* The lunch hour canoodle fest was on again today, but we had to find a new spot. The teachers' lounge had been officially cordoned off with yellow tape, with a big sign that said, KEEP OUT. Instead, we went back to the basketball court. Unlike yesterday, though, the courtyard wasn't deserted. Lower school kids were running around everywhere. Again, I suggested my place. My parents had a lunch meeting in the city, and we could go there without being observed, interrupted, or caught. Vin shook off the suggesting. He was worried about the timing. We'd consumed half of the lunch hour trying to find a place to go. Instead, we went to the top floor of the auditorium and sat in the balcony pews, the colored light from the stained-glass windows shining upon us. We glommed for the seventeen minutes we had left.

*7:00 to 7:45 P.M.:* Vin ran by my house after practice. He was sweaty and wearing smelly track pants and a sweatshirt. We sat on my stoop (he still refused to come upstairs, this time, not wanting to offend my family with his post-workout appearance, although I couldn't help thinking he had no problem presenting his sweaty self to me). I wasn't so keen to grapple with him all sticky like that. So we kissed with just our lips. It was sweet. I guess.

## Wednesday

*8:00 to 8:30 A.M.:* I saw Vin on the front steps at Brownstone when I arrived. He was with a bunch of his tracklete friends, and they were gawking openly at Sondra Fortune, Micha Dropov, Stacy Dallas, and Violet Fugg (all Ruling Class juniors or seniors). Even Vin seemed to be staring at the girls as they preened, pretending to ignore their audience. I was practically standing on Vin's toes when he finally noticed me. He grabbed me by the wrist and pulled me around the corner to Sydney Place. We ducked into the cranny under someone's stoop and made out with the fever we were lacking last night. His hands were everywhere. I was glad I wore loose jeans. I wondered why Vin was so frisky at the early hour, and he said, "Why are you always asking me these annoying questions?" I swore I wouldn't ask another question for as long as I lived. He seemed satisfied by that, and we ran back to school and made it on time to first period.

*12:00 to 1:00 P.M.:* Vin suggested we actually eat lunch today. He wanted to go to Sushi Zen, a take-out Japanese place across the street from Brownstone with no back booths or dark corners. The only seating was in the front window on stools. We'd be totally exposed (as a couple, which I didn't mind), but would have no privacy for sexual activity. The decision seemed to work in contradiction to the heat he'd shown me earlier. But I went along with it. We were sitting in the window, feeding each other pieces of California roll when Sondra and Micha walked by outside. They waved at us as they passed, and Sondra threw in an extra little winky-winky. I turned to Vin to grouse about her. He looked distracted. I asked what was the matter, and he said he'd swallowed a big piece of wasabi. We didn't kiss, except good-bye when we went our separate ways at the end of the hour.

# 18

Wednesday, 1:00 P.M.

Ms. Benet:
It is now Wednesday afternoon, and I haven't yet received your weekly
update and strategy report. Am I to assume that the task you have set
out for yourself is too difficult? If so, please plan an alternative re-
port/presentation for your term project (gentle reminder: you've got
one month before the due date).
Sincerely (not threateningly),
Mr. Sagebrush

October 5th, Wednesday

To: Mr. Sagebrush
From: Dora Benet
Subject: Begging your forgiveness and understanding

Forgive my delinquency. I had a very rough weekend. And an emotional,
trying week thus far. The difficulties were of a personal nature, or I'd tell
you all about them in graphic detail. But I'm sure you understand that
there are some private events that a student cannot describe to her
teacher (even one as intelligent and sympathetic as you are). That vio-

lates the time-honored separation of school and home, one of the values of American education we citizens prize so deeply. I fully intend to deliver an outline to you, without further delay.

Wednesday, threeish

Ms. Benet:
The amount I am interested in your personal life cannot be measured on any conventional scale, because it is less than the weight of a single grain of rice. That said, the separation between school and home is a flimsy line that can be crossed at will at the request of a parent or teacher. The separation of church and state, however, prevents me from leading prayer groups in class. It does not prevent me from insisting that students meet their deadlines. Especially students granted certain latitudes, which I'm regretting more and more as the days press on. Get me an update by tomorrow morning.
    And I mean it,
Mr. Sagebrush


"Vin and I use our mouths for more important matters than talking," I said to Liza and Eli at Grind after school. "He's not a verbal person."

"So what is he?" asked Eli.

"He's a physical person," I said. "His love of sport. His hot and puffy lips. His warm and comforting arms. We communicate with our bodies, our touch, our skin. We don't need words. In fact, I'd honestly prefer that he didn't talk at all."

Eli said, "It's optimistic to think that any conversation you had with a boy—any boy—would be as satisfying as one you'd have with a girl. Any girl. Even some girl you just met on the subway."

Liza said, "Max and I used to talk for hours. Actually, he'd tell me how brilliant he was for hours, and I'd listen."

Eli and I made eye contact. This was progress, Liza showing a flash of insight into the relationship that wasn't. Perhaps, in watching Stephanie's deference to Gary, Liza saw a bit of herself.

I said, "Much as I'd like to talk about Vin Transom and how devoted he is to me—how sexy and irresistible he finds me—I need material for my update. Mr. Sagebrush will pull the plug otherwise. So, what've we got? Minister of Propaganda?"

That was Eli. She'd been working at the *Brief* for Eric two afternoons a week—of her own free will. She reached into her backpack and withdrew a sheet of paper.

"Sondra Fortune's response to your rant. It's pretty short, sweet as syrup and just as sticky. It runs in tomorrow's paper."

"*What*?" I blurted. "You waited until now to show me?"

"I only found out about it myself this afternoon. And it's not like you've been around lately," sniffed Eli.

"Sorry, sorry. Just the idea of Sondra responding. Read it," I said.

"Aloud?"

"Sure. With feeling, if you please."

Eli cleared her throat. Then she read, trying to imitate Sondra's girlfriendese. " 'Diversity. That's what sets Brownstone apart from every other elite private school in Brooklyn, or Manhattan, for that matter. Here at beloved Brownstone, we students and teachers represent dozens of races, religions, and ethnicities. Like America, we are powerful because of our diversity. This message—that our variety is our greatest strength—has been as much a part of our curriculum as music, art and science.' "

"That is true," said Liza. "We've had mandatory diversity and tolerance seminars since kindergarten."

I sneered at Liza for interrupting. "Keep reading," I said to Eli. "We're on the verge of a big 'but.' I can feel it."

"How right you are," said Eli. "And I quote, 'BUT, for all our diversity training, our teachers hadn't prepared us for differences of another kind. Besides skin color and faith, we have other telling dissimilarities, namely, our interests, tastes, passions, ideals and personal goals. Oftentimes, one's individual goals might seem strange or perverse. For example, I question the personal goals of someone who writes an intentionally inflammatory editorial in the student newspaper. I wonder if the pursuit of a personal goal might help the individual get the attention she clearly craves, but would cause harm to the larger population of the school. As Brownstone students, united in our diversity, we owe it to ourselves to embrace all ideas, and treasure all opinions, value every goal. Just as long as they have all of our best interests at heart.' "

"That's it?" I asked.

Eli nodded. "The title she suggested was, 'We Are Brownstone. We Are One.' "

Liza said, "She's calling you a troublemaker. A rabble-rouser."

"Not to sound like a geek, but that is exactly how threatened governments try to marginalize rebellious factions. They call revolutionaries lunatics and idiots. Next, she'll insist I'm in league with the devil, or that I'm from a predatory race of aliens."

"She's got you stuck, though. Any criticism of her piece would make you seem self-serving and disloyal to the school. Unpatriotic," said Eli.

"Shit!" I said loudly, drawing the glares of several Grind customers. "Sondra outsmarted me."

"Then you have to out-outsmart her," said Liza.

"You're Minister of Intelligence," I said. "Any bright ideas?"

"Short on ideas, long on information," she said. "What if

Sondra were forcing other people to help her achieve her personal goals? Kind of bucks her 'We Are Brownstone. We Are One' thesis. That is, unless it was 'We Are One. We Are Sondra.' "

"Her personal goal?" I asked. "Other than humiliating me?"

"She wants everyone to wear a Brownstone T-shirt tomorrow."

We all had at least one T-shirt with a Brownstone Institute logo. Parents were urged to buy them for school fund-raisers. They were decent-looking: navy with a white logo, including the cute pelican mascot.

"Mr. Sagebrush is going to love this," I said. "She tries to make me seem like a crazy selfish cow while unifying the wavering masses with patriotic fervor. This is a frigging classic antirevolutionary tactic."

Putting Sondra's scheme into a historical perspective, I reasoned the best strategy would be an immediate and ferocious counteroffensive.

"Okay, here's what we do," I said.

Eli and Liza leaned forward, expectancy and excitement in their eyes.

"We sleep on it," I suggest.

"Good idea," said Eli.

"I've got to go anyway," said Liza. "Lori Dropov's ballet class ends in twenty minutes, and I have to get to Manhattan in time to see where she goes next."

"Forget her for one night," said Eli.

"No," said Liza firmly. "I want to see if she and Max have dinner plans."

"Maybe you *should* cut back on the spying," I suggested gently.

"This is going to sound nuts, so brace yourselves," said Liza.

"But watching Lori makes me happy. I feel like I'm still in-volved with Max this way."

"But you're not," I said, as Liza stood up and gathered her stuff. "For fock's sake, Liza."

"Easy, Dora," said Eli.

Liza kissed us each on the cheek. As she left Grind, Eric Brainard came in. He walked right over to our table and sat next to Eli in the chair that Liza had just vacated. He said to her, "Sorry I'm late."

Was she expecting him? I wondered. She hadn't mentioned it. I asked Eric, "In your objective professional opinion, what do you think of Sondra's essay?" I asked.

Eric said, "I told her it was brilliant. But I'll tell you that the writing is flat, and her thesis is pandering."

"Is it not too late to pull it?"

"I'm not pulling it!" he said. "Sondra Fortune in the *Brief*? I have a full-body shot of her in a miniskirt. I'll move five hun-dred copies."

"There are only eight hundred kids in the entire school," I said.

I was so focused on Eric, I failed to notice another boy ap-proach our table.

"Hey, guys."

I looked up to see Noel Kepner grinning down at me.

Eric said, "Noel! How's it going? Want a seat?"

With a fawning offer like that, how could Noel resist? He sat, and said, "I missed you at Juicy on Saturday night, Dora. I thought you were coming to see my show."

His show? "Oh, yes. Lump." I said the name of his "band" with extra tweak on top. Eric and Eli suppressed giggles. Noel acted like he hadn't heard it. "I was busy."

"You missed a great time," he said.

"I had my own great time."

He frowned. "You were with Vin Transom?"

"I was indeed." News traveled fast, and all the way up the social ladder.

Noel seemed to want to say something else. Instead, he showed uncharacteristic self-restraint and kept his mouth shut.

Eli said, "Anyway, we were just leaving. To go to Eric's house to do homework. You coming, Dora?"

I stood. "Sure."

Unless I was completely mistaken, I got the impression, based on his beseeching expression, that Noel wanted me to stay for a private confab.

More like, he couldn't go for five minutes without some groupie girl to absorb the overflow of his ego.

And so we left Noel alone (first time ever?) at Grind. The sight of him abandoned made me feel unsettled, though. Guilty. I'd been rude, after all. That bucked my training. Then again, I'd been rude a lot lately.

We walked to Eric's apartment on Pierrepont Street, only a couple of blocks from Grind. He lived in one of the largest Victorian mansions in the Heights, once occupied by a single family about a hundred fifty years ago. Nowadays, the building was divided into seven apartments. I'd never been inside this mansion, although I'd admired its spiral stoop, front porch, stone gables and terraces for as long as I could remember. I felt excited for my first peek inside.

The entryway was mirror-lined, with a thick mahogany banister that led up the steep staircase. Eric said he lived in the rear triplex on the top floors. The apartment was too big for him and his parents now that his two brothers (Brownstone grads) were in college.

"One's at Harvard and one's at Yale," said Eric as he unlocked his apartment door. "I'm expected to go to Princeton. But give me a break! *New Jersey*? I'd just as soon go to some school in Alabama where they shoot Jews on sight."

"Snob," said Eli. I wasn't ready to think about college yet. I knew my buffer of blissful avoidance was growing slim. But that was a stress I'd postpone for as long as possible. Just the idea of it made my mouth feel dry.

"Can I have a glass of water, please?" I asked.

Eric said, "Sure," and led us into the kitchen.

A window overlooking the rear courtyard between Pierrepont and Montague Street was open. Piano music poured in through it and filled the small kitchen. Even with my tone-deaf ears, I heard the sadness and loneliness behind the notes.

Eric was prattling on about the history of their kitchen renovations, but Eli wasn't listening to him. She was floating on the raft of the melody, her head bobbing slightly.

Jack Carp lived in an apartment on Montague Street. I looked out of Eric's kitchen window, across the courtyards between the buildings, following the sound. Through a square-shaped window directly across the way, I could actually see Jack inside his living room as he swayed over the keys.

"He sounds good," said Eli suddenly. "That bastard."

# 19

O ctober 6th, Thursday

To: Mr. Sagebrush (for whom patience is a virtue)
From: Dora Benet
Subject: Belated update

Read today's *Brief*. You will find an article by Sondra Fortune—an article that my sources alerted me to prior to publication. As the leader of the entrenched government, Sondra's attempt to manipulate the masses is only too obvious. That girl doesn't know the meaning of the word "subtle." She's demanded that all her friends wear clothing with the Brownstone insignia on them to whip the students into a patriotic frenzy. Her ploy to marginalize and stunt my revolution had temporarily forced me to halt proceedings. I know I'm supposed to be enlisting the masses to my side. And I will. But since the success or failure of the enemy's strategy remains to be seen, I've decided to take a day or two to evaluate, analyze and regroup. Therefore, decisive action is not, at present, prudent.

I handed the single sheet of paper to Mr. Sagebrush only moments before social studies class started. He read it and asked, "You want to stage a revolution, and you're being prudent?"

I said, "You read the *Brief*? Sondra's editorial? Ms. Shatsky called it, 'Like a Rolling Brownstone.' A title that makes NO sense whatsoever."

"Yes, I read it," he said, but his eye telegraphed a longer message: "Wimp . . . chicken . . . yellow . . . coward . . ."

"Look around, Mr. Sagebrush," I said, exasperated. I swung my arm toward the students now filling their desks. Nearly every kid was wearing a Brownstone T-shirt, or jacket, or hat. I was astounded at how well Sondra had gotten the word out. I felt like I was the only junior not dressed to order (along with Eli, Liza and a few brave and/or clueless others). Sondra herself, who'd staked out a spot in the lobby at first bell and greeted the incoming student body like a maniacally friendly stewardess, was Brownstone head to toe, in track pants (with name of school across the butt), T-shirt, varsity jacket, baseball cap. She was a walking, talking advertisement for herself.

"Can't you see what I'm up against?" I demanded of Mr. Sagebrush. "These conformists are loving it. They're giddy with the special, unique joy of following orders. So much for rugged individualism. So much for the American spirit."

He said, "All right, settle down. We'll talk again after class."

I plopped on my desk chair and scanned the room for any other kid who had a mind of his or her own. Row after row, the students were sartorially homogeneous. And then, in the sea of navy, my eyes lit on a bright red shirt. It might as well have been a red flag—or a red cape, taunting the bull.

Noel Kepner turned in my direction. The red in his shirt made his skin, usually healthy and glowing, seem pink and humble. He looked right at me and smiled.

Eli, herself in a lovely yellow cashmere sweater set, whispered across the aisle, "Noel making a fashion statement?"

I shook my head, breaking eye contact with Noel. My heart

was beating hard all of a sudden. I whispered to Eli, "He and Sondra probably had a spat. He's going against her out of spite. It's personal, not political."

"That sounds right," said Eli. "But I'm not sure if his personal motivations have anything to do with Sondra."

"Attention," boomed Mr. Sagebrush. "Today, I would like to talk about how Hitler and the Nazi Party used nationalist pride to gain power in Germany, circa 1933."

An hour of European dictatorship later, I loitered in front of Mr. Sagebrush's desk as requested, waiting for the last straggler to leave the room. The last straggler was, of course, Noel.

"Yes, Mr. Kepner?" asked Mr. Sagebrush.

"I wanted to make one last point about fascism, sir," said Noel.

"Can you make it next class?" I asked. Vin was waiting for me at Chez Brownstone. Every second that Noel espoused was one less second of making-out time. I hadn't seen Vin after school yesterday, or this morning, and I missed him.

Mr. Sagebrush said, "Yes, hold your thought until we meet again, Mr. Kepner so that the whole class can benefit from your insight."

I stifled a laugh. Noel nodded—the boy was born with an overactive earnestness gene—and split, if reluctantly.

That left me alone with Mr. Sagebrush. He said, "Revolutionaries are unafraid. They take dramatic action. They are decisive. They don't back down when faced with an organized and powerful opposition."

"Things are different now," I started.

"What, exactly, is different?" he asked. "Two weeks ago, you were begging to do this project. You had passion. Where's the passion now, Ms. Benet?"

"I don't under—"

"I've been teaching in the upper school at Brownstone for seventeen years. Did you know that?"

"Vaguely."

"I've seen a lot, Ms. Benet. Forgive me if I'm wrong, but is it possible that your passion for this project has been channeled elsewhere?"

His eyes bored into me with the message: "Please don't be just another hormonally driven teenage girl."

I said, "Dramatic, decisive action. I'm going to meditate on that later, Mr. Sagebrush. But right now I've got to go to lunch. Hunger. Food. Growing body. I'm sure you understand."

"Only too well, Ms. Benet," he said.

"Let's go under the stairs," said Vin as I sat down next to him at the Fringe Dweller table at Chez Brownstone. It'd been twenty-four hours since I'd seen him, and I was pleased that his lanky deliciousness hadn't abated. He was wearing flat-front khakis and a jean jacket, buttoned all the way up.

I said, "Five minutes," and pointed at my sandwich on the tray.

"No offense, Dora, but if you're going to eat that garlic hummus wrap, we can forget about going under the stairs."

It'd been a day since we'd locked lips. And he acted glib about passing on a lunchtime tryst? I felt a buzz of fear. Was he bored with me already? I wondered. After five days?

"Okay, let's go," I said.

Leaving my food in Liza's care (with the understanding that she could nibble), we left Chez Brownstone and walked around the corner to the back stairwell, used mainly by middle school students, but not at that time of day. The stairwell's proximity to food services and its relative privacy made it a perfect spot for lunchtime nibbling of a different, more erotic nature.

Vin plunged right in, savoring my lips as I tasted his. A day of waiting proved worth it. The magic of making out had returned, and I was both glad and relieved. The kiss had the sweet tang of romance, too, which, apart from our time on the Bridge, had been absent from our relationship. Vin—not a romantic—hardly ever called. He'd yet to give me a gift or pay for anything. Vin wasn't a poet. He wasn't big into asking me questions that would peel back the layers to discover my deepest emotional core. He showed zero interest at all in my revolution project. I doubt he heard a word I said about it. But his mouth was hot and wet, and his tongue made tantalizing sweeps across my teeth. Caught up in the kiss, I unbuttoned his jean jacket, and slipped my hand under his shirt to touch his chest.

He started breathing shallowly, and I thought he might hyperventilate. I would have asked, but he'd slipped his hand under my sweater, and let it rest on my bra.

I said, "Someone will see."

Vin said, "Shhh." And he kissed me again, his hand no longer at rest. I rubbed his chest, and felt the embossed letters of his T-shirt against the back of my hand. There were so many letters, I was distracted by what word they spelled. I pulled my hand out from under, and traced the letters with my fingers, finding a round one.

"Oh?" I said.

"Ohh, baby," he said.

"Oh, shit!" I said, pushing him back. "Take off your jacket."

"What's the matter?" he groused.

"Take off your fucking jacket."

He groaned. "I knew you'd make a big deal out of this." Vin shrugged off his covering and revealed the depth of his betrayal.

I looked at the T-shirt he'd tried to hide from me. The classic logo design: BROWNSTONE in all caps, the pelican under-neath.

And I'd given up a garlic hummus wrap for him.

I said, "Explain yourself."

"Sondra called me last night and told me everyone was wear-ing Brownstone gear today. All the guys on track are doing it."

"I called you last night and told you NOT to."

"You did?"

"Do you listen to a word I say? No. Forget it. You heard every word Sondra said, I'm sure. You stare at her. You and your friends talk about her. You even try to look in her town house windows."

Vin was flabbergasted. "That's bullshit!"

"Why did you ask me out in the first place?"

He opened his mouth, but he was clearly overwhelmed. He wasn't a talker in the most comfortable situations. This assault from me might render him mute for life.

Then he surprised me by speaking. "In the first place, you asked me out."

"So you figured you'd go for it, see what would happen with the pushy girl?" He'd make out with me, sure, but all the while he was secretly pining for Sondra, like every other boy? Vin *was* exactly like every other boy, I realized, and felt nauseated.

He said, "It's just a T-shirt, Dora."

I ran back into Chez Brownstone. Eli, Eric and Liza were laughing about something. I slid onto the bench next to them on the verge of a major crying fit.

I couldn't help noticing that my wrap was three-quarters consumed.

Everywhere I looked, Brownstone T-shirts, caps, sweat-shirts, jackets. Each piece of clothing seemed like a personal rejection, a rebuke.

"I've got to get out of here," I said to my friends.

Eli immediately picked up on the desperation behind the words. "What happened?"

Vin came rushing into the cafeteria, his jacket wide open now. Liza saw him—and his shirt. She pointed and said, "That's what."

And then it got worse. Sondra and her Slavic bookends, the Dropov twins, marched like conquering heroes into the room. Vin stepped aside to let them pass. Sondra, I saw, gave him a wink, and he smiled dopily at her.

The sight had one upside. I no longer felt sad. Now I felt mad.

"Sondra! You look so cute!" I gushed when the Ruling Class trio walked past my table. "Who knew so much Brownstone merchandise existed!"

"I love *your* sweater," gushed Sondra. "And your hair continues to amaze me. I mean, *amaze.*"

We smiled at each other. I said, "What's this about you calling my boyfriend last night?"

"I had to, Fringe! I just love the track team uniform and Vin's been on the team forever, as I'm sure you know. And he is so sweet, I thought he'd let me borrow an old pair of team pants. And of course, he did. I swung by his place to pick them up. I couldn't believe they fit me. He's so skinny and tall, and I've got all this junk in the trunk." She slapped her own ample—but by no means flabby—ass. "It's a miracle, really. I sure am glad I could get into your boyfriend's pants, Fringe Girl."

I laughed loud and hard, and smiled with such intensity I thought my face might crack. Sondra matched my smile to the inch. We must have made quite a strange sight, the two of us staring each other down with happy, toothy, beaming grins. I could hear the hush of the crowd, despite the roaring in my

ears. She'd stolen my thunder. She'd needled and picked at me
since fourth grade. She'd impugned my reputation in the
paper. She'd slurred my friends, my parents. And she'd invited
herself over to my boyfriend's house to undress. I stared and
smiled, stared and smiled, incredulous that so much anger
could fit into one person's body. This was the kind of fury that
incited war, a hot, flaming rage that made otherwise rational
people do crazy things.

"Writing that editorial. Hitting on my boyfriend. You buried
yourself, Sondra," I said. "And you put the shovel right in my
hands."

Her smile faded. "So it's war then," she said. "Do your
worst."

"No," I said, "I'll do my best."

Sondra gave me the last word. She turned around, her
booty swishing from side to side, the word "Brownstone"
slapped across it, each swivel of her hips a silent jibe. How I
wanted to kick that ass! Vin followed her and the twins on the
way out of the cafeteria. He was gone for good, and good rid-
dance.

I stomped one foot on the bench at my table. And stomped
my other foot on the table itself.

Liza, looking up at me, said, "Dora? You're standing on
school property."

"Listen up!" I screamed. "Your attention, please!"

Eric said, "I smell news!" and took out his cell phone camera.

Eli moved the trays and cups away from my feet.

The faces of the junior class turned toward me. Their ex-
pressions were a mix of surprised, bemused and sympatheti-
cally uncomfortable. Their attention focused on me now, the
room quieted enough for me to be heard.

The fire of rage still pumping inside me, I was unnaturally

calm as I scanned the crowd, making selective eye contact,
drawing confused glances. I contemplated saying, "Friends,
Brownstoners, Brooklynites," but that'd be too oblique.

"There goes Sondra Fortune," I said, pointing at her retreating figure. "She's been a leader of this class since second
grade. I remember the day her Gap Kid ad appeared on the
side of a bus. I was in awe of her then, as I am now. Sondra is
a fine example of a unifier, not a divider. We all read her editorial in the *Brief* today. She hit the nail on the head: We should
be supportive of each other."

Sondra paused halfway out the door of Chez Brownstone.
She had to come back in. She had no choice. A few of the kids
started applauding her. I continued, "That's right! Go ahead.
Clap. Whether she's been on the side of bus or at school, Sondra has always put her true face forward. She's always been honest and upfront about where she stands. She never once
pretended to, say, befriend someone she secretly despised. Or
compliment a girl's dress or a haircut, and then make fun of it
behind her back. She never ever, not once, used people to help
her with homework, or flattered for favors. Or had parties that
made everyone uninvited feel small and unwanted. Not once
that I can remember has Sondra ever stared right through a
person, as if he or she wasn't there. No, Sondra is honest and
trustworthy and so totally *there* for every kid in this class. We're
one big happy family. Just like she wrote in her editorial."

At this point, a few of the faces staring up at me began to
fall. Memories revisited, old wounds exposed. Sondra, for her
part, smiled solidly, as she had to, knowing that if she were to
show anything but perfect agreement now, she'd reveal herself.

I continued, "Sondra wrote—eloquently, inspiringly—that
we're all supportive of each other. That we be supportive of
worthy goals. And the question I have, since we are at Sondra's

service—in gratitude for her leadership—is this: What are your goals, Sondra?"

The eyes of her classmates upon her, Sondra said, "My goals?"

"Your goals," I repeated. "I'd like to know what they are, so we can all be supportive of you and help you achieve them."

Sondra aw-shucksed, "You don't have to help me, Fringe Girl. None of you do."

"But we do! We must!" I said. "For example, most of us helped you by wearing Brownstone insignia clothes to school today. You wanted it done. And most of us did what you asked without questioning your motives, or your goals. So why don't you tell us, in your own words, what the point was?"

She fidgeted. But said, "To unify the student body."

I said, "About what?"

"In the belief that our differences make us stronger."

"But if we were united in our support of each other's differences, then why on earth would you have us wear the same thing?" I laughed ruefully at the absurdity of it. I saw more frowns on the faces below me, especially on girls sporting Freestyle cuts.

I said, "See, I think that you're a loving, honest, supportive, caring, generous friend to every person you meet. But *others* might think that you have only one goal in mind and you expect all of us to stand behind you in achieving it: the goal of ruling the school, dictating tastes and style and determining people's placement in the social hierarchy we all pretend doesn't exist. If any one of us—no, not anyone—if I, Dora Benet, had a goal that ran in interference with yours, you'd stand behind me, all right. With a knife."

Gasps and murmurs of shock and disbelief floated into my ears from the tables below. Liza looked as if I'd actually been stabbed. I had just committed social suicide, unless I could get the crowd behind me (and not with a knife).

"I've had enough," I announced with years of pent-up frustration powering my voice. "I've chased your approval, and hated myself for wanting it so much. As of this day, I'm done. I'm not a member of your clone army. I'm not dressing or thinking or kissing ass for your pleasure and amusement. I'm no longer at your service, Sondra. From now on, I'm doing things my way."

Chez Brownstone hung in silence. Rapt silence. Eerie silence. Crickets-chirping-in-the-background silence.

Sondra glared at me with naked malevolence. I'd said what every girl in this room had wanted to say for years. Liza's hand was wrapped around my ankle as if she thought I might faint. My legs were shaking. I didn't think I could move.

And then someone in the back of the room started clapping. I wasn't sure who it was. Then someone joined him (or her). More people started applauding, and a few started cheering.

Sondra, meanwhile, had taken the cue to leave. Lori and Micha (who looked exactly like lieutenants in her clone army) and Vin left with her.

"Whew," I said loudly. "She's gone. At least she can take a hint."

The room erupted in laughter. I was rolling now. "It's one thing to talk. But it's another thing to act. I—we—have to make sure that we're not sheep again. We have to strip away the social structure. Strip away the pressure to conform."

Kim Daniels, a Teeming Masser, suddenly jumped up on her table and stripped (!!!) off her Brownstone T-shirt. She flung it into the air. Her circle of friends, girls I'd never befriended (but should have, given their moxie), joined Kim on the table and whipped off their shirts as well. They jumped up and down, breasts bouncing under bras and camis.

Granted, when I'd said, "Strip away the social structure," I hadn't been calling for a group streak. But more kids got up on tables and started disrobing their Brownstone vestments. Eric was whooping, photographing everything. Eli and Liza were standing next to me now, clapping and laughing.

"You've started a riot!" Eli screamed above the roar.

"A nudist uprising!" I said. "This is the greatest thing I've ever done!"

Liza said, "I should have told you about Vin and Sondra. I'm sorry."

So she knew. "Tell me now," I said.

"While squatting on a toilet in the third-floor bathroom this morning, I overheard Lori tell Micha that Sondra and Vin spent the day together on Sunday."

"The day I spent waiting by the phone."

"If it's any comfort, they didn't hook up until last night."

I nodded, surveying the nearly naked impromptu streakathon around Chez Brownstone, now spilling into the school proper.

"No comfort," I said. "No comfort at all."

# 20

"You are my hero!" said Joya after dinner Friday night. It'd been one day since the Topless Streak through the hallowed hallways of Brownstone. I'd been imagining the reaction of the building's ghosts, the nuns from a hundred years ago, the haunted look on their spectral faces as the girls and boys ran around with their shirts off. Fortunately, no one was expelled. Unfortunately, when the head of the upper school, Ms. Ratzenberger, saw Billy Bauer, a six-foot-five basketball star, storming past her open office door, his massive torso gleaming and covered with copious chest hair, his pants—fashionably though ridiculously—hanging low, his butt crack peeking from over his belt, well, the poor old woman clutched her heart and swooned. Before she completely collapsed, she grabbed her assistant by the collar and demanded to know who was behind the riot.

"I have detention every day for a week," I said to my worshipful sister. "Some hero."

"It's perfect!" chimed Joya. "Like the wrongful imprisonment of Nelson Mandela!"

"Let's not compare Adora's inciting nudity to the suffering of Nelson Mandela," suggested Dad.

My punishment wasn't too severe, and I had Mr. Sagebrush to thank for that. He interceded on my behalf, arguing that I'd overstepped my bounds but that my impassioned speech was academically related. When he joined me in Ms. Ratzenberger's office for my mini-hearing, I'd sent him a message with my eyes that said, "You asked for passion, drama and decisiveness." He sent me a message back that said, "You astonish me, Ms. Benet, but I have to pretend to be outraged in front of my boss." Without him backing me up, I might have been suspended. I should buy him a cupcake or something.

Mom said, "I thought Sondra Fortune was your friend. Didn't you just go over to her house for brunch? You've been talking about her since you were ten."

"It's complicated, Mom."

"I don't know much about her family," added Mom. "I never see her parents at potlucks or Brownstone events."

I'd met Sondra's mom a few times and had seen her dad maybe twice. But I didn't get what her parents had to do with anything.

Mom said, "If you'd like us to speak to Ms. Ratzenberger, or if you want to tell us how you feel about the incident . . ."

"Goes without saying."

If I were to tell Mom my thoughts and feelings, she'd learn that I had one foot in heaven and one foot in hell. Naturally, since I was basking in the glow of infamy at school, a rebel leader, a beacon of strength to Teeming Massers and Fringe Dwellers everywhere. I was considered to be, excuse my immodesty, something of a cult hero. I'd become a scourge to the Ruling Class, but for all their hate, I perceived an undercurrent of fear, too. I could see the trepidation in the eyes of Lori and Micha. Yesterday, they'd pulled their Freestyling hair into ponytails (which had the ill effect of making their painfully thin faces seem oblong, like horses'). Sondra had managed to avoid me completely, but I'd heard whispers from my scores of new intelligence agents that she was acting as sweet and phony as ever, pretending the Chez Brownstone political push hadn't happened.

Ring. Landline. "I'm not home," I said. The phone had been ringing off the hook since the incident. Kids I'd spoken five words to in as many years wanted to congratulate me, tell me that I'd done what they'd always wanted to do, compliment me on my bravery. I wasn't letting any of it go to my head. I was staying humble. Keeping it real.

Mom picked up. "Hello, Vin. I'm sorry. Adora's not here. I'll tell her you called. Again. Yes, she got the other fifteen messages. Okay. Good night." She hung up.

"If you ask me—but I know you haven't," said Mom, "you should call him back. Hear him out. Whatever he needs to say, it's got to be important to call sixteen times."

"Never," I declared. Vin had betrayed me for Sondra. He'd lied and cheated. And for that, he would be punished. I would not take his calls. I would let him twist on the spit for eternity. If he wanted Sondra so badly, he could have her. If she really wanted him. Which I doubted.

Dad said, "Not that I have any idea what's going on, but it's possible Vin is calling to apologize."

"I don't want to talk about Vin. Can both of you drop the subject? Please and thank you."

"Watch it, kid," said Dad. "Standing on the table and shooting off your mouth doesn't play at home."

They hadn't grounded me, by the way. Ms. Ratzenberger had called my parents and told them what happened. They sat me down on Thursday night and talked at me for a while about responsibility and self-control. But I could tell they were proud

I stood up (literally) for myself and for every other kid who'd ever felt cowed by the Ruling Class.

I said, "I'm not standing on the table. I'm sitting on the couch. And, in a minute, I'll be climbing the stairs to go to my room."

Joya said, "Can I come with you?"

"No."

"I want to show you something," she said, her big brown irresistible eyes moist and pleading.

"Okay, but only for a minute." I had some serious IMing to do with Eli and Liza, planning my next move. In one swoop, I'd questioned authority and enlisted the masses. Now I had to present an alternative government. I wasn't sure how that would work yet.

I went upstairs. Joya followed. She ran into her room first and then dashed into mine. I was already at my computer, booting up. She stood next to my chair, ants-in-pants excited, her hands behind her back.

"What are you hiding?" I asked.

"You're gonna love this," she said and presented me with one of her homemade comic books. The front cover was a drawing of me (thinner and prettier, with my new haircut) in a sexy superhero outfit (low-cut black leotard, high-heeled thigh-high black boots and sweeping cape), standing on top of a table, the torch of liberty in one hand and a whip (!!!) in the other. The title, screaming in red bubble letters: "The Adventures of Fringe Girl!"

I flipped through the pages. The story arc started with me as my alter ego, Dora Benet, the mild-mannered high school student. In the face of tyranny, I transformed into the righteous Fringe Girl, guardian of justice, defender of the meek, inciter of the partially nude. My evil nemesis was illustrated, at first, as a huge, forbidding female, who got progressively smaller and smaller until she was a dot in the corner of the last panel—a speck that triumphant Fringe Girl flicked off the page with her finger.

I said, "This is incredible, Joya." It really was.

Joya gushed, "You're an inspiration."

I didn't know what to say. The kid was hitting me right in the soft spot. I got a bit choked up and I wanted to tell her. But she was looking at me with those huge eyes, and I got lost in there somewhere. "I prefer not to be called Fringe Girl," I said.

"But that's who you are. That's what makes you strong."

"Being on the outside keeps me strong?"

"Just a bit outside," said Joya.

"My so-called strength comes from inside," I said, pointing at my chest.

"No, you're motivated by place," she said. "Placement. Where you stand, as it were. And I don't mean on the cafeteria table."

At this point, I'd had enough of Joya and her comic book insight. I said, "Provocative point. I'll have to give that some serious thought. But now, if you'll excuse me, I have IMing to do."

"Plotting the next move in your master plan for school domination?" she asked, eagerly.

"Exactly," I said. Plus, I wanted to read some of the e-mail that'd been flooding the *Brief*'s queue. Eric was beside himself—his formerly sleepy little paper was suddenly buzzworthy. He was going to devote the entire next issue to reactions from the student body re: recent sociopolitical events at Brownstone.

Joya smiled and said, "I'll leave you to it." And then she gave me a hug. I wasn't expecting it. She knocked my elbow, making the Sarcastic Ball roll off my desk and onto the floor.

She bent down to pick it up. Shaking it, she asked, "Do I have the greatest sister in the world, or what?"

The Sarcastic Ball read: "Talk to the hand, the Ball isn't listening."

Joya laughed, put the ball back in its place and left, closing my door gently, respectfully.

The girl was demented to like me despite the way I treated her. I decided then and there to be nicer to Joya. Her comic book was an astonishing work. She was a talented—gifted—beautiful loving big-hearted individualist. She deserved my respect more than I deserved hers. I shook the ball and asked, "Will I be able to swallow my jealousy and resentment and learn to love the little interloper?"

It read: "Yeah, and pigs will fly from your ass."

So I had that to look forward to.

"Did Vin care about me at all?" I dared to ask.

It read: "Yeah, right."

And then Mom called me back downstairs.

Now what?

I slogged to the first floor. Mom was waiting at the bottom of the stairs. She said, "A boy is here to see you. He's out on the deck."

So Vin had finally come crawling. I smiled. I'd let him beg for forgiveness, and then I'd make a decision based on the sincerity of his pleas (although I could say right now it wouldn't be in his favor). I thanked Mom. She retreated to her and Dad's office, and I headed through the dining room and living room, and then out onto the deck.

Night had fallen. It was dark outside. Our deck—constructed on top of our downstairs neighbor's extension—was off our living room, and, by Brooklyn standards, very large. Along the gate around the deck, my mom had hung multicolored Christmas lights. The pink and red and green bulbs supplied minimal brightness. By their rainbow glow, I saw him out there, tall, dark, slim and waiting.

He was leaning over the railing, looking down at the court-yards between Garden Place and Henry Street. I stepped on a loose deck board. It creaked. He spun around to face me.

"Jack Carp?" He was most certainly not Vin (I'd never no-ticed how similar they looked from behind)—and not Noel Kepner, either. I didn't know why I'd thought my visitor might be Noel. But his face had flitted across my mind when Mom announced a boy on the deck. Jack Carp hadn't flitted or even floated into my head. Hadn't, honestly, since he and Eli broke up.

Jack said, "Sorry for the dropby. I was in the neighborhood."

He lived on Montague Street. Three blocks away. "What can I do for you?"

Heavy sigh from him. Deep and bleating. Clearly, he'd come to talk about Eli. This would be awkward, at best. Jack and I hadn't established an outside-of-Eli friendship. When-ever we tried to have a conversation of our own, it always went awry. Jack lived in a musical consciousness, one that only other musicians (and dolphins) could understand.

He said, "I saw them just now."

"Who?" I knew who.

"Eric Brainard and Eli. I can look across the courtyards be-tween our buildings right into his kitchen. As easily as you can look into that red bedroom." He pointed over the deck at the buildings on Henry Street. I knew the red bedroom he was re-ferring to. I'd looked in it many times from my room, watching the man and woman who lived there walk around in their paja-mas, sometimes with toothbrushes in their mouths, sometimes talking on the phone. Sometimes, getting into bed together and turning out the light. They needed curtains badly. I'd thought about leaving a note on their front door.

"Eli has been working at the *Brief*," I said. "And Eric is the editor. They're friends."

He squinted at me, his expression raw. "Friends? Everyone knows about Eric's Asian fetish."

"Eli hates that."

"I saw them kissing. Right in front of his kitchen window. As if they wanted me to see."

Please don't cry, please don't cry, I chanted in my head. To his credit, given his artistic nature, Jack Carp was stronger (emotionally) than he looked.

"Why would she do that?" he asked. "To hurt me on purpose?"

"I don't know," I said. I didn't want to second-guess why Eli did anything. Maybe she thought that since he'd hurt her, she could hurt him back. Or maybe she was trying to get a re-action. She had told me that Jack hadn't called her once to try to make up.

He shook his head and kicked the deck railing with his Chucks. "At least all this pain and misery has been great for my playing," he said.

I nodded. "That makes you happy? Playing well."

He said, "Of course."

"Then go be happy." He didn't move a muscle. "That's right. Go. Go ahead," I said, fluttering my arms toward the door, encouraging him to fly away, like a baby bird.

"The piano doesn't make me as happy as Eli," he said, pawing his black hair off his forehead. The skull on his black shirt seemed to frown. "How do I get her back, Dora? I trust you. I've always liked you. Give me a hint. I'll pay you. I've got three hundred dollars back home in my underwear drawer."

In his underwear drawer? I couldn't take the money now,

knowing where it'd been. Besides, I wasn't sure whether Eli wanted Jack back. I thought of Eli's complaints about orgasm deprivation.

But a hot nugget of good advice was on the tip of my tongue. The answer to his problem was sitting right there, burning to tumble out of my mouth, into his eager ears. The impulse to tell was strong. I got a sudden inkling of what advice giving felt like to Mom. To have an itch on the tongue that could only be relieved by unloading the tips and tricks.

"Okay, Jack. You want Eli back? You have to make a grand gesture, one that proves your love," I said, buckling under the pressure. "Make a sacrifice for her. She wants you to die on the sword, don't you see it?"

He looked as me as if I were speaking Bulgarian. "A grand gesture? Die on my sword? What the fuck are you talking about?"

Argh. Boys and their thick skulls. I wish someone could explain to me why males (supposedly) ran the world. I said, "For all her cool detachment, Eli's a romantic. She's a princess in a tower. Think of her bedroom. Top floor. Highest room in the house. All that pink! The frills!"

"She hates the pink," said Jack. "She apologizes for it every time I'm up there."

"But she hasn't changed it, has she?"

"Her mom won't let her," he said.

"Mrs. Stomp begs Eli to change it! Do you honestly think Anita Stomp likes having a pink room in her house?"

He still wasn't getting my point. I wasn't speaking Jack's language. He wanted the melody and notes on paper, forte symbols on the clef. "You play beautifully, with a lot of heart and soul," I said. "You put your emotions into your music. Have you ever written a sonata?"

He said, "I tried once, when I was, like, ten. It was inspired by the movie *Galaxy Quest*. Have you ever seen it? So fucking funny. I called my piece, 'Never Give Up, Never Surrender Suite.' Nice play on words. As if the suite was *sweet*. Get it?"

"Yes, very clever. So you can write. There you have it."

"Have what?"

"An idea. For a grand gesture."

He looked at me like I'd gone screwy. "*What* idea?"

Honestly. How could someone be a genius and an idiot at the same time? I said, "Write a sonata for Eli. Play it at States instead of the piece you've been practicing."

Jack looked confused. And then the concept settled in. He said, "You're brilliant! And, by the way, nice job with the nudie parade."

Without further ado, he floated out of my apartment as if he could already hear the melody.

# 21

# DETENTION WEEK DIARY

**Monday**
*3:15 to 4:15 P.M.:* I arrived in the windowless, airless basement dungeon, located conveniently between the band rehearsal room and the *Brief* office. I took some comfort in knowing that Eli would be close, even if she was making out with Eric Brainard next door instead of being fraught with worry about my imprisonment. The other delinquents and I were seated in desks when our monitor, Ms. Ratzenberger (the head of the upper school herself), shuffled into the room.

"Please arrange your desks into a circle," she instructed us. "No reason we can't make new friends, even under these unfortunate circumstances."

Once we'd done as she asked, she said, "Now let's go around the circle. Say your name and why you're here."

Since there were only four of us, I figured her amateur-hour group therapy couldn't hurt any more than dental surgery. Ms. Ratzenberger said, "Rebecca, why don't you go first?"

The girl to my right started talking. "I'm Rebecca Janeson, a sophomore."

"Why are you here?" asked Ms. Ratzenberger, who'd taken a seat in the circle and was scribbling notes on a legal pad.

Rebecca said, "I was caught by Mr. Contralto"—custodian—"in the upper school library after closing on Friday."

"You've been caught there several times, in similar circumstances, haven't you, Rebecca?"

She shrugged. "I guess."

"With several different boys, correct?"

"Yes."

"And *what* were you doing in the library?"

Rebecca paused. "Reading?" she tried.

I laughed out loud. Ms. Ratzenberger shot me a dagger and I stopped.

"I was making out with Brian Disreal. We lost track of time! If there were clocks on the library walls, I wouldn't be here right now."

Ms. Ratzenberger turned toward the boy to Rebecca's right. She said, "Next?"

He cleared his throat. "My name is Brian Disreal. Sophomore." The boy pointed at Rebecca. "I was caught with her. And, for the record, we were not making out."

"You were reading, as well?" I asked.

"I mean, we were doing other stuff, too," said Brian, who kissed—and other-stuffed—and told.

The boy next to Brian said, "Other stuff, too? Dude!" and then they high-fived. It was a disgusting sight. Rebecca giggled.

"Next," said Ms. Ratzenberger.

"I'm Seth Wonderwall. Junior. My crime . . . honestly, I'm not sure what I'm being held for this time. Ms. R., am I still working off downloading the worm virus onto the school's Ethernet?"

"No, Mr. Wonderwall. That was last week. This week you're in detention for hacking into the school Web site and randomly inserting obscenities into the parents' association newsletter."

Rebecca's and Brian's eyes popped with awe. She said, "That was you?"

"I only did it to prove how vulnerable the system is." Seth sounded sincere, but the mischievous glint in his hazel eyes (my same color) gave him away.

Rebecca said, "You're famous!"

"My deeds are famous, not me," he said correctly. I'd never heard his name before.

I asked, "How long have you been at Brownstone?"

He checked his watch. "One month," he said.

"Mr. Wonderwall has attended a number of private schools in Manhattan. We are fortunate that he's joined us at Brownstone this year," said Mrs. Ratzenberger.

He'd probably been kicked out of every one. I wondered who his parents were and how they could get him accepted into school after school. He was clearly creative and gifted with the tech stuff. And he was cute, with the long shaggy black hair, smooth skin and sparkly eyes. I smiled at him. He smiled back, enjoying the attention.

"Ms. Benet?" prompted the proctor.

"Hello, I'm Dora Benet. Junior. I'm here because I defiled school property."

"What property?" asked Brian.

"I stood on a table in Chez Brownstone. I defiled it with the bottoms of my clogs."

"You're here because you incited a riot," clarified Ms. Ratzenberger.

"No way!" said Brian. "You're Fringe Girl! You're the balls."

I took that as a compliment.

Rebecca said, "I'm with you, Dora," and then flashed me her bra in a show of solidarity. I noticed that Rebecca did not have a Freestyle haircut. I smiled, and flashed her my bra. Just the strap. It was the best I could do.

Seth Wonderwall had not heard of my exploits. "What's this about?" he asked. "And can I see those bras again, please?"

Ms. Ratzenberger clapped her hands suddenly, stood up and started shuffling around the circle. "Today, I'd like to try a new approach to detention. I want you to discuss your deeds with the peer group, and learn from each other how to act more appropriately."

"Great idea," said Brian. "So what are you going to do next, Fringe Girl? I'd like to see you get everyone in Chez Brownstone to take off *pants*! And underwear! Total nudity! Now that would be awesome."

Ms. Ratzenberger clutched a desk corner and swooned at the very thought.

Seth said, "Total nudity? All in favor?"

"I'm not going to spur further undressing," I said. "I do want to get my message across—"

"Your message is?" asked Seth.

"Not to kowtow to the Ruling Class," I explained.

"The Ruling Class?" he asked, eyes twinkling something fierce.

Was he making fun of me? I wondered. I squirmed a little in my seat, feeling hot and liking it. "I support equality among students and freedom to pursue unconventional goals."

"Like inciting a nude riot," said Seth.

"Topless," I corrected. "Problem is, I don't know what to do next." I thought back to my original three-pronged plan that I pitched to Mr. Sagebrush. I'd questioned authority, enlisted the masses. "I don't know how to present an alternative government."

"For what purpose?" asked Seth.

"To govern."

"Students need governing? Are we having tax and land disputes?"

"We need a leader, a role model. Every society selects leaders who guide the larger group. It's only natural. Think about it. Aliens come down to Earth and say, 'Take me to your leader.' "

Seth looked confused. "You lost me at 'role model.' "

I sighed (flirtatiously) and said, "In a free society, people choose their own leaders. I'm merely suggesting that we rethink our previous choices and select someone else."

"Who?" asked Seth.

"I don't know."

"Why not you?" he asked. "If you care about it so much, why don't you present yourself?"

The roundtable detention/group therapy session had turned into a verbal volley between me and Seth. In my peripheral vision, I could see Rebecca, Brian and Ms. Ratzenberger watching us, uncertain about breaking into the conversation.

I said, "I wouldn't dare presume to install myself—"

"You've thought about the top job," said Seth. "Everyone has. I'll be your campaign manager."

"That won't be necessary," I said. "And, frankly, given your history—"

"You don't know my history," he said succinctly, "and I don't know yours. But, so far, you're the most interesting person I've met in this school. I want to be a part of whatever it is you think you're doing."

"I know exactly what I'm doing. And the first item on my agenda is . . . to throw a huge party, and invite everyone who is sympathetic to my cause."

"I love that idea!" squealed Rebecca.

"Will there be beer?" asked Brian.

Ms. Ratzenberger looked horrified at the thought.

I said, "No beer. No pot."

"Oh," said Brian, quickly losing interest.

"What about boys?" asked Rebecca.

"Boys can come, but this won't be a hook-up party."

"Oh," said Rebecca, quickly losing interest.

It *would* be a celebration of the new order, a final shedding of the old regime. Suddenly, I got a bright idea, speaking of shedding (not clothes this time). I'd have to make some phone calls. Get some money from Mom and Dad.

"I'm there," said Seth. "Regardless of what kind of party it is."

"I haven't invited you yet," I said.

"But I'm sympathetic to your cause," he said.

"I suspect you have your own cause, which has little to do with mine."

"I'm sure our causes can meet," he said. "Somewhere in the middle." His eyes fell to my hip region, and his lips curled into a wicked grin.

I felt breathless all of the sudden. Seth Wonderwall, he of the sparkling eyes and full lips and long, way-out-of-fashion hair. I'd never heard of or seen him before in my life. But I knew he was about to become a big part of it.

Ms. Ratzenberger said, "I might be old, but I can still hear a salacious double entendre, Mr. Wonderwall. For the remainder of the hour, do your homework in silence."

I composed my next update for Mr. Sagebrush. To wit:

October 10th, Monday
To: Mr. Sagebrush
Fr: Dora Benet
Subject: Stage Three

This might come as a surprise to you, Mr. Sagebrush, but I hadn't given much thought to who would head up the replacement government. As you discussed, revolutionaries, generally speaking, do not make good politicians. They're a bit hotheaded, spontaneous, temperamental, violent and therefore unsuited to lead the newly converted masses. However, this is the Brownstone Institute and not 1930s Mexico. Since the Streak, the masses have been panting, frothing at the jowls for a new leader to step forward.

I believe I am that leader. I believe, sir, that I can shoulder the mantle of responsibility, serve as a role model to my classmates while maintaining my keeping-it-real identity of the girl on the fringe. I'll be at the top, but my fringe roots will keep me grounded.

To initiate myself as the leader of a new order, I'm going to throw a party (they're called political parties for a reason, right?). It'll be a brunch. The choice is significant. Sondra Fortune used to have exclusionary brunches that made the uninvited (aka, everyone) feel like losers. Sometime tomorrow, I'll send an evite to every girl in the class, except the Ruling Classers. We'll eat bagels, lox, Krispy Kremes, drink multiple cups of coffee. And if I can convince my mom to pay for the special surprise I have in mind, it'll be the best brunch ever. Seriously. We'll bond. We'll be united! Or something close.

### Tuesday

*8:30 A.M.:* I tracked down Mr. Sagebrush in his office to see if he'd read my update yet.

"A day early," I said to him.

"And a dollar short?" he asked.

"Huh?"

"Quiet and let me read this."

He read the update. I smiled, feeling good about life, myself. I even liked his ugliest-sweater-vest-yet today. He looked up from his computer and said, "A brunch."

"I'm so excited about it!" I trilled. "Aren't you excited?"

"Ms. Benet, my excitement could only be contained in a bucket."

He gave me a look that said, "I wish with all my heart that I could be a fly on the wall at your party."

I sent him a look back that said, "None of this would have been possible if it wasn't for you."

*12:00 to 1:00 P.M.:* "A brunch," said Eli. "I like it."

"Did you get the evite?" I asked. We were at Grind for the midday break.

"Yes," she said impatiently.

"What?"

"You're all revolution, all the time."

I thought about that. "I am not."

"You never talk about Vin Transom anymore," said Eli. "Not that I prefer boy talk to politics."

"You'd rather discuss global warming or the plight of the Bengalese tiger."

Eli frowned. "Maybe we could talk about Liza. Her mom and Gary got engaged, you know, and she's not taking it well."

At that moment, Kim Daniels, the girl who'd started the Streak, burst into Grind with half a dozen former Teeming Masses girls. They descended on our table and gushed about my evite. They were all coming. The brunch was shaping up perfectly.

*3:15 to 4:15 P.M.:* Seth and I passed notes back and forth for the entire detention hour. Not personal confessions, or anything remotely emotional. I got it started, sending him a note that said, "My favorite TV show is ———."

He filled in an answer, and sent back a note that said, "If I could choose the manner of my own death, it would be ———."

I sent him: "The first rock concert I went to was ———."

He sent me: "I have erotic fantasies ——— number of times per day."

I answered every wacky, weird question he threw at me. And I was pleased to see that, for all his oddity, he liked chocolate, cats, red and daisies. Just like me.

## Wednesday

*8:30 A.M.:* A dozen copies of the *Brief* were stacked outside my locker with a note from Eric that said, "Publishing a day early due to reader demand. Congrats."

The front cover was a photo of me standing on the table at Chez Brownstone with the banner headline BREAKTHROUGH AT BROWNSTONE. The rest of the issue was devoted to Eric's eyewitness account of what he'd heard and seen that fateful lunch hour. He'd included a dozen photographs of me, students running through the halls, Sondra's retreating form with the word "Brownstone" splayed across the butt of Vin's borrowed track pants. And the letters! He'd given an entire page to commentary from readers. I was blown away. I nearly cried.

*3:15 to 4:15 P.M.:* When I walked into detention, Seth, Rebecca and Brian applauded. I bowed, just as I had when greeted with applause wherever I went today. Ms. Ratzenberger said, "Take your seats. I have a parent conference in my office. I expect you to sit quietly and do your homework. I'll be back in twenty minutes."

As soon as the door shut behind her, Rebecca and Brian started glomming on each other like vacuum cleaners.

Seth made an exaggeration of opening up his copy of the *Brief*. "Now I see why you're considered a local hero, Adora. Quote Millie Ross, Junior: 'Dora Benet spoke the truth, what every kid at Brownstone had wanted to scream, every day, for way too long. I wish I'd had her guts!'" He'd given Millie a hoity-toity English accent. "Quote Nate Wright: 'That was the most fun I've had at Brownstone in a decade! And to think that, underneath the thrill of it, we were making a sociopolitical point, too! If this is what politics are about, sign me up.'" He gave Nate the accent of a waiter in an Indian restaurant.

Seth asked, "Shall I read on?"

"I've read the letters already," I said, "but I like your interpretation. Do go on."

And so he did, giving each letter writer a distinct foreign lilt, until even Rebecca and Brian stopped making out to laugh.


**Thursday**
*12:10 P.M.:* My cell rang as I was walking toward Chez Brownstone.

"Hello?"

"Minister of Intelligence reporting in," said Liza. "I'm at Monty's, watching Lori feed Max Lindsey a slice."

"A slice of what?" I asked.

"I'm hiding in the kitchen, watching them through the fucking window."

I still bristled when Liza cursed. It sounded so wrong. "I heard about your mom and Gary. Are you okay?"

She ignored that. "Max is leaning in to lick a drop of tomato sauce off Lori's lip. Oh! My! God! She deflected him. She gave him the hand! He seems sad, forlorn. She's pushing aside her plate and opening her pink notebook. Max is taking out a pencil. What's this . . . he's writing in her notebook. He's Doing Lori's Homework! My theory is correct! He gives her answers, and she gives him sex! She's a math whore! I bet she's got him lined up to take the SATs for her!"

"You're shouting," I said. "They'll hear you."

Eli was waiting for me at the cafeteria entrance.

I passed the phone to her. "Hello?" she asked, giving me a questioning look.

"No, Liza. I don't care what they're doing! Liza! Listen to me! Stop!" said Eli into the phone. To me: "She's going to confront Max and Lori."

I grabbed the phone and said, "We're on the way. Do NOT do anything until we get there." Eli and I dashed down the stairs and crashed out the door onto the street. Monty's was only two long blocks away, and we ran, our backpacks bouncing with each stride. I was winded by the time we burst into the restaurant. Despite my heavy breathing, I could hear the shouts from the back of the joint.

"She's using you, Max!" Liza screamed.

"Shut up, Liza," said Max.

By now, Eli and I were at the back booth. Lori and Max were trapped on the inside, Liza looming large, waving her arms wildly as if she were trying to scare a bear in the woods.

Little Lori—all ninety-five pounds of her—was sufficiently terrified. In all her days, I'd bet this pampered, ballet-dancing diplomat's daughter had never been yelled at by a peer, or an adult. She was shaking with fear.

Liza *was* a frightening sight. Her eyes were round and spitting raw fury. A thick blue vein popped and throbbed under the pale white skin of her temple. Her mouth was a savage snarl. Legs planted solidly shoulder width apart, Liza tilted forward menacingly, as if she might lean closer and take a big bite out of Lori's paltry cheek meat.

Immediately, Eli and I each grabbed one of her flailing elbows. Liza struggled and screamed at Lori, "You don't know what love is!"

The twin, gaining in confidence now that Liza was restrained, said, "You're crazy! If you want Max so badly, he's all yours."

Max said, "I am?"

"You're not worth it," said Lori. "I'm tired of being followed. Tired of being spied on. I like you Max. I *love* my As in calculus. And you're not horrible in bed. But you come with way too much baggage." The scrawny dancer slipped out of the booth. She looked Liza up and down. "Get help," she said. "And for God's sake, lay off the donuts."

Liza roared and fought to break free. We held on for Lori's dear life. Once she was safely away, our blond friend stopped bucking. She turned to Max and started to say something. But then she stopped.

Her former quasi boyfriend was slumped in the booth, his head in his hands. Max appeared to be crying.

Eli said, "Let's go."

"Excellent idea," I said.

We dragged Liza out of there. The cool autumn air was a relief for us all. My mind spun, trying to think of what to do. Liza said, "I have to go see if Max is okay."

"No," I said. "Leave him alone. He's had enough of you today."

"He needs me," she said.

"He hates you!" I said, suddenly angry at what Liza had done to herself. "You just destroyed his life. You call that love? You're wallowing in this obsession. It's disgusting. It's pathetic.

Get over it, Liza. Or maybe you should waste another year on him. Gain another twenty pounds."

Eli said coolly, "Dora, shut up."

"I'm embarrassed for you. I'm embarrassed to be your friend," I said. Not my most sympathetic moment. I regretted my outburst immediately afterward. But I didn't get the chance to take it back.

With eerie calm, Liza said, "Thank you for being honest, Dora. It's good to know how you really feel."

She turned from me and walked away. Eli said, "Way to kick her while she's down," and then ran after Liza. I watched her catch up and put her slender arm over Liza's shuddering shoulders.

My reaction to the sight of my two best friends walking off together, hating me blind for what I'd said? Classic, unmitigated *shame*. My picture could appear next to the word in the dictionary.

I had to look away, only to catch sight of Max Lindsey, eyes red, head down, exiting Monty's. I approached gingerly and said, "On Liza's behalf, I'm sorry, Max."

He nodded but said nothing. I added, "I'm sure Lori will come to her senses."

"Lori *has* come to her senses," he said. "I never understood what she was doing with me in the first place." He quickly added, "Besides doing her math homework."

"Can you just tell me one thing?" I asked. "I've pieced together some of what happened this summer with you and Liza. But not all of it. She refuses to talk about it."

Max said, "What goes on between a boy and a girl is private. What Liza thinks about me is private. And what I think of her is private. It's none of your fucking business what happened. I'm glad she never told you. I hope the curiosity kills you."

He walked back in the direction of Brownstone, leaving me alone on the street. I stood still for a few minutes, people passing me on either side, bumping into me with shopping bags and pocketbooks.

**Friday**
*4:00 to 6:00 P.M.:* "Let me try it," said Seth Wonderwall toward the end of detention on Friday afternoon.

I handed him the Sarcastic Ball. I'd put it in my backpack that morning to remind me of the first day of school when Liza gave it to me. I'd asked it a million times if Liza would ever forgive me. She hadn't responded to any of my dozen e-mails. She wouldn't get on the phone. She avoided me at Chez Brownstone. Eli, too, was blowing me off.

Ms. Ratzenberger had checked out a half hour ago and would be returning any minute. Rebecca and Brian were rolling on the floor.

"You have to ask it a yes or no question," I said.

He shook the Sarcastic Ball. "Will Rebecca and Brian stop this soft-core bullshit and show us some X-rated action?"

The ball said: "Dream on."

Seth laughed. We both turned to look at Rebecca and Brian in a tight lip-lock. He kept trying to get his hand under her shirt, but she pushed him away.

I had to admit, the sight of them at it again was disturbing (in a sexy way). Seth seemed cool about our private erotica show. Or he was faking it really well.

I asked, "Why do you do it? The hacking, troublemaking and general no-good-nicking?"

"Because, Dora, I am usually chronically, colossally BORED," he said. "My entire life is one big battle against boredom. I'm not some cigarette-smoking, beer-swilling, pot-inhaling numbskull thug, though. So I do things that I find funny, even if the authority figures of the world disagree. It's a constant struggle with the forces of complacency—and I'm *losing*, Dora. At least, I thought I was."

He looked at me with the slyest, naughtiest smirk on his face. I imagined what kind of trouble I could get into if we were alone together. But since we had Rebecca and Brian as chaperones, I was safe. Not that they cared—or even were aware of—what we were doing.

I asked, "The tide is turning? No longer hopelessly bored?"

"Not when I'm with you," he said.

Rebecca let out a loud moan. A quick glance confirmed Brian had gotten under the shirt.

Seth shook the Sarcastic Ball. He asked, "Is Dora Benet a kindred spirit?"

It read: "Totally."

"You see?" he said. "Maybe I'm not as outnumbered as I thought."

I smiled. Couldn't resist. Seth's appeal wasn't only his dashing looks (although gorgeous didn't hurt), but the intensity of his attention. I said, "I don't think I'm much good to you in my weakened condition."

"Weakened condition?" he asked. "This is your shining moment. You've dethroned the biggest bitch of the school. And, I can tell you from personal experience, having attended half a dozen in the last five years, every school has a biggest bitch."

"Well, we don't," I said. "Not anymore." Sondra, incidentally, despite her threat of open war, had been lying low, going to class but staying in the background, not making public appearances at Chez Brownstone, Grind, the Juice Bar. It was like she'd made herself invisible—the polar opposite of what she used to be.

"Give it a week," said Seth. "Someone else will rise to take this Sondra's place. Now tell me why you're weakened, as you say."

"I'm in the middle of a fight with my two best friends. Or just one. I'm not sure if the other is royally pissed off or just busy with her own drama."

"Forget them," said Seth. "Hang out with me instead."

When he looked at me, it was as if he could see my heart and guts. I said, "I am hanging out with you. Every afternoon. All week."

"What about next week?" he asked.

"You'll have to wait until then to find out," I said.

"Oh, really?" he said. Shaking the ball, Seth asked, "Will the suspense of waiting until next week kill me?"

It read: "As if."

"I like this Sarcastic Ball," he said. "I like you, too."

Rebecca let out another theatrical moan. We both looked over. Brian was on top of her now, Rebecca squirming underneath.

Seth assumed a falsetto voice and said, "Oh, Brian! Oh God that's good. Don't stop, Brian!"

He moaned and thrashed—loudly. Rebecca and Brian stopped and looked over at him, clearly annoyed.

Rebecca said, "Can you please keep it down? We're trying to concentrate over here."

# 22

My brunch party was minutes away.

Mom said, "Are you sure you don't mind if I hang out?"

"Do whatever you want," I said. "As long as you don't turn this into an *Oprah* appearance."

"What does that mean?" she asked.

"Forget it," I said. "Just don't pry into anyone's personal life with a crowbar."

I could tell she was taken aback. But Mom said, "Consider the crowbar shelved."

Dad said, "I'm leaving. Too much estrogen in one place gives me cramps."

He took the Sunday *Times* and left. Mom, Joya and I finished setting out the food and picking up dust balls on the floor.

People started arriving right on time, at noon. I greeted each girl with a hug, a kiss and a virgin Bloody Mary. I remembered the one and only Sondra brunch I'd been invited to. She hadn't greeted me with affection and a beverage. She hadn't offered five kinds of cream cheese spread for bagels. The main courses on Sondra's brunch menu were gossip, conceit, slander and donuts. Not necessarily in that order of importance.

Kim Daniels, seminal Streaker, gave me an especially

generous hug and kiss when she arrived. As the unofficial leader of the Teeming Mass junior girls, Kim would be an important ally.

Our living room space filled up with the thirty-odd guests. Mom sidled up and asked, "Where are Eli and Liza?"

"Liza has a thing, and Eli has to practice," I said truthfully. As truthfully as I could. According to Eli—who'd finally called me late last night—Liza was required to join her mother, Stephanie, and her step-fiancé, Gary, to go look at dresses for their "intimate-and-dignified" (as Eli put it) upcoming Thanksgiving wedding. It hurt to have to hear about the plans secondhand. Liza was probably gagging nonstop at the notion of Gary becoming her stepdad.

Once Eli finished making Liza's excuses, she made her own. "I'm so sorry, but I can't come to your brunch, either."

"You have to come!" I said.

"States are in two weeks. I've been spending so much time with Eric. I need more practice."

"I'm sure you can take an hour break," I said. "You're my Minister of Propaganda, Eli. I need you here."

Eli didn't say anything for a beat of three. Then she said, "I've got to go, Dora. Good luck on Sunday."

As I surveyed the room of familiar faces—but near perfect strangers—I knew I'd need all the luck I could get. Joya ran up to me, practically bouncing up and down in her Sketchers. She sang, "Simone's here! Should I start drawing?"

"Yes," I instructed. This was my big idea, to have Simone from Pomme de Hair come to the brunch and give every girl a new (not Freestyle) haircut. Mom would pay her an hourly rate (I wasn't privy to that conversation, but fake French stylists weren't cheap). I agreed to let Joya do some drawings for each girl, too, so she'd be a part of the action. She was thrilled be-

yond thrilled about it. Which made Mom happy. Which softened the blow of the expense.

Mom's idea was to have Simone set up on the deck, so the
cut hair wouldn't make a mess in the living room. Kim Daniels
went first. She was sweet to Joya, and it made me feel a bit jealous, actually, much to my surprise. I kept busy passing around
trays of Fresh Direct cookies and brownies while my classmates were treated to food and beauty. The weather was perfect: sunny, no wind, not too cool. The girls laughed, ate,
watched the salon show. Simone kept the patter going, telling
funny stories about bitchy, demanding clients who thought she
didn't understand a word they said.

I should have loved every second of it. I should have been
reveling in my success. This was—by far—a better brunch than
any of Sondra's. It was egalitarian and all-inclusive, like Club
Med. The entertainment wasn't verbally beheading a prese-
lected target. I should have been having the time of my life.

But I wasn't.

As I watched a girl I barely knew eat a bagel while Simone
gave her a fabulous fresh look, I thought of a pseudo-shrinky
spiel my parents had espoused since I could talk: "Avoiding
your challenging emotions only strengthens them," I heard in
Mom's voice. "Let yourself feel the feeling, no matter how difficult, and it'll dissolve. If you're sad, be sad. If you're angry, be
angry. If you're scared, be scared."

I had no idea why that particular bit of advice—from the
endless list of their bromides—popped into my head in the
middle of my brunch. I looked across the room at Mom. She
was chatting with a couple of girls. She must have sensed that
I was watching her. She glanced over and smiled at me. I
smiled back and gave her a thumbs-up. Mom had gone out of
her way to help me with this party. Hiring Simone, buying the

food, helping me set up. She had proven—not merely stated—she was there for me, whenever I needed her.

*If you're sad*, I thought, *be sad.*

The whole thing felt wrong. Eli and Liza should be here. They should see this, the long-awaited intermingling of social groups. The dismantling of the status quo. I'd done this for everyone. But without my best friends to share it with, the victory was empty. I felt a flash of anger that Liza and Eli would deny me the complete joy I deserved.

Kim Daniels glided over to me. Her new do came with a set of bangs. I said, "Your hair looks so good!"

"Thanks," she said, flipping it. "This party rocks."

"Much obliged," I said, bowing slightly.

"If only we had a life-sized Sondra doll to burn in effigy."

I laughed. "She'd rise from the ashes."

"She probably would," said Kim.

Silence. A bit awkward. We watched another girl submit to Simone's flashing scissors.

Kim said, "Are you still with Vin Transom? Apparently, he blew you off for Sondra."

"Is that what he's saying?" I asked.

She said, "Apparently."

*If you're angry, be angry*, I thought.

"He didn't blow me off," I said breezily. "I dumped him. Like a truck."

A couple more girls were standing around me now, listening. I went on, "The thing is, Vin turned out not to be my type."

Kim said, "What type is he?"

"He's a perverted weasel, if you want to know the truth," I said. Whispering, so everyone leaned toward me, hanging on my every word, I said, "He has a fetish for public snogging. Every time we got together, it was outside, in full view of whoever walked by. Under the stairwell, in the hallway, on the basketball court. We made out for hours on the Brooklyn Bridge, and he even told me he had a fantasy about having sex up there! The guy is twisted. I hope Sondra is up for some of his red-hot-pervert action, because I sure wasn't."

The girls around me were delightfully, excitedly shocked by my tale of libidinous adventure. Although what I'd said was true, I felt a funny aftertaste in my mouth—once I'd shut it. I quickly added, "But don't tell anyone what I said about Vin. What goes on between a boy and a girl is private."

An echo of what Max Lindsey said to me outside of Monty's. My bad aftertaste got worse.

Joya said, "Who else needs a haircut?"

We looked at each other, admiring the freshly chopped locks. And then it registered: All the girls standing around me, and the girls by the food table, everyone at the party—save Simone, pixie Joya and shag Mom— had bangs. Just. Like. Mine.

I was surrounded by Fringe Girls. My heart went flippity. I was flattered, surprised, creeped out and speechless. If Eli were here, she'd say something cutting and wicked that would make me laugh. If Liza were here, she'd say how beautiful everyone looked and make me feel less guilty about the girls whose bangs were most definitely NOT working.

I said, "I guess bangs are the new black."

Everyone laughed, including Simone. Mom seemed proud, and Joya was, almost literally, jumping out of her skin with glee. I let the guests surround me, chatter at me. I started chattering back, but I don't remember a word I said.

Later that night, after dinner, Joya was still glowing. Mom seemed serene, content, as if she'd aced a pop quiz on parenting.

"Why don't you host a brunch, too, Joya?" she suggested.

"You mean it? With Simone and bagels and Dora and everything?" asked my kid sister, who sprang off the couch and hugged the stuffing out of Mom.

I smiled wanly, detached, observing the happiness around me but feeling none of it. Those girls were not my friends. Not really. They pretended to be, just as I pretended to like them. But our nascent friendships, if one could call them friendships, were hollow. I thought of Easter bunnies that looked amazing on the shelf. One bite later, you realized that the rabbit wasn't a thick chunk of yummy chocolate but rather a thin, tasteless shell. I wondered if Sondra Fortune, after one of her famous brunches, felt hollow or phony. Did she worry, as I did, that she was only a bland, brittle mold of what she pretended to be?

Dad said, "Adora? Are you okay? You look like you've just swallowed a bug."

"I'm going to bed," I said, and excused myself. "If anyone calls, I'm not home."

# 23

B
I
T
C
H
! ! !

The word was drawn on my locker with a Sharpie, letters thick and black. It was Tuesday morning, around eleven o'clock.

Ms. Ratzenberger and I stood in front of it, pursing our lips at the editorial commentary. She asked, "Was it there first thing this morning?"

I said, "I'm sure I would have noticed it."

"Three exclamation marks," she said.

"I guess she really means it," I said.

"She?" asked Ms. Ratzenberger.

"Or he."

"You suspect this was the work of a girl."

I was thinking Sondra, of course. Or henchgirls Lori and or Micha. Maybe even Liza. "I have no idea who did it," I said. Some bitch, I thought. And I didn't mean female dog. Or maybe I did.

"Here's Mr. Contralto," she said as the school custodian approached. A big man, he moved slowly and purposefully. When he saw what was written on my locker, he whistled long and low.

"Mr. Contralto, you'll have to paint over this locker immediately," said Ms. Ratzenberger.

He made a clucking sound in his teeth. "Can't. We're out of the blue paint. Remember the new budget? The one you approved? Paint and building supplies—as needed?"

"You must have put aside a small bucket," she said.

"Not a drop, ma'am."

Clearly, this was a sore point between them. "Well, I'd say that paint is now needed," she fumed, pointing at my BITCH!!!

"Special order," he tsked. "Could take a week."

"Please proceed," she ordered. He lumbered off, his gait a bit less labored. "Meanwhile," she added, "I'll make a list of the usual suspects. I wonder where Mr. Wonderwall was during morning free period today."

"He was with me," I said.

Since Eli and Liza were nowhere to be found (purposely avoiding me, no doubt), and I couldn't stand the idea of sitting with Kim Daniels and faking my way through half an hour at Chez Brownstone, I called Seth's cell and asked him to go to Grind with me.

"Too public," he said. "I want to be alone with you."

We met in the lower school gym. The little kids never used it until afternoon. Seth and I sat down on the bleachers.

He said. "Come to me, Dora Benet. We've had five days of flirting. Time to move this along."

I moved myself along and sat on his lap.

Since getting Vin under my belt (as it were), I was more confident about kissing boys. Also, I'd waited forever to get

Vin, and what a disappointment that turned out to be. From now on, I decided, if I liked a boy, I'd go for it and see what happened.

"You're right," I said. "Why waste time?"

We started kissing. Instantly, I realized from his easy, slow smooch that Seth had had a lot more experience than Vin. He gripped me around the waist and nibbled, not devoured. He held me close but gently, not in the way Vin mauled and clutched. Seth also kept his eyes open, the light inside them totally switched on.

While enjoying this new sexual experience, I wondered if Eli had had similar revelations going from Jack to Eric. And then I remembered that Eli had stopped confiding in me—ever since I'd started to rise, now that I thought about it.

Seth stopped. He said, "It's not much fun unless you kiss back."

"I think I'm going to start crying," I warned.

"For the love of God, don't do that," he said, shielding his eyes. "It burns!"

"Seriously," I said. "I've won the esteem of the Teeming Masses, but I've lost my two best friends."

"Stop whining about them and kiss me," he said, putting his hands on the back of my head and guiding me toward him. "And shift your weight. My left leg is falling asleep."

"Ms. Benet!" said Ms. Ratzenberger. "Pay attention, please."

"Yes, I'm here. Sorry. I zoned out for a second," I said, mentally returning to my conversation with the principal at my defaced locker.

She sighed (frustrated) and said, "I'm sure this is distracting and disturbing. For the record, I have never thought of you as a . . . rhymes with 'rich.' I do wonder if this is the unhappy result of your social studies project. I'll meet with Mr. Sagebrush today to discuss putting an end to this experiment. It's already caused too much disruption."

"Revolution is disruptive," I said. "That's the whole point."

"Then you've achieved your goal," she said. "I hope it's everything you thought it'd be." And then she turned on her flat heel and shuffled away.

Suddenly, doors burst open, and kids flowed into the corridor from the classrooms. I stood in front of my locker, trying to block the negative review scrawled upon it.

Vin Transom and a few of his posse surrounded me as if they'd rushed to find me here.

He said, "I see you got my message."

"You did this?"

"I heard what you said about me at your little party," he announced. His friends were chuckling behind him. Sensing a confrontation, several more kids gathered around to watch. "You trashed me. All because I dumped you for Sondra. You're a spiteful, power-mad, manipulative freak. Even if you begged on your hands and knees, I wouldn't kiss you with my dog's mouth."

The cluster of gawkers loved that line. Objectively, I found it funny, too. I wondered how long it took Vin to come up with it, or if he'd stolen it from a book. Meanwhile, I was at a loss for a comeback. So I stole something myself, a page out of *His-and-Her Dating*.

"I shouldn't have divulged personal information about your sexual preferences to my friends," I said. "It was wrong, and I'm sorry." Then I expanded on my theme. "In fact, I'm glad you graffitied my locker. Now everyone can see what gossip—even if it's true—can lead to. How it harms people on both ends. This message is really about hope, about wishing we had a school where pernicious gossip didn't exist, where everyone could live in peace, harmony and security that our sexual proclivities are private. And I totally agree with your larger point. I want to thank you for the reminder. Really, Vin. Thank you for this. So much."

Vin stared mutely at my apology, which both sounded contrite and insinuated that what I'd said about him was true, thus hitting him where it hurt most.

Without waiting for him to respond, I served up a look of what appeared to be genuine regret, and walked off, saying a polite "pardon me" and "excuse me" to clear a path.

As I got the hell out of there, I wondered which one of my new "friends" had loose lips. Kim Daniels, no doubt. I felt anger swirling to the surface of my skin. I'd specifically asked her not to tell anyone what I'd said. It was a blatant breach of confidentiality. I was pissed off, and I wanted blood.

Thoughts of revenge consumed me. As a result, I mentally dipped in and out of social studies class like a rock skimming on the surface of a glassy lake.

My consciousness came above water in the middle of Noel Kepner's recital. He was saying, "The problem with transitional government is instability."

"The American Revolution was spearheaded by the same men who would govern the newborn nation for the next thirty years," said Mr. Sagebrush.

"Thirty years! That's nothing," said Noel, all of sixteen himself. "And there's a difference between the birth of a nation and the overthrowing of a centuries-old entrenched governnment."

"Right you are, Mr. Kepner," said Mr. Sagebrush. "Anyone else have an opinion on the stability of nascent democracy?"

"One more thing," inserted Noel. "Which we see in the Russian Revolution, when the communists killed the Czar and his fifteen children. The beheading of Marie Antoinette in the French Revolution. There's a desire to annihilate the over-thrown leaders' families for symbolic reasons. But they're just people caught up in their place, just like the revolutionaries."

"Ms. Benet," said Mr. Sagebrush, "surely you have an opinion on *that*."

"On what, exactly?" I asked.

"Sympathy for the oppressor." He sent a message via eyeball that said, "Save me from having a one-on-one with bombastic Noel Kepner."

I shrugged. "I have sympathy for the oppressor," I said. "If I were a rebellious Frenchwoman, I would have let Marie Antoinette eat cake before she was guillotined."

The class tittered. Noel shook his head, but he smiled, too. I continued, "Whether it's the outgoing or incoming government, history proves that both sides eventually get what they deserve."

I didn't know what history would do to Sondra Fortune. At this point, no one was trying to behead her.

Noel said, "So you agree that oppressors are also victims of an oppressive society."

"They *are* victims," I said, "when they're dead."

The class laughed again, loving my ribald frippery. They were on my side. They supported me—not Noel and his Ruling Class pedigree. They rejected his sharing and caring. They smelled change in the air, and they supported it. They supported ME. They loved me.

"Everyone deserves sympathy and understanding," said Noel.

"That's so naive," I said. "Does Saddam Hussein deserve sympathy? Does Osama bin Laden deserve understanding?"

Noel said, "Maybe not sympathy. But we need to understand them."

"Why? So you can get all the tips and tricks on sticking it to the little guy? A how-to guide on kicking the underdog?"

The classroom full of little guys and underdogs applauded. Mr. Sagebrush quieted them down, clearly enjoying a spirited discussion but trying to maintain some control. I looked around the room, catching the eye of some of my brunch guests, basking in their deferential, respectful nods and grins. Eli and I made contact, sustained, and I took that as a sign she was open to a rapprochement. I beamed at her, and she couldn't help smiling back. When my gaze fell on Noel Kepner, though, he was not a happy camper. He frowned aggressively at me, as if he was a mix of pissed off and wounded.

I looked away, spooked. I got the feeling Noel wouldn't invite me to any of his shows again. Despite my loathing of his "music," I had to admit I felt a bit pissed off by his expression. Wounded, too.

# 24

Octber 19th, Wednesday

To: Mr. Sagebrush
From: Dora Benet
Subject: Recent events

I'm sure Ms. Ratzenberger has spoken to you about the upper school locker situation, and blamed me. Although I can (and will) take credit for provoking the graffiti artist, I cannot (and won't) be the fall guy (girl, whatever) for the rash of copycat graffiti that is only too evident in the upper school locker hallway. For one thing, I don't even own a Sharpie. For another, I could hardly say, let alone write some of the slurs that decorate the two dozen lockers that have been hit since this morning. I suppose one could argue, since I'd made a heated speech that praised the use of selective slander, that I might have inspired some kids to take pen to metal.

All revolutions have to deal with the acts of misguided extremists. As their leader, I will try to squash this rebellion within the rebellion by . . . well, I'm not sure how. Some brilliant idea is sure to pop up.

Meanwhile, my brunch was a huge success. I am now recognized as the leader among the junior class girls. The boys will have to find their own replacement, if they too crave change. I have a candidate in mind that is creative, smart, gifted in the computer sciences and well traveled through the world of private schools. He's a new student at Brownstone, but his mysteriousness could add to his standing. Timing is of the essence. I heard from Kim Daniels, my new Minister of Intelligence, that Lump played at Juicy on Saturday night—and no one showed up.

Thursday, noonish

Ms. Benet:
I've had a very long conversation with Ms. Ratzenberger. She is quite upset. Of the three dozen lockers that have been vandalized, your BITCH!!! seems to be one of the tamer slurs. You've certainly started something. Now you'd better put a stop to it. The *Brief* was suspiciously boring today. No mention of you, at all. Do you still have influence there, or has that dried up?
With respect,
Mr. Sagebrush


"The Dropov twins have been grounded," said Kim, slurping a latte at Grind. We were having Friday lunch with a few other Teeming Masses (not that distinctions mattered anymore).

"By their parents?" I asked.

"Apparently!" she screamed.

She did that. Screamed. Kim, I was fast learning, was a loud person with her voice, clothes, gestures. In hindsight, it made perfect sense that Kim would take off her shirt in the middle of the cafeteria. It also made sense why she'd been the leader of the Teeming Masses. Her compulsive lack of volume control both demanded attention and intimidated any challengers.

I pinched the bridge of my nose. A headache usually set in whenever I spent more than ten minutes with Kim. "Okay," I said, "why were they grounded?"

"You will LOVE THIS!" Kim hollered. "The day Max Lindsey and Lori broke up, Mr. Swenson gave a pop quiz in advanced calculus, and Lori got every single question wrong! She failed so stunningly, despite her flawless homework history, that Mr. Swenson assumed she was having some emotional trauma. He called Mr. and Mrs. Dropov, and they came in to discuss if there was anything wrong with her home life. It turns out that the Dropovs are having marital problems, and were going to tell the twins about their plans to separate. And that was how Lori found out her parents are getting a divorce! CAN YOU BELIEVE IT?"

"That's horrible," I said.

"It gets BETTER!" shouted Kim. "Lori started crying and cursing, and blaming her parents for putting too much pressure on her. Apparently, Mrs. Dropov was unhappy with Lori's grades, and wanted her to quit ballet to study more. That's when Lori called Max, initially to tutor her over the summer, but then she realized it would be quicker and easier to get Max to do her work for her. So it all came out. And now Lori has to quit ballet!"

I thought of how passionately—and beautifully—Lori performed in school dance recitals. "She loves ballet," I said weakly.

"I KNOW!" screeched Kim. "No more boyfriend, no more ballet, no more happy family. Her life is OVER."

Had I been responsible, somehow, for destroying Lori Dropov's life? And, more importantly, would she see it that way and attempt to retaliate? And, meanwhile, I was beginning to suspect that Kim Daniels was a bit of a sadist. She seemed to have no sympathy for Lori, not even one drop.

Noel had said, "We should have sympathy for the oppressor."

*When you're guilt ridden, be guilt ridden*, I thought.

I said, "Kim, you're enjoying Lori's downfall a little too much."

"Why shouldn't I? Lori Dropov has called me a fat shit since I was ten. I wasn't even fat then. Or now. But every time she passes me in the hallway, she oinks. I hate her. I'm glad she's miserable."

Truth was, Kim Daniels was pink and flabby with big nostrils like a pig.

"How's Micha taking the divorce news?" I asked.

Kim snorted. "She has, apparently, taken to her bed."

The cluster of girls started laughing, tickled pink by the Dropovs' pain. I smiled along with them, but truth be told, I felt sorry for the twins. Even though I knew they were sniveling, scheming Ruling Class lackeys for Sondra, I didn't wish divorce on their parents. I remember the hundreds of e-mails that flooded my parents' Web site after *His-and-Her Divorce* came out. Many of them were from lonely, desperate kids whose parents had split up.

Kim added, "Both twins have, apparently, gained five pounds!"

Why did Kim have to say "apparently" in every sentence? I wondered. And why did I have to listen to it?

*When you're annoyed, be annoyed.*

"I've got to go," I said abruptly, standing. The gang of girls (all with bangs) around me stood up when I did, as if I were a departing dignitary. I half expected them to salute.

They sang, "See you later," as I walked out of Grind, suddenly hating the place I'd once loved. I hadn't seen Liza or Eli in there for over a week.

Not wanting to go home and face Mom, Dad and Joya, I decided to take a walk along the Promenade, check out the view of Manhattan, remind myself that I was only a speck, a fraction of a speck, compared to the city, the country, the planet, the universe. Readjustment of my perspective was much needed. My backpack squarely on my shoulders, along with my head, I trudged down Montague Street as far as I could go.

The Promenade was crowded, as always, with dog walkers, people on benches reading the paper, a few joggers and nannies with strollers. I walked slowly, alternately looking at the skyscrapers across the East River and my clog-clad feet.

About halfway along the Promenade, I heard someone calling me, "Hey, Fringe Girl! Over here!"

I turned to the right. Sondra Fortune was sitting in an Adirondack chair on the back deck of her town house. It abutted the Promenade, separated only by a fenced-in garden. Sondra put down her *magazine* and waved. She seemed peaceful, enjoying the simple pleasure of an autumnal evening.

This was the first I'd seen of her in a while. She'd been lying so low, she was practically underground. I said, "Sondra. Hello."

"How's the view from the top?" she asked wryly.

"Better than the middle."

"Is it really?"

"You would know," I said. "And how's the view from . . . wherever you are?"

"I'm exactly where I want to be," she said. "It feels good, taking a rest. I feel like I'd been running since I was ten years old."

"I'm so happy for you!" I enthused. "But, I must admit, it is odd to see you sitting alone, without a buffer of friends around you. And the line of boys groveling at your feet."

She said, "It's a relief to get some private time."

"And your parents?" I asked, digging deeper. "Are they keeping their distance, too? Respecting your private time?"

I could see her sharp eyes darken from ten feet away. "That's right," she said. "I've got this big old house to myself."

I waited a beat. For a crazy moment, I thought she might invite me to join her on the deck. To strip away the pretense and have an honest conversation about what had happened to pit us against each other, where the animosity came from, why the hostility flowed hot as magma between us. Maybe, I fantasized, she'd propose a truce. We could fashion a treaty, giving her back her position—on restrictive, modified terms, of course. But Sondra just sat there, saying nothing, smiling quixotically.

"Nice day for a stroll," I said.

"Sure is," she agreed.

"Care to join me?"

She laughed (heartily, ruthlessly) at the invitation, then said, "Over my dead body." She picked up her magazine and went back into her house, closing the deck door quietly behind her.

# 25

Sunday morning. One week since my brunch. One week since I'd assumed my place at the top of the new order. Ten days since Liza or Eli last spoke to me. Thirteen days since I met Seth Wonderwall, six since I took him as my canoodler.

I lay in bed, thinking about the cosmic spheres of life spinning in the right and wrong directions at the same time, judiciously preventing complete happiness—or sadness. My pillow started ringing. I answered it.

"Is this the lovely and talented Dora Benet?"

"Seth, can't you give a girl a rest?" I asked into my cell. "You kept me up until two last night." We'd talked on the phone for hours. Mom had insisted I stay home last night to help Joya prepare for *her* brunch party, scheduled for this afternoon.

"You should talk about keeping someone up all night," he said.

Seth was referring to my refusal to have phone sex with him. Since I'd yet to have actual sex, with Seth or anyone, phone sex seemed like skipping to the advanced pages before reading chapter one. I said, "What time is it?"

"Eleven."

"Joya's party is at one," I moaned. "I have to be here for it. She's convinced that her guests are coming to meet me."

"That means you have two hours to spend with me first," he said.

I'd give this to Seth: He was persistent. Since we'd met in detention, he'd been chivalrous nonstop. He wanted to be with me all the time, and he always asked what he could do to please me. I smiled and said, "What did you have in mind?"

"I've always wanted to see a competitive eating event," he said.

"The Atlantic Antic is today," I remembered. The Antic, Brooklyn's biggest street fair, stretched for miles along Atlantic Avenue, promising food, fun and frolic for the entire family. I'd been every year of my life, and used to count the days until. But the lure of Scooby Doo balloons, belly dancing, and greasy Italian sausages wasn't as tempting at sixteen as it had been at twelve.

He said, "The world-famous Brooklyn cheesecake-eating competition starts at noon. I've been told that if Brooklyn is known for one thing, and one thing only, it's cheesecake eating. I must be there. I can't miss it. How much cheesecake can one man eat?"

"I can't begin to imagine," I said.

"So you'll join me?"

"I'll meet you at the grandstand at eleven thirty, but then I have to come home," I said.

"Excellent! See you there. And wear protective clothing. You don't want to get puked on."

I got dressed quickly. No one was home; probably they were out shopping for fresh lox and bagels. I left a note, promising to be back in time for the brunch.

"That gargantuan white guy is the favorite," said Seth. He was pointing to a man mountain seated, along with his competitors, in front of a table on the grandstand stage.

"What's his T-shirt say?" I asked.

Seth recited, "I ate cleveland."

The borough president of Brooklyn began announcing the contestants who would be eating an unlimited supply of Junior's cheesecake, known o'er this vast land as the greatest edible to come out of Brooklyn since Nathan's Hot Dogs.

The other competitive eaters were a three-hundred-pound black man who, in an attempt to intimidate his adversaries, removed his shirt and let his flopping, jiggling, Volkswagen Beetle–sized belly hang out; a skinny Japanese guy who'd won last summer's clam-roll-eating competition at Coney Island; Miss Brooklyn, a model in an evening gown who was the weight of Cleveland's forearm; a bearded, mustachioed white man who had a lean and hungry (and scary) look on his face; and a Russian guy named Oleg who wasn't much bigger than Seth but had, reportedly, won the national linguine-eating contest in Little Italy.

The crowd cheered as each contestant was announced. Seth and I applauded and hooted along with them, getting into it. He'd somehow maneuvered us into the front row, just behind some journalists and photographers. We could see everything.

"I'd love to watch you eat cheesecake," said Seth. "I'd like to feed it to you."

I must have blushed or something. He liked it, and he leaned down to kiss me, licking the inside of my mouth with his tongue as if it were already stuffed with cake. I melted, felt dizzy.

He pulled back and asked, "Are you a virgin?"

"*What?*"

"It's okay if you are," he said. "It's good."

"And if I'm not?"

"Then my instincts are way, way off."

"No, they're right on the money."

"Let me be your first," he asked as casually as if he needed change for a dollar.

"I've known you for less than two weeks."

"Didn't you tell me there was no point to wasting time?"

The borough president said, "The rules are simple: Each contestant has a tray of fifty half-pound cheesecakes. Whoever eats the most in eight minutes is the winner."

"I'm not going to make that kind of decision right now," I said.

"We don't have to do it this minute, as long as I can count on doing it eventually. Soon."

He kissed me again. But this time, my lips didn't open to him. He pushed his tongue against them, frustrated but undeterred.

"Counting down. Five, four, three, two . . ."

A whistle. Seth pulled away and aimed his laser of attention at the eaters. Flustered, crushed in the surge of the crowd, I felt hot and light-headed, as if I might faint.

The men onstage were cramming baseball-sized cheesecakes into their mouths with their hands. Miss Brooklyn gamely used a spoon.

Cleveland had consumed about ten cakes (five pounds of food) in two minutes, and then he slowed significantly. The Japanese guy was methodically inhaling cake, his skinny arms moving like pistons. The bearded guy had chunks of white matter all over his facial hair. The shirtless black guy was using both hands, his face right over the tray, his lips coated with mush. The Russian linguine champ was keeping up with Cleveland, but after a too quick stuffing, he gagged a bit and his eyes bugged.

I thought I might be sick. I looked down at my clogs, but the air was thick and stifling. I looked up at the sky, and got woozy from lifting my head. Seth slapped a hand on my ass and screamed, "Swallow, swallow, swallow," joining the chanting crowd.

Thank God the whistle blew. Two more minutes and I would have lost my digestive composure. Seth was jumping up and down, cheering and applauding. He said, "That was the most disgusting, glorious, horrible, beautiful thing I've ever seen."

He kissing me yet again, pawing me (where was the gentle Seth of yesterweek?). In his excitement, he didn't notice that my skin was clammy or that my body was stiff as a corpse. Despite his rapt attention, Seth seemed oblivious to my plight. I began to wonder if he was seeing me at all, or just seeing who he wanted me to be—a kindred spirit, a virgin who'd let him get inside.

Cleveland was announced the winner by the slim (if anything about him could be described as slim) margin of half a cheesecake. The crowd broke up, some people staying to purchase Junior's goods, the rest dispersing along Atlantic Avenue. Seth tugged me away and tried to lead me down Hoyt Street to find a "secluded spot."

"I have to go home," I said. "Joya's brunch." I checked my watch. It was nearly one, and the walk home would take at least fifteen minutes.

"You don't care about that brunch," he said dismissively. "Come with me."

I tugged loose of him. He said, "So now you're scared of me, right? Because I said I want sex. Now you're a trembling prude?"

His words were caustic and harsh. I was afraid; he was

right. Not about having sex. I'd touched two boys by now, and I had a better understanding of what I would be dealing with. I was scared that Seth was changing on me. As sweet and flattering as he'd been all week when I did what he wanted, I feared he'd be a cruel and unrelenting enemy if I didn't.

I said calmly, "Seth, I warned you that I had an obligation at home."

"Don't talk to me like I'm a child," he said. His formerly sparkling eyes had turned to stone.

Okay, now he was freaking me out. I started walking home, moving as fast as I could. Almost at a jog. My spidey senses told me he hadn't followed, and I let myself slow a bit as I walked toward Henry Street. A stage was set up at the corner of Atlantic and Henry. It was smaller than the Hoyt Street grandstand, really just a riser with some amplifiers. A band was up there. From half a block away, I could hear the fuzz of feedback.

The Brooklyn Lager keg truck was parked next to the stage. The long lines of beer guzzlers in front of it blocked my view of the stage until I was practically right in front of it.

The band up on it was Lump, of course. A month ago, were it not for the downfall of their regime, the stage would have been surrounded by Ruling Class kids, also aspiring Fringe Dwellers, hopeful Teeming Masses. Today, Noel and Stanley performed for an audience of passersby. People turned to check them out as they walked along, but no one stopped to listen, or even pretended to enjoy the music (using the word loosely). Despite being ignored, even scornfully so, Noel and Stanley were jamming their hearts out, seemingly into it, having fun, smiling, laughing. At the side of the stage, Sondra bobbed her beautiful head along with the offbeat. Beside her, looking bored but willing, was Vin Transom. Sondra and Vin were holding hands.

I dashed behind the beer truck to spy. Their fingers intertwined, Vin lifted their hands and kissed Sondra's knuckles. She watched his lips at work and then returned the gesture with what appeared to be genuine affection and kindness. Instead of plunging in for a maul as he'd done with me, Vin brushed the Freestyling strands from her forehead and smiled lazily, sweetly—*lovingly*—into Sondra's eyes.

The song ended. Noel spoke into the microphone. "All right! Thank you, Brooklyn! That was a number we call 'Cat with Hair Ball.' Before we get into the next tune, I want to thank Sondra and Vin for coming today. You're true friends, guys. Okay. We call this next one 'Twisting Metal.' One, two, three, four . . ."

And then the crash of bad music started again.

*If you feel dejected, be dejected*, I thought.

I plodded along, realizing with bitter, humorless irony that it was miserably lonely at the top.

When I got home, though, my torment increased.

Expecting to find the place overrun with eighth-grade girls, I walked into a nearly empty apartment. Mom, Dad and Ben were the only people in the living room. They were comforting Joya while she sobbed on the couch.

Mom looked up first. "Hello, Adora," she said in her angry, clipped voice. "You finally showed up."

"What's going on here? Where is everyone?"

Dad said, "The girls came an hour ago. But they didn't stay."

Joya sobbed a bit louder.

"They wanted to meet you," said Mom. "And you weren't here. You promised to be back by noon. Look what you've done to your sister!"

"The brunch was at one!" I insisted. "You said one!"

"No, Adora. I told you noon at least ten times!"

"Gloria, it isn't Adora's fault that those girls are horrible," he said.

"All thirteen-year-old girls are horrible!" shouted Mom at Dad. "Of course, it's not her fault that they're vain, selfish brats. But by sixteen"—she was glaring at me—"most girls learn to be more considerate of the people they're closest to."

"You're fifty," said Dad to Mom. "What's your excuse?"

"I'm not laughing, Ed."

"I'm sorry," I pleaded, anxious as always when my parents raised their voices at each other, which didn't happen often. "I messed up. I blew it. How can I fix this?"

Ben yelled, "You can't fix it! You broke Joya into a million pieces today. Not that she deserves it. She's never done anything to hurt you, Dora. She worships you! I can't see why. All these years, I've nodded and kept silent about my feelings. But I won't anymore. This is the straw that broke my back. You're awful to Joya. You take her for granted. You talk to her like she's stupid, insignificant. She's brilliant and beautiful and very important to me. I won't have you treat her like this." He paused to catch his breath. "Wow, I feel *a lot* better now."

The savage takedown from not-gay Ben. I was impressed! I was also full of shame and self-loathing. He was absolutely right. As dismissive as I'd been to Joya, I always knew she'd forgive me. Or we'd just wait until we were twenty-five and twenty-eight, when we'd laugh about how we didn't get along as teenagers. But now I feared I might have severed the connection—tenuous as it was—for good. That we would never be close, in our teens, or our twenties. Some ideas felt like a stab wound to the heart.

"I don't deserve your forgiveness, Joya. I'm a shit. A steaming shit. I hate myself right now. I hate everything. Seth is a wacko. Sondra has Vin. Liza and Eli hate me. And now this ugly scene. Why can't I catch a break?"

Mom, Dad and Ben stared at me in disbelief. Even Joya seemed shocked by my self-absorption in the face of her large-scale social rejection.

Joya said, "None of those girls would have agreed to come here if it weren't for you." Her irresistible face with the huge eyes (puffy and red-rimmed) hit me full force. "Why don't they like me?" she wailed.

She might as well have asked, "Why don't *you* like me?"

To that question, I gave her the best answer I could. The honest answer. The one I'd been trying to suppress for thirteen years, since the day Mom and Dad brought her home from the hospital. "They're jealous of you," I said. "Of your beauty and talent and your peaceful soul."

And then I started sobbing, for her and myself. I ran upstairs, Mom calling after me, and locked myself in my room.

Once I got the tears under control, I called Liza on my cell. Her mom answered. Voice cracking, I said, "Hello, Stephanie. It's Dora."

"Dora," she said hesitantly. "Hello."

"I heard you got engaged. Congratulations."

"Thank you," she said.

I suddenly remembered the last time I'd seen her and had so offended Gary. "Look, I'm sorry for the way I behaved when you were over here for dinner. I've been apologizing all day long, actually. I need to talk to Liza."

Her voice softened. "Liza isn't home, sweetheart."

The "sweetheart" got me. Stephanie Greene had been my surrogate mother on Hicks Street. Anita Stomp had been, too (to a lesser extent). As Mom had been for Liza and Eli. Had I alienated my entire surrogate family, too?

I started crying again. "She's home, right?" I asked. "She just won't talk to me, right?"

Softly, Stephanie said, "She'll come around, honey. Just hang in there."

We said our good-byes and disconnected.

I called Eli. Mrs. Stomp answered. "Eli may not come to the phone. She's practicing. She's going to practice from now until the States competition tomorrow night—without interruption from you, Liza or Eric."

"States are tomorrow night?" I'd completely forgotten. "I'd like to come."

Mrs. Stomp gave me the time and the address in Manhattan. The competition would be held at the High School for Performing Arts in Manhattan, located close to Lincoln Center in the West Sixties.

"You can come only if you promise not to be a distraction for Eli," said Mrs. Stomp.

"I swear!"

"Then I'll see you tomorrow," she said.

Clicking off, I felt better than I had all day. States would be my opportunity to make up with Eli. I'd bring her flowers. Shower her with love. She'd be in a good mood since she was sure to win—again. I fantasized about our celebrating together after her victory, the two of us, arms around each other's shoulders, running through the night, howling.

# 26

I couldn't wait for the school day to end. It'd been a rough one. Started bad, and stayed that way.

First thing, as I walked to my BITCH!!!-y locker (passing SLUT, LOSER, LAME-ASS and GEEK—and those were the PG-13-rated ones), I found Seth Wonderwall loitering in front of it.

"Dora, babe," he said, trying to kiss me. As if nothing had happened. As if we hadn't screamed at each other on the street less than twenty-four hours ago. "How's it going? Want to blow off school with me?"

"Not today, Seth," I said nervously. "I have a test in biology."

"Sure, no problem. I'll see you later. We'll have lunch together."

"I'm having lunch with Kim."

"Okay, cool. That's great," he said, his voice getting high and squeaky. "I can wait. I've got the patience of a Zen monk. We can hook up after school."

"I'm going to watch Eli compete in the States piano competition after school," I said, praying he'd take the hint.

But Seth, I was beginning to understand, wouldn't take a hint if it were wrapped in gold. "Sounds like fun," he said. "So, we can meet for coffee at Grind before school tomorrow."

It went on like this for five solid minutes before I could

break away. I managed to avoid him all morning. And then, at lunch, Kim Daniels dropped both her lunch tray on the table and a bombshell in my lap.

"You'll never guess what I just heard from my friend at Trinity," she said, referring to a private school in Manhattan.

"Just out with it," I said a bit rudely, but I was, by then, tired of Kim and her lengthy windups.

"Apparently," she started, "Seth Wonderwall went there last year. And he got kicked out for STALKING A FRESHMAN GIRL! My friend told me that they dated for a few weeks, but then he started getting in her face. She tried to break up with him, but he went nutso on her. Refusing to listen, showing up at her house. Staking out her locker. Waiting for her after each class. And my friend told me he'd done the same thing at the school he went to BEFORE THAT. He's CRAZY. But his father is the chief lawyer in New York for MICROSOFT and he got his company to donate new COMPUTERS to the entire SCHOOL so Seth wouldn't be LOCKED UP, and to make sure he got a decent RECOMMENDATION to get into Trinity, and then BROWNSTONE!!!"

My head started throbbing. I didn't know if it was from Kim's ear-bleeding shrieks, or the fact that I'd been tagged by a whack job. Kim's friends clustered to hear this tale, not that they needed to since her voice could be heard in Korea. They all seemed eager for my reaction. My relationship with Seth had been discreet. My instincts, thank God for them, had kept me quiet about him to my new "friends." But since I was the opinion maker at school now, I was expected to say something so everyone could agree with me.

"I feel sick," I said, which was my raw reaction to the news. "I need to find a bathroom."

I ran out of there and down an empty hallway into the middle school section of Brownstone. It was the fastest way out of the building.

I hadn't intended to spy on Joya, but I spotted her as I tore by the art studio. She was in Ms. Gligman's invitation-only drawing class, seated at one end of a large table, completely absorbed in her work. The five other kids in the class—all older than Joya—sat together at the other end of the table, chatting, sharing paint, and completely ignoring my sister.

The unexpected glimpse into Joya's loneliness made my stomach lurch again. I crashed into the bathroom next door, splashed cold water on my face and tried to calm down. The sound of opening doors and a fresh influx into the ladies' room alerted me to the change in periods. I had to run to make it to my biology class on time. Mr. Gouter locked the door of his classroom at the tick of the hour, and he wouldn't let students enter one second late. If I didn't make it on time, I'd fail the test.

Legs pumping, I ran back to the upper school. My heart thudding in my chest, I was sure I'd make it. Just as I rounded the last turn, the classroom door in view, I was stopped in my tracks by the looming figure of Seth Wonderwall. He smiled and waved and blocked me for that extra two seconds I needed to get my foot in the door and scramble inside.

The biology class door shut. I heard Mr. Gouter turn the lock, guaranteeing me a goose egg on the test.

"Hey, Dora. I thought we could grab some pizza," he said cheerfully.

"Listen closely, Seth," I said. "I know you've been kicked out of two other schools for stalking, and I will get you kicked out of this one, too, if you so much as look at me ever again. Do I make myself clear?"

"Maybe we should talk about it over coffee," he suggested sunnily.

"I would never have a cup of coffee again if I had to have it with you," I said, surprising myself with my venom.

But the poison tones seemed to penetrate Seth's dense skull. He said, "I hate you! You *are* a BITCH!!!" and then he ran away from me, his elbows flying.

As I watched Seth throw his books down the stairwell, it occurred to me that my judgment in boys might be severely flawed.

I took the subway to the High School of Performing Arts in Manhattan that evening. The lobby was packed. Who knew there were so many parents and grandparents and aunts and uncles who wanted to watch an amateur piano competition? I came alone in the hope that I'd find the Stomps, or Liza. I'd be happy to sit with Eric, assuming he and Eli were still together, whatever "together" meant for them. Since I was sure that Eli had been using Eric to get Jack's attention and/or spy on her rival's piano practices, I wouldn't have been the least bit surprised if Eli had dumped Eric on the eve of the States competition.

I was having these somewhat nefarious thoughts when I felt a tap on my shoulder. I spun around, and lo, there stood Eric Brainard, fluttery and shaking like a poodle after a cold bath.

"What's the matter?" I asked, assuming he was sick, or had just been mugged. Or dumped.

"I'm just nervous for Eli," he said, wringing his hands. "She's been practicing so hard for this. And she's performing *last*. Did you see the program?"

He handed me a folded piece of paper. Before opening it, I said, "She always goes last." As the defending champ two years running, Eli was the showstopper. The show ender. Hell, she *was* the show.

Perusing the program, I noticed that Jack Carp was scheduled second to last, right before Eli. He was going to play Rachmaninoff's Third, exactly what Eli had accused him of practicing on the sly. Eli was going with Beethoven's *Waldstein*. Fifteen other kids would be performing that evening, too, and I groaned inwardly. I wasn't sure I would be able to pinch myself awake for that long.

"I'm going to leave, get some coffee, and then come back in, oh, an hour. Want to join me?" I asked.

"No thanks," he said. "Eli will know I've left the building. She'll sense I'm not here. I can't do that to her."

*O-kay*, I thought. "I wouldn't want to break your mind meld."

"I'm glad to hear that, Dora," he said, looking at me with the earnestness of a politician. "Eli has been worried for some reason that you don't support our relationship."

"I've been worried that Eli doesn't support *our* relationship," I said, mystified by his confession.

"Our relationship?" he asked, equally mystified.

"Mine and Eli's," I said. "We haven't been speaking."

"That might be, in part, because Eli thinks you thought she was wrong to break up with Jack Carp."

"I don't care who Eli goes out with, as long as she's happy," I said, increasingly floored by this conversation. What had I said to Eli to give her these misconceptions?

He smiled. "You should tell Eli."

"I will. As soon as this is over."

"I'm going to find the Stomps. They're saving a seat for me. There might be space for you, too."

"You go," I said.

And he did. Flitting off in search of Eli's parents as if *he'd* known them his whole life, which he certainly hadn't.

Unsettled and confused, and miffed, too, I left the Per-

forming Arts lobby and walked toward Lincoln Center to find
a Starbucks. Which was easy enough, since one could stand on
any street corner in Manhattan, swing a dead cat, and hit a
Starbucks. I went into the one on Broadway and Sixty-sixth,
had myself a latte and a blueberry scone. Then I headed back
to see the end of the concert.

Just in time. Watching from the back row, I waited for a
pudgy girl in pigtails to finish some Mozart number. Jack Carp
came on next.

He looked thinner, and darker (if that was possible), than
the last time I'd seen him. Whenever that was. When he and
Eli fought in her room the day they broke up? Through the
window in Eric's kitchen? Our paths rarely crossed at school.
Oh, well. The point was, Jack looked skinny and bleak in black,
including way-too-big trousers and a vintage tuxedo jacket with
satin piping. He lurched onto the stage, flipped his tux tails to
sit and plopped down on the bench.

He started playing. The music sounded pretty good to me,
but immediately, audience members to my right and left
started murmuring. I had no idea what was so shocking about
Jack's piece. It was lovely, melodic and tonal, with a catchy little chorus that made me feel happy and sad at the same time.
The music didn't even seem "classical" per se. It was far more
accessible to people like me. I wondered if he was playing
something by Leonard Bernstein or another composer of that
era. Whatever the piece, Jack was clearly moved by his choice.
He rocked back and forth on the bench, leaning in and out, really feeling the emotions. I was moved. His performance was
powerful. Not studied and sweated over like most of the piano
machines who'd been whipped by their parents to play.

When he finished, I applauded heartily. The audience
clapped, too, but still acted uncertain. Jack stood up, bowed,

and then he spoke. Shouted, actually, since he had no microphone. "That was an original composition, written by me, called 'Eli, I Love You, Come Back to Me.' I'd like to thank Adora Benet for her support and advice during this time of emotional upheaval. Thank you all."

My lungs compressed, and suddenly, sickeningly, I remembered the last time I saw Jack Carp. He'd shown up at my house. On my deck, I suggested he make a grand romantic gesture to win back Eli. As I checked out the audience's hushed reaction to his speech, my eyes fell on the Stomps and Eric Brainard, seated about ten rows up, to my left. Dr. and Mrs. Stomp were in shock. Eric seemed on the verge of tears. He was glancing around self-consciously, and, of fucking course, he spotted me. His eyes turned black as tar. If he could have killed me with his stare, he would have.

And I'd just told him I didn't care who Eli dated.

The master of ceremonies came out to announce Elizabeth Stomp, two-time New York State piano sonata champion.

Eli stumbled onstage. To say she looked embarrassed would be the understatement of the year. Her face was bright red. And Eli never blushed. Her movements were jerky, as if she was forcing herself out there. After two steps, she dropped her head so her hair fell around her face, obscuring it. I flashed back to when we were little kids and Eli would hide her face behind her long, sleek hair whenever she'd been reprimanded. She thought that if she couldn't see anyone, no one could see her.

I won't go into the ghastly details about how well she played. Or, more accurately, how not well she played. Eli tapped out the notes as if the piano was a computer keyboard. I couldn't say if she made technical mistakes or not. But even a layperson like me could hear the tinny, tentative sounds tumbling from the piano.

I didn't bother staying to find out who won. Or to attempt to explain myself to Eli, her parents or Eric. There was no point. Whatever she believed, I couldn't possibly undo the damage. She would lose tonight. It was—indirectly—my fault. I'd screwed over my best friend in the worst way possible, destroying what she held most dear. Just as I'd done to Liza, re: Max. Just as I'd done to Joya, re: the sham of our sisterhood.

As the audience politely applauded Eli's performance, I crept out of the theater and ran out of the school. I hailed a taxi, crawled inside, bleated my destination to the driver and started bawling like a baby.

In the course of my ruthless climb to the top, I'd hit rock bottom. The higher I got, the less grounded. The metaphor could go on and on. Joya had been right to say my greatest power came from existing just a bit outside.

It was only too obvious to me now. I was not a leader. I was not a visionary. I wasn't a born advice giver, either. I was a fuckup. A complete and utter fake. Which would be okay. I could live with my inauthentic self. But I'd killed my friends and my sister along the way.

And that made me a bona fide bitch. With a capital *I*.

# 27

T HE FALL OF FRINGE GIRL WEEK DIARY

**Tuesday**
*8:30 A.M.:* I arrived in school to see that someone added fifteen more exclamation points to my locker.

11:00 A.M.: In social studies, Eli moved to a desk at the opposite corner of the room.

*6:00 P.M.:* A schoolwide e-mail arrived in my queue, warning parents, alumni and students: "The Brownstone Institute Web site is temporarily out of order. Someone has hacked into it, changed the content and written a program that prevented the changes to be deleted. The school's technical team is working on the problem, and we advise everyone not to visit the site until further notice. Thank you."

I thought of Seth Wonderwall immediately, and went to brownstone.edu. Instead of the school calendar on the home page, what popped up was a photo of me with buck teeth, horns, a jagged scar on my cheek, drool, boogers clinging to long nose hairs, red crusty eyes, and too many pus-filled zits to count. I had to give Seth his props. The pixel editing was flawless. He would soon be kicked out of Brownstone—might never graduate high school—but based on this one example, he could probably get a great job at Pixar. What bothered me the most about this: No one called me to commiserate.

**Wednesday**

*Noon:* Kim Daniels rushed up to me at Chez Brownstone. "You won't BELIEVE what Micha Dropov is telling everyone about your parents!"

Oh, what new torment was this? "I don't want to know," I said.

"She's saying that Gloria and Ed Benet got their start writing PORNOGRAPHY! Their first book was called *His-and-Her Fucking.*"

I said, "Imagine the impact if she'd said it was called *His-*and-HIS *Fucking.* Or *Her-*and-HER *Fucking.*"

Kim blinked. "Are you not getting this? Micha Dropov is trashing your family."

I thought about the family of Romanovs who'd been rounded up and shot in their palace during the Bolshevik Revolution.

I said, "Shut up, Kim. Just SHUT UP. I can't stand to listen to you yell in my ear for one more second." I re-Saran-Wrapped my turkey and Swiss and split.

On the way out, Liza was coming in. I waved at her, smiled, and said, "Liza! Hi!"

She acted like I didn't exist, freezing me completely. I felt the chill for hours.

*3:00 P.M.:* Seth Wonderwall was escorted through the front door of Brownstone by two school security guards, in full view of half of the junior class. Throughout his dramatic exit, Seth asked anyone who dared to make eye contact with him, "Have you seen Dora Benet?" or "Why isn't Dora Benet here to say good-bye?" Not getting responses from the horrified students, he started yelling, "Dora Benet was the best girlfriend I ever had!" alternating with "Dora Benet is evil! She's the devil! This is all her fault!"

**Thursday**
*8:30 A.M.:* The *Brief* came out. I was back in it. But not in a good way. This was the cover story, in full.

### Cast the First Brownstone
#### *by Max Lindsey*

I play chess. The game is about power and manipulation. The master moves his pieces around the board, sacrificing pawns, if necessary, to clear a path for the stronger players to crush the opponent. Great players visualize the pieces as actual people. The pawns are the nameless, faceless masses, pieces that represent the majority of the population (there are far more pawns than any other piece). But pawns are limited in their movements, virtually powerless, and easily plucked off. Call pawns the Masses.

The knights, rooks and bishops are the pieces that surround the King and Queen. They are on the fringe of royalty, but not royal themselves. Usually, the function of these pieces is to protect, surround and defend the King and Queen. They can go on attack, but are still vulnerable.

The King. This piece has severely limited movement. He is a figurehead. He represents power, but has little. And yet, the entire game swirls around him as if he's the center of the universe.

The Queen. She's got all the moves. Every piece on the board is easy prey for her. She is a target, too, and has to defend herself with cunning and the blunt force of a hammer. If she's smart and wily, she survives. If she is stupid and reckless, if she alienates her Fringe pieces, sacrifices too many of her Masses of pawns, she'll be taken down. She'll wind up alone in the middle of the board, enemies gunning for her from all directions. Such an ineffective leader deserves to be destroyed, since she is responsible for the pillaging of the players on her own side. She has manipulated *herself*, placed *herself* in a dangerous position. The bludgeoning should be fittingly ruthless. Her enemies will cheer as she bounces on the board when she falls.

*3:00 P.M.:* By the end of the day, two dozen copies of the article were taped to my locker. At least they covered up the !!!!!!!!!!!!!BITCH!!!!!!!!!!!!!.

**Friday**
*8:30 A.M. to 3:00 P.M.:* I was shunned and laughed at as I walked the halls. By end of the day, I was a veritable leper. *Apparently*, even Kim Daniels wouldn't scream at me.

## HOW TO BE CHEERFUL
### by Gloria and Ed Benet
#### (excerpted from His-and-Her Divorce)

Dumper or dumpee, a bad breakup puts you down in the . . . dumps. Short of expensive psychopharmacology or self-prescribed beer and/or *mojitos* (which, says Ed, are only a temporary solution), depression, regret, guilt and loneliness are part of the package when you end a relationship. Process the sadness in order to dissolve it. This doesn't happen quickly. You might be looking at months of down (in the dumps) time. Here are a few ideas for getting yourself through it.

### Gloria's Soul-Nurturing Suggestions

1  Friends. Remember your friends? The people you blew off in the early days of your relationship, had double dates with in the middle of the relationship and then called in the wallow of your self-absorption at the end of the relationship? Now is your big chance to make it up to them. Take them to dinner. Buy them drinks. Better, buy them small but meaningful gifts. Giving will make you feel better, get you out of your head and grant you at least two more hours of whine time.

2  Beauty. As the relationship waned, you might have tried to make yourself gorgeous in a last-ditch effort to keep love alive. Such desperate measures were bound to fail. No matter how much makeup you slapped on, your sadness showed through. But, since you are starting afresh, and are in need of pampering (and you've got some free time on your hands), devote all your excess hours to your own vanity. The point isn't to prettify for your next love. It's to indulge. Submit to the massage therapist. Yield to the fa-

cialist. Lift high your thigh for the bikini waxer. Why? Here's a surprising little secret: When your grandmother told you to "put on some lipstick, you'll feel better," *she was right.*

3 Plants. Green thumb or black, flowers or a flowering potted plant will put a bloom in your cheek. Research from the University of Berkeley says that people who have fresh cut flowers in their homes describe themselves as "happy" 43 percent more often than those who have no photosynthetic friends. Not having a man around to buy you roses should only inspire you to buy some for yourself. Better yet, get daisies. They last longer.

## Ed's Tough Self-Love Tips

1 Nudity. At least once a day, take off all your clothes and stand in front of the mirror. Find some body part that makes you think, "Hmm. Not bad." Find another body part that makes you think, "I've still got it." And then find a body part (look hard) that inspires the thought, "Always room for improvement." Then, busy yourself improving. One day, you will date again. And how convenient it'll be for you to have made positive adjustments during your romantic confinement.

2 Play all the sad songs. Do it. Force yourself to play the song you heard on your first date, when you first made love, on your wedding day, etc. Listen to them over and over again, and eventually, the music will lose its power. You'll wear down the groove of memory, and you won't be so devastated next time the song comes on the radio or is piped into Target.

3 Sex. No time like the present for some life-affirming action. I don't mean with just anyone. Every woman can

think of one ex-boyfriend, or a sex-willing friend. I only recommend this for women with the wherewithal not to get immediately attached to any sex partner, those who can simply enjoy the contact, and the erotic reminder of one thing relationships are good for.

# 28

I stayed in my apartment all weekend. Not that anyone called me or begged for my company. On Sunday night, Mom and I rinsed the dinner dishes together at the kitchen sink.

I said, "I need your advice."

She dropped a plate on the floor.

"Sorry," she said as we picked up the pieces.

"Forget I asked," I said testily.

"No! I want to help. I live to help. Come," she said, putting her hands on my shoulders and steering me to the living room. Joya had stepped out with Dad to Tasti D-Lite, so we didn't have much time.

As we settled onto the couch, I started to have a few pangs of concern. For one thing, Mom was looking at me as if I were a frog in biology class. She had this creepy grin on her face like she was imagining what color my innards might be. For her, advice giving was a dissection. For one night only, I would be her subject.

Before I said a word, she asked, "Is it about Joya?"

My knee-jerk reaction was to yell, "No, this is about ME. Not HER." But all this was, in part, about Joya.

I said, "I've gotten myself into a spot of trouble at school. Relax. Nothing with academics. No police involvement. At least, not yet. I think the problem started—years ago—with a kernel in my head that just grew and grew and kind of took me over. I wanted something so badly with no chance of ever getting it."

"Wanted what?" she asked.

"I wanted to be listened to," I said. "I'm not blaming you and Dad, not really. But the whole world, from Oprah Winfrey to the butcher, wants to hear what you have to say. What pearls of wisdom you can offer like little free gifts to anyone with a functional pair of ears. I remember going to a teacher conference with you in third grade. Mrs. Stanhope just sat there, beaming at you, asking question after question about book publishing. I don't think a single word was said about me."

"That's not true, Adora," she said. "Your memory is selective."

"I'm sure you're right," I admitted. "But the lasting impression—and it's been building for a long time—was envy. I wanted to be looked at with respect. For people to clamor for my ideas and opinions. This whole mess at school started because I knew that if I had to swallow my ideas and bite my tongue for one more second, I'd explode. Which is what happened, anyway. I started talking, and the result is a big bloody disaster."

"I've always listened to you. Even when I was bored to tears with your incessant prattle about American Girl dolls."

"But you're required to listen to me. It's in the mother-daughter contract. I wanted attention from people who aren't related to me."

"Tell me what happened," she prompted.

I gave her the Cliffs Notes version.

After which she exhaled and said, "Interesting. Maybe Dad and I should do a book called *His-and-Her Revolution*."

"Good one, Mom," I said. "Now make with the advice."

"That was terrible, what you did to Liza and Eli."

"I'm aware."

"Should I call Ms. Ratzenberger about this boy, Seth Wonderwall?"

"He's gone," I said. "Hopefully, he's moved to a rubber room somewhere far, far away."

Mom put her arm around me and pulled me close. She stroked my hair, and cupped my cheek. I hadn't let her hug me like this in years. Naturally, I started crying. I'd been crying so often, two tear tracks were now etched in my face.

"Perhaps you should view this pragmatically," suggested Mom. "That Max Lindsey might be on to something, comparing the social movement at school to a chess game."

"He is a very bright boy," I nodded, wiping away salty droplets.

"You have two moves," mused Mom. "And you should do both. Number one: Appeal to the King. Ask him to cast the light of his benevolence upon you. Who is the King, anyway?"

"Noel Kepner," I stated.

"Noel? I remember him from kindergarten playdates. He came over once, took all the clothes off your Barbie dolls and lined them up in a row. You ran into my office crying because Noel was paying more attention to your dolls than to you."

"That was Vin Transom," I said.

She shook her head. "I'm positive it was Noel. His mother, Ida, and I still laugh about it at potlucks."

"Are you sure?" I asked, suddenly breathless.

"Noel Kepner is the King. He's a sweet boy," she said. "He'll do what he can for you. Unless you've alienated him, too."

I gulped. "What's the other move?"

"Appeal to the opposing Queen," she said. "Who, I assume, is Sondra Fortune."

"I can't."

"If you can swallow your ideas and opinions for years and years," said Mom, "you can swallow your pride for one day. Talk to Sondra. She might surprise you."

"What do I do about Eli and Liza?" I asked. "They hate me."

"They'll forgive you," she said soothingly. "You'll have to humble yourself—rightly so—but if you're sincere, they'll give you the free pass."

"How can you be sure?" I asked, praying Mother knew best.

"I'm their surrogate mother," she said. "I didn't raise those girls to be unforgiving."

# 29

I'd been waiting, crouching, at Noel Kepner's neighbor's stoop for twenty minutes already. I had no idea when Noel walked to school, so I went there early to make sure I would catch him.

My plan: Walk to Brownstone with Noel. Enter the building with him, gain renewed status and acceptance for being in his exalted presence. Even if Lump didn't draw the slavish fan support it once had, even if Noel's rank had been rendered irrelevant by the social upheaval I'd engineered, he would always carry weight. He was handsome, a star in every category. He could be knocked down only so far. I hoped that if we were seen together, we could float both our boats.

Okay, that was the political justification for crouching at a stranger's stoop since seven thirty a.m. I also had a personal reason. The picture wasn't exactly clear yet. But ever since Mom told me that Noel had been my kindergarten love interest, I searched my mind for some misty, foggy memory that would explain the transfer of my affection from Noel to Vin. I flipped through school class pictures until late last night, pining nostalgically for those long-ago years of innocence and ignorance.

Looking at the pictures of seven-year-old Vin, nine-year-old Vin, I felt nothing. I couldn't recall caring about his face, wanting to be on his team in gym. But the smiling faces of eight-year-old Noel and ten-year-old Noel did ring some distant bell in my memory. I also noticed he was always sandwiched between Sondra and a procession of other girls who'd go on to form the nucleus of the Ruling Class by middle school.

I was both amazed and shamed by the evolution of my own face in the class pictures. My six-year-old smile, eight-year-old smirk and eleven-year-old scowl. In one shot, I was looking right at Noel, snarling.

The door to Noel's apartment building opened, and he stepped onto his stoop. He inhaled the day, oblivious to the goofy earnestness of the gesture, and jogged down the steps. Hiding, I waited for him to get a few steps ahead of me on the sidewalk.

And then I rushed to catch up with him.

"Noel!" I said, coming up alongside. "Hey. How's it going?"

He was surprised to see me, since I lived five blocks in the other direction. "Dora. What are you doing up here?" he asked.

"I decided to take in this beautiful morning before school," I said, and heard how lame that sounded. "That's a lie. I was waiting for you. We need to talk."

He seemed as taken aback by hearing my confession as I was making it. "You want to talk to me? You usually want to talk at me. Or talk down to me. Or try to embarrass me."

"I'm sorry, Noel. I've been possessed by the devil all year."

"I don't mean just this year," he said. "You've been angry at me for as long as I can remember."

"I know. Again, I apologize."

He stopped suddenly and faced me. "Name one instance in the twelve years we've known each other when I was mean to you, or rude, or forgetful or *anything*. I feel like I've been trying to win your forgiveness forever, and I don't know why. I deserve an answer."

"And you'll get one," I said. "What was the question, exactly?"

"Here are two. What have I ever done to you?" he asked. "And, why do you hate me?"

I got a flash suddenly of that playdate with the naked Barbies, watching six-year-old Noel methodically arranging them in a row, turning to me and smiling with pride. In the years to come, flesh-and-blood Barbies clamored to line up for him.

"I don't hate you," I said. "And you've never done anything wrong. I'm sorry I've fucked up everything. Your heart is soft and big and open, and mine is a tiny black rock. I'm deeply, regretfully, humiliatedly—if that's even a word—*sorry* for everything. And I hope that one day, sometime before college, we can be friends."

Then I took off, holding the straps of my backpack tightly, toward Brownstone. If I stayed with him, and walked alongside him, I might tell him the awful truth: I was jealous of the Barbies—plastic and human—because I wanted Noel's attention.

My plans had to be abandoned. Using Noel seemed wrong now. Arriving at Brownstone alone, shaken and stirred by my revelation, I walked in a daze to my locker. It had—finally— been painted over. Every locker in the upper school had been redone. The hallway smelled like paint, but I didn't mind. I sniffed the scent gratefully, hoping that the fresh paint could mean a fresh start, too.

I opened my locker to unload my books, and a note dropped out. Someone had shoved it through the slats. Picking it up, I wondered, in this post-postmodern age, why the writer hadn't called my cell, or sent me an e-mail. Why would someone scribble a mysterious, anonymous . . . okay, that was why.

The note was short. Just two sentences: "Go to the lower school gym bathroom as soon as possible. I'll be there until 8:20."

I checked my watch. It was just after eight o'clock. Slamming the locker shut, I ran down the hallway and picked my way to the lower school gym bathroom. The note writer must have known that it would be deserted at this hour. I felt a sudden blast of panic. That the gym was *too* deserted. That, in the bathroom, no one could hear me scream. Nonetheless, I took the risk, and arrived at the rendezvous quickly.

Standing in front of the bathroom door, I had no idea who would be waiting on the other side. Would it be my best friend—or worst enemy? Would the meeting be good—or awful? If I went inside, would I regret it for the rest of my life—or . . .

"I can hear you breathing," shouted the voice inside. "Just get your ass in here."

I got my ass in there.

"Sondra!" I gasped.

"Dora!" she mocked. "Shut the door. Come *on*, we don't have much time before class."

I did as I was told. It felt right, as if obeying Sondra's commands was the way life should be. Or, at the very least, it felt familiar and reassuring.

"I got your note," I said.

"Obviously." Sondra looked gorgeous, as always, but even more confident and composed than ever. She sat down on the radiator cover and smiled. "Looks like your time at the top has come to an end."

"Sadly, yes. No, not sadly. I'm accepting."

"Good for you," she said. "But we have to put things right. We can't have anarchy. No one's happy this way."

"What do you suggest?" I asked, relieved she wanted to take control. If I'd proven one thing to myself, it was that a Fringe-Dwelling cynically optimistic individualist such as myself did not make an effective leader.

Sondra frowned, paused, then asked, "Have you ever wondered why I put myself forward? Why I act superior in the way that so offends you?"

Because you're a bitch, I thought. "I just assumed you like to boss people around."

"No, Dora. No, no, no. Look at me," she demanded.

I looked.

"What do you see?"

"Fishing for compliments, even now?" I asked.

"Honestly," she said softly. "What do you see?"

I saw a stunningly beautiful rich girl, who'd been the star of the class since second grade. A superconfident girl who had looks *and* brains, was street *and* wise. I envied her, but I didn't like her.

I said, "I don't understand what you're getting at, Sondra."

"Come on, Dora. What is different about us?"

"A million small things that add up to a larger—"

She sighed impatiently and said. "Are you *blind*? I'm BLACK, Dora. I am a black American."

"So what if you're black? That doesn't have anything to do with anything."

She shook her head. "You can say that, Dora, because you're white. You don't feel like you have to prove yourself constantly. As if society—including the so-called 'diverse' Brownstone society—is just waiting for you to slip up to fulfill your racial destiny. Acting superior is the antidote to the assumption of inferiority. You can't possibly understand what I'm talking about. You're a Jew in New York. The city bows at your feet. Everyone expects great things from you. From me, they hope I do well. And it's so white of you not to believe that a rich black person feels racism. I feel it every day. Even in a school like this, in a neighborhood like this."

I was speechless. Sondra never talked about this stuff. Most—not all—of the Ruling Class was white. Then again, most of the students at Brownstone were white.

I said, "I'm floored. Absolutely blown away. I had no clue you felt this way. I mean, I assumed you were insecure, because all bullies are insecure. It's a given. But I thought it had something to do with your parents."

She laughed, shaking her head. "That's because *you* have issues with *your* parents. You like to turn *your* insecurity into anger. Just because you do it doesn't mean I do it. Your problems are all in your head, Fringe Girl. I struggle with everything on the outside. For me, it's all about appearances, how things look. How *I* look. You don't seem to care much about that."

Was that metaphorical, or a slam on my style? Was she saying I was a shallow twit? "Whether you believe it or not—I do hate to flaunt my clueless whiteness—every girl in this school envies, admires, or fears you. Sometimes all three," I said. "If you're motivated by being black, so much the better, because you're going to be black for the rest of your life. And beautiful, and a born leader."

Sondra smiled. I could tell she was flattered, even though she already knew what I'd said was true. Reassurance didn't hurt, even for Sondra, who I'd thought didn't need anything from anybody.

The air in the bathroom thinned. This, I realized, was the second honest exchange I'd had with Sondra in ten years (the first being our grinning, pissing confrontation at Chez Brownstone the day of the Streak).

Sondra said, "One other thing."

"Vin Transom," I said, nodding. "I was hurt, Sondra. I felt betrayed. Losing my first boyfriend in such an underhanded way—that could leave permanent emotional scars. It could affect every romantic relationship I'll have for the rest of my life. I might never marry, you realize."

Sondra rolled her eyes at my speech, and then she said, "Oh, please. You never liked him that much anyway."

"I did!" I countered, but even I heard the hollowness of my plea. "I did before I had him, anyway."

"But then once you got him, the feeling disappeared, right?"

"Exactly. Although I liked the making out."

"You'll like it even more with someone else."

"Who?" I asked, Noel flashing before my yes.

"How should I know?"

"What about you and Vin?"

"I like him," she said. "And he likes me. Before, during—and after. Even more after. Do you understand?"

I assumed she was talking about sex. So I said, "Oh, totally. I can totally relate to that."

She laughed. "Okay, Fringe Girl. If you say so."

I laughed along. What the hell. A truce had been reached. I felt lighter and more relaxed than I had in weeks.

Sondra said, "Now we have to put things right."

"Any ideas?"

She nodded. "You might not like it."

"Will it grant me universal forgiveness?"

"Probably."

"Then I love it."

# 30

We hashed out the details and then waited until Thursday, wrap sandwich day at Chez Brownstone, to enact our plan. At noon, Sondra and I met outside the cafeteria and waited for nearly the entire junior class to get their lunch and commence eating.

She said, "I talk. You nod and smile."

"I am shutting up forthwith."

We walked down the center aisle of Chez Brownstone, arm in arm. Since our classmates were seated, we were visible to everyone in the room. Two known enemies, walking together, *touching*. If I'd been watching, I would have dropped my hummus.

A few people did. Kim Daniels gasped loudly (as she was wont). Sondra and I continued walking until we were in the middle of the room and then, without stopping or slowing, we stepped up onto the center table. Our movements were in perfect sync, as if we'd practiced (we hadn't). Lunchers moved their trays away so we could stand together, still arm in arm. I scanned the room, and found Liza, Eli and Eric Brainard seated together over to my right. Noel and Stanley were at their usual table to my left.

We didn't have to wait for silence. A hush settled over the

cafeteria as soon as we climbed onto the table. It was as if the entire class had been waiting for this moment, been primed for it.

Sondra said, "Dora Benet and I have an announcement to make."

I nodded. I smiled. I could take orders.

"For the last six weeks, the two of us have been working on a social studies experiment together called 'Project Revolution,'" announced Sondra. "The goal was to see if, by subtle manipulation, using whatever means necessary, we could create social unrest and, eventually, chaos and anarchy in the microcosm of the Brownstone Institute."

There were some rumblings, but most of the kids just listened. "We kept our project—and its objectives—secret from everyone, including our closest friends," said Sondra. "The plan was to stage a war between us. We wrote the dueling editorials in the *Brief* together. We scripted our confrontation here at Chez Brownstone. But then the revolution took on a life of its own. The Streak incident. Dora's detention. The *Brief* coverage. The locker graffiti-ing. We hadn't anticipated that feelings and friendships would be hurt because of our experiment. We both realized about halfway into this that we were in over our heads. We're terribly sorry for any pain we caused."

I looked at Liza, Eli and Eric. They were the only kids in the room who knew the truth—that Sondra had nothing to do with Project Revolution. I wasn't sure how my erstwhile friends would react, if they'd stand up on their table and scream "Lies! All lies!" I hoped they would appreciate the gesture, the sacrifice on my part of sharing my (granted, misguided) brainchild with Sondra.

Who was still talking. "We understand that some changes brought on in the past six months can't be undone," she said.

"But we both hope that in the weeks to come, we'll all return to a semblance of normalcy. Thanks for listening. And, again, we're sorry. Right, Dora?"

I nodded and smiled. She whispered, "Now we go." She took my arm, and we stepped off the table, onto the bench, onto the floor, down the center aisle and out of the room. We kept walking until we reached the garden courtyard, where we sat down on the granite steps.

"What now?" I asked.

"We wait. See how the news settles."

"How are Lori and Micha?"

"Not so good," she said. "What's happening with Liza and Eli?"

"They hate me," I said.

We'd suffered blows in this battle. There'd been losses on both sides. But, I thought, as I sat next to Sondra Fortune in companionable silence, maybe we'd both made some gains, too.

# 31

November 7th, Monday

To: Mr. *Sage*brush
From: Adora Benet
Subject: Final report

It's been two weeks since I joined forces with the enemy to suppress the rebellion I (myself alone) initiated. It's also been weeks since my last report, which you have been waiting for with the patience of the Buddha. Hand to God, Mr. Sagebrush, I've been busy taking notes, recording the fallout from our joint announcement at Chez Brownstone (what I'm calling "The Treaty of Versus I"). So far, so good, for everyone—excluding myself, for the reasons enumerated below.

1   Ms. Ratzenberger has had the pleasure of enforcing a "no standing on tables" rule for Chez Brownstone. She takes great pleasure, as we can all see, patrolling the two aisles in the cafeteria, admonishing students to keep their "feet on the floor, at all times." If a sneaker comes into contact with, say, the table *bench*, it's a warning. Crossing one's legs in the "Indian-style" position is banned in Chez Brownstone. My

revolution has served, at the very least, to create stupid restrictions on how to sit at lunch.

2   Sondra Fortune has resumed her place at the top of the social heap within days of telling the junior class that my revolution, the one I conceived from nothing, was partially her idea. The lesson here, as politicians have known for time immemorial: Throw yourself on the mercy of the people for being bad, or wrong, or stupid, or a swindler, or gay, or an adulterer, and you'll not only be forgiven, you'll be heralded for your bravery. Sondra's gambit—to take the blame for my wrongdoings—has won her even more envy, admiration and adoration than ever before. What sticks in my craw about it: I wonder what would have happened had I taken the hit alone. But it never occurred to me to do it. And that might be the number one reason Sondra is a born leader and I'm a born cynically optimistic individualist.

3   Sondra's reflected restored glory is cast upon her immediate circle of cronies only. The Dropov twins have regained their place of prominence, although, I suspect, their family problems (have I written about these to you before?) have left permanent smudges upon their glittering veneers. I heard that Lori is taking ballet again, and I'm glad for her, even though I don't—and will never—like her. As far as Sondra's rising star shining down upon me, well, it ain't happening. When we see each other, we smile, say hello, compliment (falsely?) each other's hair and clothes and move on. I am no closer to her, despite what's happened, than I was before. I'm relieved, to tell the truth.

4   Eric Brainard, meanwhile, has transformed the *Brief* from a boring summary of sports scores to a hot sheet of editorial opinion and criticism. He's basking in his own glory and has risen to Ruling Class status. I hope his accession won't go to

his head. I fear it will. I've tried to tell him that the view from the top makes everyone below seem small and insignificant. But they're not. Unless, they are. Like Kim Daniels, who has started about five million rumors about me and Seth Wonderwall, including some that are true (blast that loudmouth). The girl has no discretion. One of these days, she'll get a dose of her own medicine. Ideally, I'll be holding the needle.

5  Speaking of guzzling one's own medicine, Max Lindsey continues to follow Lori Dropov around school in the same way Liza Greene once trailed after him. Now he knows how it feels to be the neglected puppy at his master's heel. I hope Liza has observed this, and come to the conclusions any intelligent person would make in such an enlightening situation. I wouldn't know. She ignores and avoids me like the plague. Eli Stomp continues to ignore and avoid me, too.

6  Which is my final point, and perhaps the most relevant (to the social studies project, and my life): Revolution is bound to fail unless the revolutionaries (a) know who they're up against, inside and out, (b) keep their friends close and (c) resist quick alliances with questionable and untrustworthy factions.

   As far as point (a) goes, Noel Kepner hit on this idea repeatedly in class, to have sympathy and understanding for the oppressors. I ignored him to my peril. Instead, I made assumptions about Sondra based on jealousy, envy and vanity, which, correct me if I'm wrong, are three out of seven deadly sins. So I'm fast on the way to hell. Noel Kepner, however, deserves a medal or something for speaking out, being righteous, if a little insufferably so. I regret how I've treated him in class. I wish I could take back every snide, smug comment and eye roll. Noel is the smartest kid in school. I'm sure you know that. You should give him an A.

Regarding point (b), I continue to pay with my hide for pissing off my two best friends. This part is just too sad to write about. I'll skip to point (c). No word from Seth Wonderwall. Plenty of words from Kim Daniels, none of them good. I'd love for her to go suddenly mute.

7  I'm a failed revolutionary, with no friends, no boyfriend and overly concerned parents who ask if I'm "okay" every five minutes. And yet, I have myself. I have my family. And I have way too much homework to make this report any longer than it is right now.

Monday, 2:00 P.M.

Dear Ms. Benet:

Thank you for such a detailed final report on your revolution term project, although I could have done without the gossipy sections. I'm impressed overall with the scope of the project. I read over the collection of your reports, and I came away with a sense that history—your personal history—has been written in the last six weeks (a history that—we all hope—won't repeat itself). Revolution always comes with a price (usually, payable in blood), which you seemed oblivious to at first. I trust you'll be able to rebuild your damaged relationships. You have more power than you realize. It comes from who you are, as well as where you stand. Not to sound too much like the Buddha you compared me to: All power in the emotional realm comes from within.

Oh, before I forget: Somehow, in haste, I mixed up some papers, and mistakenly slipped the Project Revolution folder into the folder containing Noel Kepner's term project. He returned the folder with your reports to me this afternoon. He may have read your updates. Sorry for my mistake.

I look forward to seeing you in class tomorrow. You are indefatigable, Ms. Benet. And if you don't know what "indefatigable" means, look it up.
Sincerely,
Mr. Sagebrush


Thursday, November 10, 5 A.M.
To: *Adora.Benet@brownstone.edu*
From: *Swonderwall@rr.fla.com*
Subject line: back on the meds


I write from Coral Gardens, Florida, where I'll be living with my grandparents for the rest of the school year at least. New York is safe from me for the time being. I'm also back in therapy, back on my medications. I won't go into detail because talking about the state of my mental health is so *boring*, and you're probably waiting for me to get to the point. Here it is: I am sorry. I regret the way our friendship ended. But it did end. I'm not coming after you. I don't expect an e-mail back, and you probably shouldn't send one. But I do want you to know that, of all the girls I met in New York, I liked you for real. You are an actual human person with feelings—both raw and cooked—and a mind of her own. I shouldn't have imposed my psychosis on you.
Stay cool,
Seth


I got Seth's e-mail when I logged onto my computer first thing Friday morning. I was hiding out, as I'd been doing for weeks, in the upper school library (I was still jittery about going into Chez Brownstone and being blatantly ignored by my former friends and acquaintances). I'd claimed a table by the stacks as my own, spending breaks, lunch hour and free minutes before and after school in this very spot. I wasn't used to spending so much time alone. But, I'd come to realize, I was adaptable.

The e-mail from Seth definitely freaked me out. On his meds? Was he psychotic? Was I an insensitive jerk for treating him so harshly when he was not operating on all cylinders? I felt sorry for Seth, for his problems, being sent to Florida, for his loneliness, which had to be deeper than mine would ever be. I pictured Seth that first time we met, in detention with Rebecca the slut and Brian her swain.

As fate would have it, just as I was having these thoughts, my eyes drifted into the stacks, where I saw the very same randy couple going at it, her back against the rows of books, him grinding into her belly.

I said, "For God's sake, people! Get a room."

Rebecca looked at me and waved. "Hey, it's Fringe Girl! Brian, say hello."

Brian grunted, "Hey," and then went back about his business.

I couldn't sit there, watching. Class was starting soon anyway. I gathered my laptop and books and rushed out of the library into the hallway—where I blindly collided with someone. My computer and notebooks scattered all over the carpet.

"Dora!" said the person I'd smashed into.

"Vin!" I said, in shock, and then started laughing. I'd actually bumped into him by accident. By real accident.

"Let me help," he said, kneeling to pick up my property. Together, we got my stuff organized. My laptop seemed to be functioning just fine, to my relief.

We stood up. Faced each other. He said, "For the record, I tried to apologize. I called like fifteen times."

"I didn't want to give you the satisfaction," I said. "It was childish of me."

After that, he didn't speak so I didn't either. It was exactly like old times, when we stood awkwardly in deafeningly loud silence. The picture was the same, but the vibe was different. The silence wasn't so loud, for one thing. It was just there. Like Vin. He was simply, benignly *there*. And I didn't feel the slightest desire to not listen to him anymore.

We nodded at each other with tacit understanding and walked off in opposite directions.

# 32

"Do I have to go?" I whined.

"I'm not forcing you," said Mom, but I could hear the iron chains of guilt in her voice, the ones that would drag me to Grind for a Saturday spot of latte with her, whether or not I felt like moving off the couch.

"All right," I agreed, heaving myself up.

Mom beamed and rushed to her room to change. Although I wasn't sure why her track pants and T-shirt wouldn't cut it at Grind. They didn't have a formal dress code.

Dad and Joya were on the way out to one of their stoop sale hunting missions through other people's garbage. It'd been a month since I ruined Joya's brunch. We were still tense around each other.

Dad sat next to me on the couch. He was already wearing his coat. "So," he said. "Nice grade on your revolution project. Mr. Sagebrush seems quite impressed with you. I had no idea you were so good at social studies."

"I was never good, Dad," I said. "I was *great*."

"And now?" he asked. "After you get an A, it's all downhill?"

I said, "I'd give it back. If I could . . ."

"Could what?"

"Forget it."

He frowned and gave me a hug. "They'll forgive you, Adorable. Just you wait."

Joya came bounding down the stairs. Her pixie haircut had grown out, and it looked EVEN BETTER a bit shaggy. "Ready, Dad?" she asked him. To me, she said nothing.

"Let's go," he said, heaving himself off the couch. "Dora, be nice to your mother. She's been working hard and deserves a peaceful afternoon."

"But I had my heart set on being obnoxious," I said.

After they left, Mom bounded down the stairs, looking just like Joya, if twenty-six years older. Same cuteness, same enthusiasm. Mom didn't seem too strung out, for all her hard work. I almost said, "If you're stressed, be stressed."

We walked the short blocks to Grind in relative quiet. I was glad. I was sick of talking. Especially about my feelings. I was still waist deep in emotional conflict, even if the fireworks had stopped at school and at home. I desperately wanted to stop feeling disjointed. But the weirdness wouldn't let up. Not much, anyway, in weeks.

Eventually, I was sure, I'd feel better. I remembered a page from *His-and-Her Dating*, on the half-life theory of breakups: However long the relationship, one needed half that long to recover from its demise. If my relationship with power and glory lasted six weeks, start to finish, I'd need at least another week to get over the crash and burn.

I'd consulted the Sarcastic Ball about this repeatedly, asking it, "Will I ever feel normal again?"

Last night, it gave the same response four times in a row: "What do you think?," which was an insulting cheat, answering a question with a question. The balls on that ball.

We walked to the door of Grind. "Here we are!" Mom sang, as if we'd arrived at the palace to meet the prince.

"We sure are!" I sang.

Mom patted her hair and smoothed her coat, and I wondered if we *were* meeting with a prince. I asked, "What is *up* with you?"

"Shhh," she said, opening the door. "Let's get coffee!"

The prospect of coffee always made Mom jolly, to be sure. But never had it made her quite so giddy.

As soon as we walked into Grind, I knew why.

Sitting at a back table, I spied Liza and Stephanie Greene, and Eli and Anita Stomp. They were at a table for six, with two empty chairs.

I'd been set up. By my mom. From the looks on Eli and Liza's faces, they'd also been set up. By their moms. It was almost too embarrassing to contemplate, like the three of them had arranged a playdate for us, as if we needed parental upkeep with our social calendars. As if we were still seven years old. I could not believe Mom would put me on the spot like this.

But, goes without saying, I was glad she had.

"Come along, Adora," she said.

I followed her toward their table. She said, "Have a seat. I'll get us a couple of lattes."

Stephanie Greene stood up and said, "I'll help."

"Me, too," said Anita Stomp, who quickly added, "For the record, Adora, in my opinion, Jack Carp deserved to win States. His composition was beautiful, even more so because he'd been inspired by love for my daughter. That said, regarding the States competition next year, if you don't mind terribly, Adora darling, *stay out of it.*"

"Yes, Mrs. Stomp," I said. "And I'm truly sorry."

The women left the table. I heard Mom gushing to Stephanie about her engagement, and then the three women started blabbing about the wedding plans and making Liza look sicker than she already was at the mere sight of me.

I said, "I had no clue you guys would be here."

"Obviously," said Eli.

"Jack Carp came to me," I said. "He showed up at my apartment. If I'd had any idea he'd make a big announcement at States, or that you were really into Eric Brainard, I wouldn't have said anything. At the time, I was locked in a mortal struggle with my own egomania. I was crazy! Mad and drunk with power. But even in total delusion, I never wanted to hurt you."

"I know, Dora," said Eli flatly. Her eyes flitted over to Liza.

"Liza," I said, "what I did to you was even worse."

"No, it wasn't," she said, which were her first words to me in a month. "I understand what happened at Monty's. I was crazy myself. You gave me the verbal slap across the face. I should have said, 'Thanks, I needed that.' "

"I had no right to tell you how to behave. I'm not your mother! I'm your friend, and friends should support each other. In fact, if you asked me right now to stalk Max Lindsey every spare minute and provide you a detailed report of his movements, I'd do it. I will do it. I want to. Let me make it up to you."

Liza laughed, a sound I'd missed terribly, and I loved her so much right then. "Max Lindsey?" she asked. "Why would I ever want you to stalk that loser?"

"My thought exactly," I said, a bit confused.

"She doesn't know," said Eli.

"Know what?" I asked.

"I'm so over him!" announced Liza. "I'm seeing someone else now."

"That's amazing," I said. "I haven't heard . . ."

"Well, we've kept it quiet. We didn't know how you would feel about it."

How I would feel? What did I have to do with it? I wondered. And then, Noel Kepner's face flashed across my brain.

I said, "After what's happened with Jack and Max, I vow never to interfere in anyone's relationships again."

"Good," said Liza.

"And, you know, we haven't exactly been talking. I can only pray to one day have the privilege of just being informed about your relationship . . ."

"Oh, Dora. Don't be ridiculous," blurted Eli. "Like we weren't going to forgive you? Did our parents—all of our surrogate parents—raise us to be hard-assed bitches?"

I laughed, and almost cried. "I didn't think so," I said. "But why haven't you called me? I've been twisting in the wind, you know. And it hurt. A lot."

"Well, you deserved some twisting," said Eli.

"And after that freaky Sondra Fortune hand-holding freak show, we weren't sure you wanted us anymore," said Liza. "We were waiting for you to call."

"Aren't we just a bunch of phone-shy idiots," I said.

"So do you want to know the secret identity of my new boyfriend?" asked Liza.

"Do tell," I said. Not Noel Kepner. Not Noel Kepner.

"Noel Kepner," she said, "fixed us up. I'm dating Stanley Nable!"

"He's so not Max Lindsey!" I rejoiced. And so not Noel Kepner!

Liza said, "Eli, tell her about Eric Brainard."

"What? You didn't break up?" I asked.

Eli smiled. "The opposite." One eye on the moms, she whispered, "We had sex. And it was fucking fantastic!"

"Literally," I said. "Does this mean you had an orgasm?"

"Oh, no," she said, shaking her head. "Not a single one. I had three, Dora. With many more to come."

"As it were," I said.

We all laughed, and the relief was like knocking ten elephants off my shoulders. I felt like I might fly to the ceiling.

The moms returned. Stephanie Greene asked, "And what are you girls laughing at?"

"Nothing," said me and my two best friends.

# 33

On Sunday morning, I set out on a very important shopping expedition to Manhattan. I woke up early and was out the door by ten o'clock.

I got about half a block from my building when I heard fast footsteps coming up behind me.

I turned around.

"Dora! Hi," said Noel Kepner.

"Were you . . . hiding by my neighbor's stoop, waiting for me to come out so you could pretend to run into me on my own block?"

He turned bright red, and said, "I can explain."

"No need," I said. After all, I'd done the same to him.

"I read your revolution reports. All of them. Mr. Sagebrush gave them to me—by accident."

"By accident," I muttered. Mr. Sagebrush might be more attuned to his students' personal lives than he'd care to admit. The wily genius. No wonder he was supreme master of social studies.

"Giving Sondra Fortune credit for what you did, that's a lot of pride to swallow. A ton. That must have hurt."

"It would have hurt more not to do it," I said.

"I think I understand," he said. "About what happened with Sondra. And also why you've been so harsh to me."

My turn to go red of face. He couldn't possibly have figured out the hairpin turns of my feelings for him. It wasn't possible. It was all so convoluted. I hated him because I loved him? It was like opposite day, every day. For a decade.

I said, "I hear you're responsible for fixing up Liza and Stanley."

Puffing with pride, he said, "Yeah, well, Stanley has liked her for a while. They had a brief thing once, a while ago."

"I remember."

"I encouraged him to start it up again. It didn't take much."

"I guess you'll have a new regular at your concerts."

"Yeah, we could use the fans," he said. "You should come, check us out. One of these nights."

"Yeah, well, it could be awkward, with Sondra there. And Vin."

He nodded. "Or maybe we could hang out. One of these nights."

"Just us?" I asked. "I don't think we've been alone together since we were six."

"That's a lot of lost time to make up for," he said.

And then, Noel Kepner leaned toward me, eyes closed, puckering. I was so shocked by the sight, that I started laughing—with nerves, mainly. The sight of him coming at me with the lips did seem a bit comic, too.

He instantly bolted upright, looking sheepish.

I said, "I'm so sorry! I want you to kiss me. I want you to—badly. But seeing you move in for the smooch, I wasn't ready. I went a little daffy. You have to forgive me. I mean, SHIT! That behavior is inexcusable. It's pathetic. It's—"

He held up his hand. And then Noel Kepner, of all people, said, "Don't you know when to stop talking?"

And then he kissed me.

It was fortifying, nutritional, like I could survive for months on a desert island if I could feed off his lips. The kiss filled me up and made me hungry at the same time. But just as it was getting serious, expanding to include other body parts, Noel broke it off.

"This is going to sound odd, but I've got to go," he said.

"Okay."

"I told my parents I was running out to buy eggs two hours ago."

"And you've been waiting for me the whole time?"

"I needed to talk."

I smiled. How wonderful it was to hear that. "I'm glad you waited."

"But now that we're straightened out, I've got to go or my parents might call the police."

"I understand."

"Later?" he asked.

"Sooner," I said, and we kissed good-bye, and walked in opposite directions, backwards, looking and waving at each other until it got a little stupid. But only a little.


Three hours later, I was in my room. My heart lighter than marshmallow, my shopping expedition a success.

Knock on the door.

"Enter," I said.

Joya opened the door tentatively, holding a piece of paper. She held it up and said, "You wanted to see me?"

I'd left an invitation to my room on her bed. "Have a seat," I said.

With a moment's hesitation, Joya sat next to me on my bed. I smiled, and she wanted to return it. I could tell. But she didn't.

I reached behind my pillow to retrieve a small square wrapped with a pretty pink bow.

I handed it to her. "For you," I said.

"Really?" she asked, suddenly the old Joya, open, eager, excited, tearing away the wrapping with delicious abandon.

She stared, eyes wide, at my gift, the one I'd gone to three stores in the Village to find. "You bought this for me?" she asked.

"I gave it to you, didn't I?"

"Does this make me a member of the club?" she asked. "I can have coffee at Grind with you guys, too?"

"We're not a club," I said, irritated. "That's so middle school. But, yeah, whatever. Consider yourself in. On a limited basis."

"Should I ask it a question?" She was smiling wide as a river.

"That's what it's for."

Joya opened the box lid and removed her very own, brand-new Sarcastic Ball. She shook it hard and asked, "Will Dora and I be best friends when we're twenty-five and twenty-eight?"

I said, "Don't ask it that."

"What should I ask?" She sounded deflated.

I said, "How about this: 'Even if she doesn't act like it, are Dora and I already best friends?' "

Joya repeated the question and shook the ball.

It read: "Abso-friggin-lutely."

Read on for a preview of
Valerie Frankel's next novel starring
Dora Benet and friends

# Fringe Girl in Love

Coming from
NAL Jam
in April 2007

A pivotal first: Eli, Liza and I all had boyfriends at the same time. More importantly, we were excited about these guys. And they were excited about us (or, I should say, each to his own specific girlfriend). As a subset, the three boys reveled in each other's company. And we were enchanted (platonically) by each other's boyfriends. If one were to visually conceptualize the six of us on a piece of paper, we'd make the shape of a hexagon with lines connecting each individual dot, forming not three or six different relationships, but *fifteen* unique, whole and satisfying pairings. In the span of two weeks time (even to me, that seemed brief; the slipping of one grain of sand through the hourglass of my continuing existence), I'd transformed from being a friendless, boyfriendless, pathetic loser who hung her sorry head in shame, to having the giddy, slamming social life of a girl in a shampoo commercial.

"Makes you worry though. Too much happiness," I said to Eli and Liza at Grind, our usual spot for an afternoon jolt of pumpkin spice latte and lemon cake.

"Makes *you* worry," said Eli Stomp, wiping her lips with a napkin. Only she, with her tidy sweater set, pin straight black hair and perfect porcelain skin, could make slurping seem dainty.

"I get what Dora means," said Liza, a strand of blond hair dipping accidentally into her cup as she drank lustily from it. If Eli made coffee consumption seem like a subtle, ancient art form, Liza's earthy delight in her beverage made me think of Roman orgies. "If you're too happy, then God notices and turns you into a salt sculpture," she warned. Despite her sunshiny demeanor, Liza Greene was the most sensitive—and superstitious—of our threesome.

"Can we leave God out of it?" asked Eli, who was born in communist China and raised in Brooklyn by her adoptive Catholic mother and Jewish father.

"I'm not a hundred percent happy," said Liza, chomping her third almond cookie. "So I guess I'm safe."

I assumed Liza was referring to her mother, Stephanie's, imminent wedding to Gary "The Whitest Man on Earth" Glitch. Since I'd listened to Liza moan about the dreaded upcoming ceremony every day for hours at a stretch (time I could have spent playing Snood or probing my beloved Noel Kepner's dental work with my tongue), I steered the conversation in a more upbeat direction.

"So Mrs. Barbaloo needs hip replacement," I informed the table. "She's taking a medical tourism vacation to Thailand to have surgery and convalesce. Should be months before she comes back to terrorize Brownstone." I spoke of an older-than-bedrock blue-haired, evil-eyed nasty harridan English teacher and our private school, the Brownstone Institute, a place of higher (ahem) learning in Brooklyn Heights, New York City. Attendees called themselves Brownstoners.

"I heard that hip replacement is an absolutely gruesome surgery," said Eli, daughter of a physician. "The Thai doctors will use a circular saw to cut through the bones of Mrs. Barbaloo's pelvis."

"Nice sound effects," admired Liza of Eli's violent whirring.

"Can you not use 'Mrs. Barbaloo' and 'pelvis' in the same sentence ever again?" I asked. "The replacement English professor arrives today from some WASPy prep school in Connecticut. She's, allegedly, a Shakespearean scholar."

"I think Mrs. Barbaloo might have actually met Shakespeare himself in her youth," said Eli.

"Love themes in literature," sang Liza. "New teacher, sexy stories. This class might actually be good."

I was counting on it. Otherwise, my course load for the semester ran the gamut between deadly and fatal. Ideally, this English class would be romantic—not necromantic like the rest of the school day. And the love theme would play nicely into my personal schedule, too. English Lit was the only hour—except lunch—I would spend with Noel this term. I let myself imagine reading the required passages to each other while sitting on the bed in my room, faint lava light flickering across our faces and the open pages our books. Leaning close to kiss, the volumes sliding off our laps, hitting the floor with twin thuds.

"I'm outie," said Eli suddenly. "I've got to meet Eric at the *Brief* office." Her boyfriend, Eric Brainard, was editor of *The Brownstone Brief*, the school's student run and published-scalding-hot broadsheet.

I checked my watch. How time flew when sucking down coffee and cookies.

The three of us walked the four blocks back to school. The sidewalk should have the indentations of our feet, we've walked the same route so often over the days and years. We passed the Tandoori Palace, Soulvaki Hut, Sushi Den, Pagoda House and Burger Heaven. One could circle the globe cuisine-wise on Montague Street. It was all so predictable and routine, I thought as we walked. No surprises along the way.

And then a big shock when we finally got to the huge twelve-panel oak front doors of Brownstone. Right there, on the steps leading up, I spied Noel Kepner, my dear heart, laughing with his hand on the shoulder of my sworn enemy (or lifelong friend—our relationship was a one massive gray area), Sondra Fortune. Sondra, it bears mentioning, used to go out with Noel. And not a million years ago. Just the one.

My hazel eyes changed color, depending on my mood. When I saw Noel touching Sondra, however innocently, my eyes turned a roiling, boiling green—the thick murky jade of jealousy that was hard to see through. But he saw me. He smiled and waved in his shamelessly unironic way. The gesture was earnest, big, loveable. It defused my jealousy somewhat. But not enough. As far as Sondra went . . . well, actually, Sondra never went as far (away) as I wished she would.

At my side, I heard Eli say, "Steady, Dora." My full name, FYI: Adora Benet. But I preferred Dora, as anyone with shame would.

I ascended the steps toward Noel, my teeth locked in a plastic smile. He pulled me into a tight hug. When he let me go, Sondra was gone. So were Eli and Liza.

He said, "You smell like pumpkin."

I thought I was rank with jealousy.

I said, "Noel, as a personal favor to me, I wish you'd make just one small gesture, not to prove your love, but to acknowledge a flaw in my character, a charming flaw, a loveable quirk. Just, please, don't be so friendly with other girls."

"Sondra is my friend, Dora," he said. "I've known her since we were seven."

"You've known me since we were five," I said. Whispering, I added, "But you know her better than you know me, in one sense, anyway."

"Come on," he said, his long arm over my shoulder. He led me inside the building and down the carpeted corridor toward the upper school annex. He talked while we walked. "How many times do I have to tell you," he said. "I'm like a dog, Dora. Loyal. Faithful. I've never cheated on a girlfriend in my life."

"You've never kept a girlfriend long enough to cheat on her," I said.

As we approached the door to English Lit, he gently nudged me into the space underneath one of the corridor's vaulted archways (the building was rife with gothic touches; it was originally constructed a hundred plus years ago as a college for nuns in training). Then he pressed his body against me and kissed my forehead. Instantly, from just that much contact, my breathing quickened and blood raced. It was a primal power, what Noel had over me.

"Jealousy is a charming quirk," I said, my resolve melting.

"You don't have to worry!" he said. "I'd never cheat on you. If Angelina Jolie walked down this hallway and begged me, I wouldn't do it."

"Of course not," I said. "Not in front of all these people."

"If she appeared magically to me in private, forced a powerful aphrodisiac on me, and hypnotized me, too, then, yes, I'd oblige the lady."

"I would understand, in that case," I said.

The bell rang.

"Love themes in literature," said Noel, waggling his eyebrows. "Promise you'll be my study partner."

Together (heavy sigh) we walked into the half-full classroom. Eli and Liza were seated in back already. I put my bag on the floor and took out my laptop. I'd only just pushed the start button when Angelina Jolie walked into the classroom.

Not the real Angelina Jolie. A blond version, with bigger

boobs in a tight pencil skirt and a knit short-sleeved red sweater.

The bombshell—she couldn't have more than 25—picked up the cursor pen and wrote her name on the digital white board.

"Ms. Matilda Rossi," she wrote. And then she spoke. Her voice was the equivalent of hot chocolate. Not the mix you stir into boiling water. Her voice was dark, smooth, bittersweet, as if the heat of passion had liquefied the richest center of a thousand cocoa nuts.

"This month, we'll be reading *Romeo and Juliet*," she said. "To start, I'll read the part of Juliet. Do we have any willing Romeos? How about you? The tall, brown haired boy in back."

Naturally, Ms. Rossi was pointing at Noel. His jaw, completely unhinged, rested squarely his desk, like that of every other boy in the class.

Never thought I'd miss Mrs. Barbaloo. Curse that crone and her brittle hip.

# About the Author

Valerie Frankel is the author of nine previous novels, including *The Accidental Virgin*, *The Girlfriend Curse*, and *Hex and the Single Girl*. She writes often for magazines including *Self, Glamour, Marie Claire,* and *Allure*. When not working, Val plays Snood, blogs, jogs and takes amateur-quality digital portraits. She lives in Brooklyn Heights with her husband, two daughters and three cats. All of them are extremely photogenic. Go to www.valeriefrankel.com and see for yourself.